"If you're so bad at bull riding, why do you keep trying?" Ellie teased.

Tate heaved a very weary, very fake sigh. "If at first you don't succeed, try, try again." But instead of smiling at the cliché, he frowned, seeming to pause and consider the meaning of the words.

"I like your boyfriend, Mom," Della announced.

"Let's marry him," Lulu added, giving a firm nod.

Tate laughed loudly.

"Nobody is marrying anybody," Ellie said shakily, feeling as if she was standing on the beach while a wave rolled back out to sea, taking the sand beneath her feet with it. "I don't know where you kids get these ideas."

"From Gigi," Lulu said cheerfully. "She says we have to find you a job or a husband if we want to stay in Clementine."

Tate made a noise suspiciously like a stifled laugh.

Ellie scowled at him. "Don't encourage them."

Dear Reader,

I'm going to share a secret with you. Someone in my family had a high school crush on his best friend's girlfriend. He kept that crush hidden through the years, through his best friend's marriage to the object of his affection, trying his darndest to be a true and loyal friend. Until they divorced.

Meet Tate Oakley, rodeo cowboy, former foster kid and a man who knows a thing or two about loyalty. Yes, he's had a decade-long crush on his foster brother's childhood sweetheart. And yes, his family doesn't want him to rock the boat now that Tate's foster brother and Tate's crush are divorced. But sometimes you have to rock the boat to find smoother waters.

I had fun writing Tate and Ellie's romance, taking liberties with the original couple who inspired this story for me. I hope you come to l ove and root for the cowboys and cowgirls of The Cowboy Academy series as much as I do. Happy reading!

Melinda

HEARTWARMING

A Cowboy for the Twins

—

Melinda Curtis

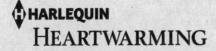

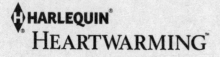

HARLEQUIN®
HEARTWARMING™

ISBN-13: 978-1-335-47571-8

Recycling programs
for this product may
not exist in your area.

A Cowboy for the Twins

Copyright © 2024 by Melinda Wooten

For questions and comments about the quality of this book,
please contact us at CustomerService@Harlequin.com.

TM and ® are trademarks of Harlequin Enterprises ULC.

Harlequin Enterprises ULC
22 Adelaide St. West, 41st Floor
Toronto, Ontario M5H 4E3, Canada
www.Harlequin.com

Printed in U.S.A.

Award-winning *USA TODAY* bestselling author **Melinda Curtis**, when not writing romance, can be found working on a fixer-upper she and her husband purchased in Oregon's Willamette Valley. Although this is the third home they've lived in and renovated (in three different states), it's not a job for the faint of heart. But it's been a good metaphor for book writing, as sometimes you have to tear things down to the bare bones to find the core beauty and potential. In between—and during—renovations, Melinda has written over forty books for Harlequin, including her Heartwarming book *Dandelion Wishes*, which is now a TV movie, *Love in Harmony Valley*, starring Amber Marshall.

Brenda Novak says *Season of Change* "found a place on my keeper shelf."

Sheila Roberts says *Can't Hurry Love* is "a page turner filled with wit and charm."

Books by Melinda Curtis

Harlequin Heartwarming

The Cowboy Academy

A Cowboy Worth Waiting For
A Cowboy's Fourth of July
A Cowboy Christmas Carol

The Mountain Monroes

The Littlest Cowgirls
Caught by the Cowboy Dad
A Cowgirl's Secret

The Blackwells of Eagle Springs

Wyoming Christmas Reunion

Visit the Author Profile page
at Harlequin.com for more titles.

To Cari Lynn Webb,

who always seems to know what
my characters should be thinking.

PROLOGUE

In High School...

"BE MY COWBOY VALENTINE?"

"Shh." Tate Oakley refolded the small slip of paper in his hand and then held it away from his twin brother, Ryan, who, having uttered the words, was trying to snatch it.

Other kids passed them in the narrow hallway, including a cowgirl with long, reddish-brown hair and freckles.

She was the same cowgirl who'd slipped the note into Tate's locker. The cowgirl who'd won his heart. The cowgirl who was dating one of his former foster brothers.

"Come on, Tate." Ryan kept trying to steal Ellie Rowland's homemade valentine from Tate's hand. "I didn't see who signed it. There were too many hearts in the way."

"Stop it, Ry." Tate swatted at his brother with his straw cowboy hat, noting that Ellie had rounded a corner at the end of the corridor, likely heading toward the science lab.

Ryan took a step back. "Tell me it's not from Nia Plevins."

"It's not." Tate settled his hat back on his head and leaned forward to whisper his all-burning question: "When did Ellie break up with Buck?"

Buck, who was one of the few foster teens who hadn't fit in at the Done Roamin' Ranch with the Harrison family. Buck, who blamed everyone else for his problems, scorned the advice of and spurned the love from Frank and Mary Harrison. Buck, who'd been dating Ellie off and on this year.

"I don't know when they broke up, but..." Ryan's eyes widened. "Remember what Dad said about no love triangles? And what he said about treating Buck like he's still a member of the family? All to keep the peace?" Ryan referred to their foster father. No good advice was ever to be had from their biological dad, who had disappointed his boys in more ways than one.

"It's not a love triangle. Ellie and Buck broke up for good this time." Tate assumed. He tried to reason it out in his head. "Because she asked me to be her valentine. She wouldn't do that if—"

"She didn't want to make Buck jealous?" Ryan was always glass half-empty. He frowned. "Or maybe Buck knows you've had a crush on her forever and he had someone write the note for him. Or—"

"I get the idea." Tate shoved a wayward notebook back into his locker. But what he couldn't shove away was his compulsion to be near Ellie. "I'll be careful. But Ellie might need a friend right now." Even if his heart hoped she wanted more.

Tate closed his locker and headed toward science class.

Ryan fell into step next to him. "Okay. But your idea of careful and my idea of careful are two different things."

CHAPTER ONE

Present Day...

"GET YOUR LOVE fortune told!"

"And your Valentine's Day cookies!"

Two little cowgirls with reddish-brown hair and freckles ran up to Tate on his way to the stock pens during the first rodeo of the season, kicking up plenty of dust with their sparkly pink cowboy boots.

"Hey, mister!" The cowgirl in the pink dress planted herself in front of him. "You aren't married, are you?"

"He don't look single." The cowgirl with a frilly pink shirt and blue jeans plunked her hands onto her hips. "Do you need a present for your valentine?"

The traffic in the merchant aisle flowed around Tate as he digested the disparate pitches of the two little salesgirls.

He was used to attracting female attention, but not from cowgirls this young. They couldn't be more than eight or nine. "Howdy, ladies."

"Bring him over here, gals." An old woman with long wild white hair beneath a straw cowboy hat sat behind a table with a blue-and-purple paisley tablecloth. She wore a flowing bright orange dress belted with leather and silver. A display of individually wrapped heart-shaped cookies sat before her. She gestured for Tate to come closer, metal bangles jingling on her wrists. "Good work, girls. He looks like a lovelorn cowboy, for sure, for sure."

Clearly she doesn't know me.

Tate was a much sought-after bachelor, but a confirmed bachelor, having lost his heart years ago. "What are you selling today, ma'am?"

"*Ma'am?*" The old woman scoffed, reaching for his hands, while the little sales prodigies watched intently. "You may call me Gigi." She worked her fingers over his palms and fingertips. She wore big rings on every finger, and every ring had a different color stone.

Smiling, Tate carefully extricated his hands. "Okay, Gigi, what are you selling?" He was willing to humor her for five bucks. Maybe ten if it included a cookie.

Gigi laughed, making the dangly earrings swing over her shoulders before settling back against all that long white hair. "I'm going to do you a favor and tell you the truth. You, my friend, are pining after a woman you think you can't have."

"Do tell," Tate murmured, his smile feeling strained.

"Your hands say you're a hardworking man," Gigi continued, pushing a cookie across the table toward him. "And that smile of yours… You smile far too much at far too many women."

Well, you did say I was pining after an unattainable woman, so why not smile at the rest of them?

"How much for the cookie?" Tate asked, holding on to his smile by a thin thread.

"Five dollars." Gigi peered past him as the girls trapped another cowboy. "I can tell you how to win her over for another five. That's a bargain, all things considered. How long have you been pining over her?"

"I'll just take the cookie." Tate handed her a five.

"Gigi! Girls!" A commanding female voice rang out behind Tate just as the little cowgirls delivered Gigi another cowboy. "I asked you not to hard sell this time."

"We're making friends is all." Gigi was already in possession of the next cowboy's hands. It was Cord Malone, a young, struggling bull rider who was also popular with the ladies. "You let the wrong girl get away, son. For sure, for sure."

At least Cord isn't pining after the woman he couldn't have.

"Good luck, buddy," Tate told Cord. He un-

wrapped his cookie and turned to go, unexpectedly crashing into a cowgirl wearing an apron
and smelling like smoked barbecue. Dropping his
cookie, he reached out to take her arms, steadying
her. "Sorry. My fault." But shoot. He'd stepped
on his cookie.

"Tate? Tate Oakley?" The cowgirl's features
came into focus. Deep green eyes, pert little nose
and a smile that had always made him long for
something more, much to the detriment of his
friendship with her and his relationship with Buck
back in the day. "It's me! Ellie Rowland."

Tate didn't know whether to whoop or vomit.

Before he settled on a reaction, Ellie threw
her arms around Tate's neck and hugged him so
enthusiastically that her cowboy hat fell to the
ground.

I'M HUGGING TATE.

Ellie stumbled back in wonder because she'd
latched on to him tighter than a starfish did a
rock in low tide.

I hugged Tate.

Ellie picked up her hat and slapped it against
her thigh, dusting it off before putting it back onto
her muddled head. She'd never dared hug Tate so
completely before.

She stared at the cowboy in front of her, drinking him in. "I'm so happy to see you."

"Hey… Ellie…" Tate took a step away from her and into the friend zone.

And not the BFF zone. No, his was the *barely know ya* zone.

Thoughts about hugs disappeared, and the need for words pressed down on her.

Words. The right words…

I miss being good friends, Ellie wanted to say.

I made a mistake, Ellie wanted to say.

I'm sorry I hurt you, Ellie wanted to say.

"I was just thinking about you the other day," she said instead, touching the scar on her lip briefly, self-consciously. "I drove by the high school and all these memories came flooding back." The good and the bad. The things she regretted. The smile of a kind young cowboy when she'd needed it.

She hadn't been thinking that Tate would mature into such a good-looking man. Tall, broad-shouldered, features more defined. He had the same sweet brown eyes and swoon-worthy, thick, dark eyebrows. But his smile… His smile was guarded. Or perhaps it was just diluted by the beard he'd grown.

No. Ellie hadn't been pondering what a handsome man Tate would turn out to be. She'd been thinking her life might have taken a different path had she handled Tate's answer to her Valentine's Day note like the adult she was today. Because…

Ellie's gaze brushed over Tate's whisker-fringed lips, drifting up to meet his gaze, which was trained on her face.

He caught me staring at his lips!

Her cheeks began to feel hot.

The silence stretched between them. Ellie needed to say something, not just stand there in front of Tate. "Um… I'm sorry my family roped you in." She made a half-hearted gesture toward the cookie table.

Tate glanced at Gigi and the girls while an announcement was made over the loudspeaker about contestants needing to show up for the team roping competition.

A handsome young cowboy behind Tate chuckled and gave Gigi a friendly wave before moving on, cookie in hand.

"He's not mad at us, Mom. He bought a cookie." Della sidled closer, hitching up her blue jeans on her slender frame and stepping on what must have been the remains of Tate's Valentine's Day purchase.

"Do you know him, Mom?" Lulu scurried to stand in between Ellie and Tate, swishing the skirt of her pink dress and staring up at him. "My name's Lulu Rowland Jones, and that's my twin sister, Della. Have we met before, mister?"

Tate blinked and seemed to come out of whatever stupor seeing Ellie had put him in.

I still have the power to knock Tate speechless.

A small thrill wound its way through Ellie, a thrill she hadn't experienced in a long time.

"Miss Lulu..." Tate straightened Lulu's cowgirl hat, as if he was used to interacting with kids, although there was no ring on his finger. "You and I haven't met before. I'm Tate, and I'm pleased to know you and your fine sister."

Ellie hurried to introduce him to her maternal grandmother. "I went to school with Tate," she told her family, unable to keep her eyes off him. "It's been a long time, Tate. We should catch up." *So I can apologize.*

"I'd like that." Tate's gaze may or may not have drifted in the direction of her ringless left hand.

Another small thrill energized her.

Tate smiled a little. A very little. "But I've got to get my horse for the team roping event."

And yet, his boots didn't move.

"And I've got to get back to the barbecue booth." And yet, Ellie's boots didn't budge either. But her mouth sure did. "I was hired to cook for a company that has food booths at various fairs and rodeos in eastern Oklahoma. I wasn't really looking for a job, but they liked the fact that I'm a chef and could just step in and take charge. Plus they let me fiddle with their sauces and make them my own. It was kind of a last-minute thing. And Dad wanted us out of the house at least one day a week. He says he needs his peace and quiet, although I'm not so sure. But the job...my job...

it's a great job because it's mostly weekends. Plus Gigi can rent a table to sell cookies, and…" *I should shut up.* "I'm babbling. I'll stop." Before she spilled the reason why it had taken her so long to get up here after Dad had his stroke.

Tate always unsettled me.

Tate continued to give her that reined-in smile. "No need to apologize for that. Or for…for anything."

Including my Valentine's Day mistake?

Tate wasn't a mind reader. He didn't answer her question. Instead he said, "See you around." He tipped his straw cowboy hat and left them.

I will not watch him walk away.

I will not watch him…

I will not…

Tate looked almost as good walking away as he did just standing in front of her. Familiar. Safe. A real friend.

Ellie frowned. She wasn't watching him the way she would a friend.

"Ellie, I'm going to do you a favor and tell you the truth." Gigi flung her thick tangle of white hair over her shoulder. "You let the wrong man get away."

I did indeed.

Ellie faced her outspoken grandmother. "You need a few new ideas for your act. I'm either pining for someone or I let the wrong one get away."

"Pish." Gigi waved Ellie's teasing aside and

then leaned forward, beckoning the twins closer. "Girls, what your mother *doesn't know* is that those two sentiments—*pining for someone* and *letting the wrong one get away*—sum up almost all the world's love problems."

"Girls, what your mother *knows* is that there is work to be done." Ellie picked up her girls' hats by their crowns before plopping them back on their sweet heads. "We want the goodwill of rodeo contestants, not to be a nuisance. Don't drag folks over and pressure them to buy. Promise?"

"We promise." Lulu nodded solemnly.

"Yep." Della shook her head vigorously in agreement.

Neither one was believable.

Ellie waggled her finger at them. "Tonight we're going to have to talk about sincere promises on the drive home."

It didn't escape Ellie's notice that Gigi didn't promise anything. But she had no time to argue. She had barbecue to make, and the day was flying by.

CHAPTER TWO

"You LOOK LIKE you've seen a ghost." Ryan pressed Prince's reins into Tate's hand, having been waiting for him in the arena's staging area behind the cattle chute. "What's wrong?"

Tate's twin could read him too well. They were identical, after all. Same height, same build, same dark hair and stubborn jaw. It was just Tate's beard that made it easy to tell them apart.

"I just saw Ellie Rowland." And Tate still wasn't sure what to think about it.

"Oh." The way Ryan said *Oh* made it sound as if he'd seen her already. "I was going to tell you about her."

That she looked like a field of spring wildflowers and smelled like a hearty picnic lunch? That she had two precocious kids and hugged him like she'd never let go? "She's working one of the food booths."

"Uh-huh." Ryan turned away and led his horse, Pauper, toward the entrance that led into the rodeo arena. He was dressed similarly to Tate in blue jeans, a blue button-down shirt with the Done Roamin' Ranch logo on the back and a working man's straw cowboy hat.

"*Uh-huh?* What's that supposed to mean?" Tate hurried to catch up to his brother.

"She's back in Clementine." Ryan gave Tate an assessing glance, no doubt trying to gauge Ellie's effect on him. "Her dad had that stroke a few weeks ago. I thought you knew." Ryan was plugged into the gossip grapevine because his *mother-in-law-to-be* served on various committees in Clementine. "She's a chef now, I think."

"We drove ninety miles out here and this is the first time you thought to mention Ellie to me?" Tate wasn't mad. Exactly. "I literally ran into her. She threw me for a loop." He still felt numb, an unusual feeling for him. But it was kind of a happy numb, if such a thing existed.

"This is a good test for us, then." Ryan nodded briskly.

"What are you talking about?" The woman he'd been hung up on since high school was back in town. "It's not a test. It's mind blowing."

How was he supposed to react to her? They couldn't just pick up where they'd left off before that valentine. He'd turned her down, quashing their friendship. Then she'd married Buck and followed him to Texas for his military career as an airplane mechanic.

End. Of. Story.

"It's a test," Ryan insisted. "This year is going to be tough, tougher than last year." When Tate had wanted to quit. "We need to make the postseason this fall so we can buy Prince and Pauper instead of leasing them."

Since they couldn't afford to buy them outright, Jo Pierce had agreed to lease the talented competition horses to them for the rodeo season, payments due monthly. Their foster parents had signed on as sponsors in December, helping Ryan and Tate afford the big down payment Jo required. Their lease ended this December, at which time they'd have the option to purchase them. And the only way to take advantage of that option was to win. A lot. And then win in the postseason, where all the largest purses were up for grabs.

"The next few months are going to be full of ups and downs," Ryan continued, tone turning serious. "But we need to be steady in the saddle. So...let's see how you do after having been thrown for a loop. Ellie always had a way of messin' with your head."

"I'll be fine." Tate hoped, swallowing back nerves. He didn't like to think about everyone's expectations—Ryan's, their parents', even Jo's. He slowed down as they neared the rest of the roping competitors and their mounts. Ellie represented a different kind of stress. And it had to be managed. "It's not like Ellie's going to stay in Clementine. She's probably just here to help her dad until he gets back on his feet, and then she'll return to Texas."

Except she got a job.

A job where he'd be seeing a lot of her, since he worked for their father's rodeo-stock company and competed in team roping. A man had to eat while rodeoing, didn't he? And Tate was fond of barbecue. And, of course, he'd see Ellie around town. Picking up groceries, grabbing coffee, or having a beer.

There'd be no escaping her. Or more accurately, no escaping Tate's feelings for her.

Tate took a deep breath, putting a halt to his growing panic. Her job was temporary. Seasonal, like the rodeo. She'd made a life for herself in Texas for over a decade.

She won't stay.

The thought allowed him to breathe easier. If he didn't expect people to stay, he didn't get hurt.

Recently, that axiom was proven true. He and Ryan had reconnected with their biological mother, helping her repair a small ranchette in nearby Friar's Creek. Tate had expected her to stay and for them to finally become a family. And then, she'd disappeared without warning.

And during her absence…

Tate's stomach had been tied in knots and Ryan had recited multiple versions of *I told you so.*

I told you not to believe a word she said. I told

*you not to give her money. I told you she'd leave.
I told you not to care.*

Tate found that last bit impossible.

Thankfully, their biological mother had returned home a few weeks ago, sober and with a small herd of alpaca. She'd also had another long list of things she wanted to do at the ranchette. Or more accurately, a long list she wanted Tate and Ryan to do for her. And although Tate was trying to be a good son, he worried that she'd fall off the wagon and take off again, perhaps for good.

People leaving was the story of Tate and Ryan's life. It's what folks they cared for did to them before they'd been placed in foster care at the Done Roamin' Ranch. And Ellie would be no different. Her life was in Texas and had been for years. She hadn't come home, not even for Christmas. The best Tate could do was smile and keep her at a distance, which was a different kind of heart-break.

Prince nudged Tate's shoulder with his nose and then nibbled on his shirt collar, demanding attention.

Tate chuckled, turning to scratch beneath his horse's forelock. He and the playful brown speed demon had bonded since the lease agreement had been signed before Christmas. "You're just as much of a mischief-maker as..."

Ellie's family.

Her grandmother and those two girls were a handful. Selling cookies and love advice?

Tate smiled, imagining Ellie trying to wrangle that trio.

Back in school, Ellie had wrangled whoever wanted to be in her universe, which was practically everybody. She'd been active in student government, on the yearbook committee, in the Future Farmers club. And whatever she spent her energy on, Ellie made sure her friends chipped in, too. Rallies, fundraisers, dances.

Tate had been smitten from the moment she'd told him, *Don't just stand there taking up air, make yourself useful.*

He'd tried to make himself indispensable to her after that. Because making himself useful to Ellie meant all that sunshine was directed his way. Since his parents were more like fast-moving storm clouds, Tate was drawn to Ellie's warm and steady sunbeams. But the move to Clementine and a foster home on a rodeo-stock ranch meant Tate couldn't always stay in Ellie's sphere of light. He had rodeos to work and chores to attend to. Homework and other friends to keep up with. He had a life he liked, because his foster parents actually made sure he had decent clothes to wear, a clean bed to sleep in, and food in his belly. For once, Tate and Ryan fit in. And Tate wanted to make sure they fit in everywhere. Forever.

But as much as Tate smiled and participated in

every activity or offer anyone made to him, he couldn't quite make himself the one Ellie relied on. That was the boy who had once been his foster brother, Buck. The boy who needed a friend badly because he could never make the right choice. The boy whose only friend was Tate because Tate was the one who couldn't say no.

Back then, Ellie had driven a wreck of a truck with rusted-out fenders and a sticky carburetor that sometimes stranded her when she had no time to be stuck. Buck was handy with anything mechanical. He was the one Ellie turned to for help with engine trouble. It made sense that Ellie and Buck would start dating. And given Buck's roving eye, it made sense that they were on-again, off-again.

And then somehow, without Tate realizing it, he became Ellie and Buck's go-between when they were off-again.

Torture.

His foster family at the Done Roamin' Ranch told him to choose a side, but Tate couldn't hurt either one of them. He didn't want to *make* anyone leave him. He'd had enough of that pain to last him a lifetime.

And then came the Valentine's Day note.

Tate had shown up in the science lab and sat down next to Ellie, his lab partner. *Everything okay?*

I think we should go out, Ellie said without

looking at him. The frog they were due to dissect sat on a tray in front of her. *Tonight*.

At the time, Tate hadn't said a word. Not a yes. Not a no. What could he say? His moment with Ellie had finally rolled around, but if he said yes, he'd drive Buck away. And if he said no, he might lose Ellie. Forever.

"You ready?" Ryan shook Tate's shoulder, bringing him back to the present, to rodeo dust and the constant noise of the crowd. His twin nodded in the direction of the Pierce brothers, who'd been killing it on the Prairie Circuit for years on horses trained by their sister Jo, the same woman who'd trained Ryan and Tate's horses. "Those guys don't know it yet, but this is our year."

It's safer not to try than to fail.

That was his mother's voice, drifting into Tate's head along with the memory of a weak hug.

"You can do this, Tate," Ryan said, just on cue. "Just like in practice."

"No pressure." Tate forced himself to smile as if he hadn't a care in the world. Not one worry about beating the Pierces for the next six or seven months and proving to his foster parents that he was worth the investment. Not one worry about making a quick, accurate throw so Ryan could do the same, earning enough money to make Prince his permanently. Not one worry about Ellie living in the same zip code as he did.

It *was* safer not to try. But he'd made a commitment to do just that.

No pressure. No pressure at all.

Still, Tate's mouth was as dry as a July prairie.

And maybe his twin didn't know Tate as well as he assumed because Ryan returned Tate's smile and said, "Postseason, here we come."

"As I LIVE and breathe. It's Ellie Rowland!" Bess Glover practically stuck her head through the order window at Curly's BBQ Shack, long red hair, blue cowboy hat and all. "I heard you were back. Didn't expect to see you at the rodeo."

"Why not?" Ellie resisted touching her scarred lip. "I used to rodeo."

"Yeah, but you didn't used to *cook*." Bess grinned, looking just as friendly as she'd been back in high school. Or perhaps it was just that her blue cowboy hat and red hair brought out the freckles that dusted her cheeks and nose.

They had freckles in common.

"I learned to cook." Ellie told her, not without a goodly dose of pride. "When I got to Texas, I was guilted into putting more effort in the kitchen by the other military wives. And then I realized that I loved it. I'm a formally trained chef now." She gestured toward the side door of the booth. "Do you have a minute? I'd love to catch up." Business was slow. And Bess might spill some details about Tate.

"Sure." Bess came around, looking cowgirl chic in her black-denim duster over her frilly white blouse and blue jeans.

"What brings you to the rodeo?" Ellie asked, indicating that Bess should sit on a stool near the door. Aubrey, her teenage coworker, was on break, so they'd have a few minutes alone.

"I teach at the high school and coach the rodeo team. I'm here to watch some of my former students try to make it to the big time." Before Bess sat on the stool, she leaned back out the door. "Hey, Katie. Come say hi to Ellie Rowland." That sparked a wave of spreading enthusiasm.

Katie called Dinah.

Dinah called Ronnie.

Ronnie called Jen.

And soon, a group of Ellie's school friends were crowded outside the booth's side entrance.

Ellie gave them the short version of why she was back in Oklahoma, although she stopped short of saying she was home to stay. She wasn't quite sure of that herself. And her friends? Her friends had a range of tales to tell.

"I'm getting married to Wade Keller the Sunday before Valentine's Day." Ronnie Pickett flashed her engagement ring. "Less than two weeks away."

"I went away to college, had my heart crushed and came home with a business degree," Katie said with a laugh. "I'm working at the brewery while my degree collects dust."

"Married. Divorced. Married again. Divorced again," Dinah said, smiling happily. "I've got two kids, a good horse, a loyal dog, and I'm content."

"I rodeo, therefore I am." Jen grinned. "I'm still horse crazy. Still single. And still looking for who knows what."

They all laughed.

Ellie felt welcomed back to the fold. There were stories of failure, of survival, of love and triumph. But there were no stories of Tate.

As the women dispersed, promising to meet up at The Buckboard soon, Ellie stopped Bess. "I saw Tate Oakley earlier. Why isn't he married?"

"That is the million-dollar question." Bess chuckled, adjusting the tilt of her blue cowboy hat. "He's still single, but it's not because he isn't looking. He's dated more than his share of single women. More even than Griff." Her mirth vanished, an indication that she still bore a grudge against the guy who'd stood her up on prom night. "Tate is the most sought-after bachelor in town. And yet I can't remember him ever having a long-term relationship. But this year, he's dated even less. Folks say it's because he's saving every penny to buy that competitive horse he's leasing." She shrugged. "But that doesn't explain the last decade."

Before Ellie could ask more questions, Gigi and

the twins arrived. Apparently, the girls ran out of energy about the time they sold out of cookies. Bess was happy to meet everyone and then left them to watch the next rodeo event.

"Mom, we saw Mr. Tate rope a cow." Della pretended to throw a rope, going through the motions with over-dramatic flair. "*Wah-pow!* So fast!"

"And do you know what?" Lulu twirled a lock of her reddish-brown hair, the way she did when she was tired. She yawned, not even pivoting to make her skirt sway. "Mr. Tate has a twin who looks just like him."

"Except for the beard." Della hitched up her blue jeans.

"I'm partial to the beard." Gigi stood in the doorway. "And the way this place smells. So good. For sure, for sure."

Ellie set about feeding them. But all the while, she wondered why the nicest, most handsome cowboy in Clementine was still single.

"THESE OKLAHOMA COWBOYS are suckers for love advice," Gigi said to Ellie as they neared Clementine long after the sun went down. "Handsome, too. Especially that cowboy you hugged. What was his name again?"

Ellie wasn't fooled. Her grandmother had the memory of an elephant. "Don't get any ideas about Tate," Ellie glanced in the rearview mirror to make sure her daughters were still asleep. "We were friends. *Friends.* And then we weren't. Not exactly a happy ending. He's a dead end romance-wise. And besides, you know I don't date."

But I hugged Tate.

And it had felt like the best of homecomings.

"Hard to understand why you live like an old maid." There was eye-rolling impertinence in Gigi's tease. "I know the length and tone of your lonely sighs when you watch a sunset. You want to be in love."

Ellie pressed her tongue against the back of her top front teeth. She hadn't told anyone why she chose not to date.

The truth was Ellie wanted to find someone special to share life's daily ups and downs with. She'd always dreamed of having a big family, and that family included a loving, faithful husband.

But every time she let herself dream about such a life, Ellie remembered the day after her calf-roping accident eighteen months ago. She'd been banged up pretty bad—stitches in her lip, her two top teeth loose, her eyes black and blue. Ellie had looked like a hockey player who'd been on the receiving end of a brutal body check.

She'd taken the day off to recuperate and see the dentist. While the kids were at school and Buck was at work, she'd opened her front door to an intervention of sorts. Two women who worked with Buck at the military base entered the house, each with a story about romances with Ellie's husband.

She'd been sucker-punched.

Even though Buck hadn't been the most faithful of boyfriends, she'd never imagined he'd break their wedding vows.

What a fool she'd been.

After the women left, Ellie had felt as bad on the inside as she looked on the outside, her confidence in herself shaken. There was a scar on her lip and the suspicion that she wasn't enough… *something*…to make her man stay faithful.

Later, after the divorce papers had been signed, that feeling of self-lacking had stuck in her head, not receded like her scar. And as for dating…

Ellie hit a pothole in the road.

A new man? Nope. She wasn't going to hope. Years ago, she'd thrown herself at Tate. And he'd backed away, almost like he had today. Proof that she wasn't enough for him. Heck, if what Bess said was true, no woman was.

Ellie had other places requiring her energy.

She had to be strong enough for Dad, who was still mourning Mom two decades after her passing, and who'd never be able to run the family sheep ranch alone again. She had to be loving enough for the twins, who were still adjusting from the divorce and were gamely going with the flow of their impromptu move from Texas. And she had to be supportive enough for Gigi, who'd come from Sedona to help Dad, her son-in-law, when Dad had his stroke and Ellie couldn't get home right away. Gigi was a retired nurse who loved her life in Sedona. But she'd agreed to stay as long as Ellie and her father needed her.

And once this crisis was past, Ellie had to decide what the next phase of her life would hold and where that would be. She had a nest egg, a combination of funds from her savings and the divorce settlement. In an ideal world, she'd open a restaurant. Food was her passion, after all. But restaurant ownership and head chef jobs weren't conducive to being a good mother. It had taken Buck to point that out during their divorce.

Why did it matter that Ellie wasn't enough for a man? She had no space in her life for one.

Ellie shook her head. "If I were to date someone, it would be a man who thinks I can hang the moon, a guy who can be true to me." And that wouldn't be Tate.

Oh, he respected her enough. And he was loyal, all right. But Tate was loyal to his foster family, not her.

CHAPTER THREE

"WE SHOULD BE CELEBRATING," Ryan told Tate the morning after their first-place finish at the rodeo.

They'd won a decent purse and a pair of lariats. Professionally, things were looking up. That didn't mean Tate's confidence was anywhere near solidified. He was already half-dreading next weekend's competition. Forget it being safer not to try. It was less stressful, too.

"Why am I getting out of bed early?" Ryan yawned from the passenger seat of Tate's truck, tugging the brim of his cowboy hat low to shade his eyes from the bright winter sun. "It's my day off."

"Mom said there's a problem with the alpacas. We need to check in on her, and I only have the morning off." Tate sipped his coffee, one hand on the wheel as he drove them toward Friar's Creek, the next town over from Clementine. The narrow, rural two-lane road passed by cattle ranches, empty fields and the occasional orchard, not a high-rise or an interstate freeway in sight. "She texted me in the middle of the night."

Two words: Alpaca emergency.

Her texts were rarely longer than two words, as if saying more might give her carefully guarded emotions away.

Ryan shook his head. "You checked your messages in the middle of the night?"

"Yeah." Actually, Tate hadn't slept well. He'd been plagued by thoughts of Ellie, past and present.

What was he going to say to Ellie the next time he saw her? He didn't want to hurt her feelings but… She wasn't going to stay. She was a chef. There were no chefs in Clementine. He wanted to keep her at a distance. The problem was that he'd never been able to keep her at a distance, the same as he'd never been able to refuse his biological mother anything when she asked. Because he wanted more from both women. But he was afraid his mother could never give him the stable relationship he wanted and if he pursued something with Ellie, he'd never recover if it didn't work out.

"Alpacas are trouble," Ryan said, derision in his voice. He scuffed his cowboy boots against the plastic floor liner. "I can only hope her text means they've been stolen."

"Ry…" Tate's twin and his mother were only newly on speaking terms and had a long way to go before they'd be comfortable with each other the way true family was supposed to be. Not that Tate's relationship with her was leaps and bounds better. Still, Tate held out hope for the three of them.

"What? You don't hope the alpacas are gone when we get there?" Ryan scoffed. "Last week, she called because she couldn't figure out how to reboot her garbage disposal after she clogged it with carrot tops. And let's not forget that she was gone for over a month without answering your calls or texts. Mom isn't, like…our *mom*." Mary Harrison, their foster mother. "And on that note, if she's going to stay around, we need to start calling her something else."

"Agreed." They'd been calling Mary *Mom* for nearly twenty years.

Donna Oakley, their biological mother, hadn't earned the title even for the twelve years they'd "lived" with her, although she was trying now. In her own way. In a sense that wasn't enough for Tate. He kept trying to draw her out, to encourage the fragile mother-son bond that he had with his foster mother.

They drove a few more miles in silence. And that silence allowed memories of Ellie to return, as bright and vivid as if they'd happened yesterday.

Ellie ran up behind Tate in the high school hallway, looping her arm through his. It was as if they'd always been close. "Why are you dating Nia Plevins? She's not your type."

"She asked me out, sunshine." Tate shrugged.

And the girl who was exactly his type was taken. "Besides, Nia has a car." Tate had given the money he'd been saving toward buying a truck to his biological mother the last time she'd passed through town.

"You don't date someone just because they have transportation." Ellie laughed. "I have wheels, and you haven't asked me out."

"You're spoken for," Tate said gruffly.

"Most days anyway." Ellie had laughed again, although this time without much humor. "Can I count on you to help decorate our homecoming float? You're the best with power tools."

He'd agreed, just like he agreed with anything she asked.

"Pinkie swear?" Ellie extended her hand, pinkie out.

Tate shook it.

He liked being needed. People who needed you were less likely to disappear.

Ellie and Buck disappeared. To Texas. And hadn't looked back.

That hurt. Still did.

The sight of an old swayback mare in a pasture to his right brought Tate back to the present and the onset of their turn.

"Can we just call her mother?" Ryan asked in obvious frustration. "I mentally vetoed calling her ma, mommy or mama."

"Calling her mother will hurt her feelings,"

Tate felt compelled to say. And hurt feelings made her disappear, sometimes for years.

"Like it didn't hurt ours when she and Dad left us alone, hungry and in the cold so often when we were kids? For days? Even on Christmas?" Ryan sipped his coffee while Tate fought images of frigid nights spent in the cold back seat of a car parked at some dive bar. "If you're worried about hurt feelings, I suppose calling her Donna is out."

"Yes." Tate made the turn onto an even narrower road and approached the small ranchette their mother rented.

"This is why you're known around town as the nice Oakley." Ryan smirked. "I would have settled on *Mother* and been done with it."

Tate parked his truck behind their mother's car. "I think we should call her Ms. Alpaca, like it's a fond nickname." Who knows? In an ideal world, it might become one if she stayed.

If she stayed.

Tate didn't like it that he had doubts.

"A *fond* nickname?" Ryan got out of the truck just as their mother opened the front door of her one-story blue cottage.

But even if Ryan was sometimes jaded where their biological mother was concerned, he'd recently bent when it came to dealing with her, as evidenced by his cheerful greeting. "Hey, Ms. Alpaca, what's the issue with your flock?" Ryan leaned back into the truck and said to Tate, "You owe me breakfast for this."

"Sure." Tate got out of the truck and politely hugged their mother after Ryan dutifully did. "Now, what's the problem with the alpacas?"

Their mother was short and nonathletic in both build and movement. She wore a floppy hat, a lightweight coat and blue jeans. No cowboy boots for her. She preferred sneakers, walking with the slow, stilted gait of someone in her eighties, not her fifties. "I need someone to give the herd a haircut."

"You mean *shear* them?" Ryan frowned. "I thought you were partnering with a guy who was going to take care of all that and in exchange you were going to spin the wool from your alpacas and his."

"Oh, that." She waved Ryan's comments aside. "My so-called partnership dissolved after the first of the year. It seemed destined to fail, so why bother? Sometimes it's safer not to try."

"Why bother?" Ryan muttered, shaking his head. He caught Tate's eye. "No pain, no gain."

Tate nodded as if he shared Ryan's philosophy one hundred percent, as if he harbored no self-doubt.

Their mother blinked her big brown eyes, seemingly unfazed by Ryan's sarcasm. Since she'd sobered up, she'd lived life in a bubble of sorts, never rising to anger or falling into tears. Or anything in between. There was a distance to her, like she was floating above the world, cradled in the puffiest of clouds. Tate wasn't sure if that was a good or bad thing.

"Do you know a sheep shearer?" she asked.

Ryan shook his head.

"I...do," Tate said unevenly, feeling as if he'd had the wind knocked out of him. "Ellie Rowland."

She'd been proud of her skill back in the day, showing her scrapes and bruises from helping her family shear to anyone willing to stop and see.

"Bad idea." Ryan shook his head again. "We'll find someone else."

"Ellie sounds wonderful," their mother said in that far-off way of hers.

"Tate didn't say anything about her," Ryan muttered.

Their mother led them around the side of the house to the pasture where six alpacas of different sizes and shades grazed. "It's what Tate *didn't* say, Ryan. His words carried weight, as if he believes in Ellie."

Tate couldn't argue with that. Whatever Ellie set her mind to, she did a good job of.

Almost as one, the alpaca herd raised their heads when the trio appeared, curious about their visitors. Their eyes were so big and their fur was so thick that they looked like huggable, stuffed animals. Cute and cuddly. Simple and relaxing.

Every time he saw the alpacas, Tate understood why his mother wanted to raise them.

Tate felt his breath come easier just taking them in. "Admit it, Ry. Cows aren't this cute."

"I'll give you that," Ryan said, smiling a little. He wasn't immune to the alpacas either.

A black alpaca, taller than the rest, joyfully skipped over, mouth curled as if she was smiling.

That was another positive characteristic of alpacas. They bounced and pranced happily. Their spirits never seemed to flag. To them, every day was the best day ever.

"Hello, Sheila." Tate reached over the five-foot-tall fence to scratch the black alpaca's head. Her fur was as soft as her personality. Sheila was the friendliest of the lot. She followed them around on the property like a devoted canine.

"If you're not shearing them yourself or entering into a partnership to have it done, what did you decide about processing their wool, Ms. Alpaca?" Ryan asked, chucking a small gray alpaca beneath its chin. "Are you going to wash and dry the wool yourself? Along with spinning it into yarn?" That had been her plan at first.

"The co-op will offer me a handsome price for their wool." Their mother opened the gate and entered the enclosure, greeting her charges with more effusive affection than she had her two sons. "And then I don't have to do any of that washing and spinning. Just the raising and the loving."

"And the shearing," Ryan muttered. He was always touchy when their mother talked about love for something other than them.

Tate elbowed him. "It seems like the raising is what makes you happy. Maybe you should stick to that. It'll be warm enough to shear them soon. I'll ask Ellie if she's interested in the work."

Ryan rolled his eyes. "He'll take any excuse to talk to her."

Tate elbowed him again, even if it was true.

"Yes, send Ellie my way. I'm sure she'll be perfect." Their mother gestured to the young, bare trees lining the fence that separated the backyard from the pasture. "I'd like to trim the trees today. They need cutting back before the buds appear."

Tate looked at Ryan. Ryan looked at Tate.

Tate didn't think either of them had ever trimmed a tree before. The Done Roamin' Ranch always hired a professional tree trimmer when the need arose.

"I've got everything right here." Their mother walked to the back porch, where she'd assembled a variety of saws, loppers and clippers.

Ryan gave Tate a friendly slug to the shoulder. "Breakfast and lunch. That's what you'll owe me for this."

Tate nodded.

The trees were slim and only a few years old. But there were a lot of them. By the time they were finished helping Ms. Alpaca, Ryan claimed that Tate owed him breakfast, lunch *and* dinner.

"WHAT ARE YOU…up to today, Ellie?" Dad asked slowly late Monday morning. He sat at the kitchen table in an oak captain's chair, his walker within easy reach, his speech not as flowing as it had been before the stroke. "Prepping…to make us another…fantastic dinner?"

"The fact that I'm getting out your toolbox after breakfast should tell you." Ellie poured him a small cup of coffee. "I'm surveying the pastures and sheds for needed repairs." Cooking was the least of her worries. To the trained eye, the ranch was falling apart. It had been neglected long before Dad's stroke.

"You need to leave…repairs to Robbie." Dad's features were a bit lopsided, impacted by the stroke, as were his limbs. But he'd been lucky. He could still walk, if slowly and assisted, and talk, although the words were sometimes elusive. "Robbie said…he'd be down…this weekend."

"He said he'd be down *last* weekend," Gigi muttered into her tea mug without so much as a jingle in her bangles.

Yes, Ellie's older brother had said he'd be down this weekend. And the weekend before. And the weekend before that. And the weekend *after* Dad's stroke.

Ellie sighed. It didn't matter how many times

Robbie was a no-show or that she'd arrived in Clementine with two kids and three horses, her father assumed Ellie would be going back to Texas soon.

To be fair, Ellie hadn't come home at all during her marriage. She'd flown Dad down to Texas for holidays and birthday visits. Things with Buck hadn't been easy, even in the beginning, and she hadn't wanted to put on a brave front during visits home to Clementine.

"Robbie will…take over the ranch," Dad said with utmost authority.

It was the same tone he'd used after Mom had died and they'd fought over preteen Ellie helping on the ranch. Back then, Dad and Robbie had needed an extra pair of hands. Back then, she'd proven she could do it. Had the stroke taken those memories? The ones where Ellie had proved helpful around the ranch? Or was Dad just being the curmudgeon he'd become after being widowed?

"Dad, until Robbie takes over, I'm going to handle things," Ellie said firmly. She poured herself a cup of coffee. She'd made it just the way she liked it—thick as mud, strong as a gut punch. "I plan to run errands when I pick up the kids from school later. Make sure you add whatever you need to the list."

She kept a running list on the refrigerator. It included a variety of items from a head of lettuce to a box of half penny nails.

"You should…ask Robbie…what needs doing."

There went Dad again, touting Robbie as the family savior.

Ellie loved her older brother, but Robbie was the first Rowland to graduate from college. He worked in the marketing department of a national fast-food chain based in Oklahoma City. He was never going to move back to Clementine and run the sheep ranch.

"*I* don't need to ask Robbie," Gigi said crisply, nose in the air. Her thick white hair tumbled down her back. "I'm doing a cleanse of the barn with sage. I feel a presence when I go in there."

"Rats," Dad said straight-faced, making Ellie laugh. "No barn cat. Not since last summer."

"Or a dog." Ellie missed having a dog. Buck had kept the family's German shepherd in exchange for Ellie keeping her horse. Not exactly the fairest of exchanges.

Don't go there, girl.

She'd much rather think about Tate in her arms before he'd retreated to the friend zone yesterday.

Don't go there either.

Ellie moved restlessly around the kitchen, sipping her coffee and reminding herself that she wasn't looking for romance. She was looking for a place to settle down. And it didn't feel like it would be Texas.

But standing in her mother's kitchen, taking in the things her mother had loved, like the antique salt-and-pepper shakers shaped like a Victorian couple and the rose-trimmed tea kettle on the top shelf, this house didn't feel like her destination either.

Maybe it was because of unsettling memories. She'd stood at this stove after Mom died, trying to make dinner, only to have Dad kick her out, telling her gruffly, *Your mother wouldn't want you to feel tied to this ranch or this kitchen.*

That had never made sense to Ellie. Dad was so proud of being a third-generation rancher. Who did he think would carry on the family legacy? Robbie had always talked about college. It was Ellie who'd wanted to stay back then. At least, until she'd felt unwanted.

Sighing, she took stock of the contents of the refrigerator.

"It's almost spring. There'll be lots of kittens looking for homes soon," Gigi predicted with a shake of her bangles. "You should get a pair of cats. You never know what might happen to one."

"That's dark." Ellie noted, adding broccoli to the list on the refrigerator.

"We should wait…for Robbie…before we make…decisions." Dad removed a small rose quartz from his breast pocket, examined it and placed it with a shaky hand on the table. "What's this?"

"You need to keep that rock close to your

heart." Gigi snatched up the quartz and rubbed it between her palms. "It'll help your heart chakra."

"I...don't believe in...that *woo-woo* stuff... Gigi," Dad said in a slow cadence. "And nei-ther...did Irene." Gigi's daughter. His wife. El-lie's mother.

"*Woo-woo?*" Gigi fairly trembled with agita-tion. Her bangles clanked. Her dangly earrings jingled. Her chair creaked as she leaned forward and said in a hard voice, "My darling son-in-law, you don't know what my daughter believed. And since you're not in the best of health, you should be thankful of any extra energy I send your way." She dropped the quartz on the table. It clattered and bounced toward Dad before coming to rest within his reach.

He didn't touch it.

Ellie sipped her coffee. Her father and grand-mother poked and prodded each other. Always had. Always would.

"You know, visualizing the future has power," Gigi snapped. "If you see yourself recovering, you'll recover. And if you don't, you don't. It's not *woo-woo*. It's the power of positive thinking amplified by the natural energy in things, like that quartz."

With a lopsided grin, Dad leaned toward Ellie, nearly falling over before she caught him. "*Woo-woo.*"

They all laughed, even Gigi.

"You're as stubborn as the day Irene married you." Gigi shook her head with a smile.

"Woo-woo," Dad repeated with that off-kilter grin.

"As fun as this is, I've got to get moving." Ellie finished her coffee.

A few minutes later, she drove Dad's ancient red ranch truck past the corrals with her horses. Then she drove through the metal gate leading to the road that cut between a series of sheep pastures.

She glanced around. "You're not in Texas anymore, Ellie."

The smogless blue sky. The brownish-green prairie grass dotted with small white wildflowers. The occasional scrub oaks. The sheep wandering the fields, bleating as she drove past. Even the cracked dashboard of her father's ranch truck, its worn leather seats and the eight-ball handle on the stick shift. It all called to her in a way that said, *You belong here.*

For the first time that day, Ellie breathed easier.

Texas had never been home. There, she'd been career focused and had little time or energy to really plug into the network of military spouses and make solid friendships. When she and Buck divorced, Ellie had quit her job as a head chef. She'd found work in a fancy lunch bistro. But she'd been adrift, as if waiting for something to happen before making a decision about what came next for her and the twins. Because she wasn't happy.

She didn't think she'd been waiting for Dad to have a stroke. But upon hearing the news, she'd quit the bistro, packed up the girls and loaded the horse trailer, more than ready for a change. But was this the change she needed? Returning home to the ranch and past friendships?

Something fluttered in her chest as she remembered how good hugging Tate had been, how satisfying it was to wrap her arms around those broad shoulders. She could almost imagine his whiskers brushing her cheek…

Ellie rolled her eyes.

"I need to get a dog," she said out loud. A loving, furry creature to cuddle up to her. A release for all this pent-up, misplaced longing.

Ellie forced her attention back to the out of doors and the Rowland Ranch.

Pipes ran underground on either side of the dirt road she was on, delivering well water to a watering trough in each pasture. Ellie parked next to the first two pasture gates and shelters, right in between two watering troughs. She got out, tugging on worn leather work gloves.

First, she checked that the self-filling watering troughs were working properly and that the salt licks didn't need replacing. Then she grabbed a hammer and entered the pasture, approaching the first sheep shelter. It was three-sided with a metal corrugated roof. The same style was erected in each pasture. Each structure offered respite from Oklahoma's hot summers and inclement weather for most of that pasture's herd. The shelters were the least favorite place of hers on the ranch.

Because of the spiders. They gave her the creeps.

Black widows, brown recluse, jumping spiders, tarantulas. Sticky webs woven at just the right height to cling to her face as she passed. Flies wrapped up for snacking later. Skittering movement where her hand was about to land. Finding a spider on her arm, her shoulder, in her hair.

Ellie shuddered. She'd seen and experienced all kinds of spiders at one time or another in sheep shelters.

She pulled the sleeves of her jeans jacket over her wrists and pressed her cowboy hat more firmly on her head. "Not today, arachnids."

She hefted the hammer. Spiders may be her worst enemy, but wood rot was the shelter's.

Ellie walked around it. Snippets of sheep wool clung to wood here and there. She banged the hammer on anything that looked as if water had done damage or where a nail had worked its way loose—on posts, siding and beams. She'd been taught that was the best way to find damage, but she'd learned it was the best way to scare spiders into their hidey holes. After a good hammering, Ellie tested the structure's sturdiness, pushing and pulling vertical beams. Finally she checked the roof to make sure the corrugated panels were securely fastened.

This one was in good condition.

Ellie moved on to the opposite pasture and shelter, repeating the process. Still no spiders. *Yay!*

She drove to the next set of gates, getting out for inspections and feeling lucky, so very lucky, that no spider wanted to dance with her today.

A little over an hour later, Ellie reached the last set of pastures. She had a phone filled with photographs of weather-worn shelters and a running list of needed supplies. She had to keep moving so she could finish and have a late lunch before it was time to pick up the girls from school. But she hesitated, taking in the vista before her.

Here, for a mile, the Rowland property bordered the mighty Done Roamin' Ranch. There were cattle on the other side of that fence. And somewhere over the next rise, the D Double R Ranch proper. And Tate.

At least, she assumed he still lived there. It was foolish to dwell on thoughts of him. To dally and dream. He'd turned her down before. Why torture herself when she'd only receive another rejection?

Ellie hopped out of the truck, trying to leave the past behind.

Sheep moved away when she entered the field, calling out to each other. As she conducted her last inspection, she was grateful that the hammer and the chill in the late morning air seemed to have made the spider population hunker down, out of sight.

A sound in the distance—a welcoming whinny—had her looking up.

A rider on a brown horse approached from the D Double R. He wore a red hoodie beneath a jean jacket, had a beard and a set of broad shoulders. She suspected—or wished—who was coming toward her.

And then a familiar greeting removed all doubt. "Hey, sunshine!"

The flutter in her chest returned.

"Tate." Ellie casually dropped her hammer to the ground, removed her leather gloves and tucked them in her back jeans pocket, moseying toward the fence line. Not too fast. Not too slow. Just the way she would if a so-called friend had greeted her.

Tate brought his horse to a stop near the fence, smiling and leaning on the saddle horn. His handsome face was a welcome sight, bringing that same sense of home she'd felt when she first started out this morning. "I'm riding fence. You?"

"Checking shelters. Sadly, most need maintenance." This was good. Small talk. They could pretend Valentine's Day never happened.

"Any spiders?" He glanced toward the shelter.

She shook her head. "None, thank heavens."

"Good. I remember how much you hate them."

He smiled a little. Despite its size, it was still a wonderful, magnetic smile. A *come closer* smile.

It should have felt more like a friendly smile. It shouldn't have made her heart *ka-thump, ka-thump.*

"I won't be so lucky with spiders when I do the repairs." Ellie dragged her gaze away from his wonderfulness and surveyed the nearest flock of sheep. The ewes were plump and pregnant, wearing thick coats of wool. "Soon they'll be dropping lambs. And then it'll be sheep-shearing season. I hear spring is coming early this year." If she stayed, she'd have plenty of work on the ranch to keep her busy for months. "It's going to be short-sleeve weather this week, even if it is barely February."

Tate tipped his hat back, brow wrinkling. "Are we talking about the weather?"

The prairie breeze kicked up.

Ellie nodded, pushing her straw cowboy hat down and more firmly on her head. "The weather and animal husbandry." Wasn't that what you did with *barely know ya anymore* friends?

Tate's frown didn't exactly disappear at her words, but he wasn't smiling when he absently said, "Don't forget we talked about spiders, too."

"Don't remind me." Ellie shivered.

They stared at each other for a few moments, neither speaking.

Ellie wanted to say something. She wanted to

talk about the past and her regrets or Buck and what he'd done. But she bit her lip, suspecting that Tate preferred to keep the past firmly in the past.

But to her, the past was still raw and fresh...

"I can't go out with you," Tate had told Ellie at the end of high school science lab.

He might have said no, but his eyes told a different story. His eyes were filled with longing and regret.

That look had her touching his arm, closing her fingers around his bicep, gently keeping him close so she could whisper, "It's over between Buck and me. I want a different kind of boyfriend." You, she wanted to say. Someone who sought out her company. Someone who wasn't focused on where the next party was being held. Someone she could trust her heart with.

"I can't do that to Buck," Tate said, not moving, still drinking her in with his beautiful brown eyes. "We have a code at the D Double R. No family drama. No love triangles. Even if he no longer lives with us, I can't break the code." Tate spoke this last bit softly, as if he'd wanted to add, Even for you.

A code? That explained so much. Like why Tate always helped Buck win her back. But this... Did it mean they could never be together? Ever?

Annoyance filled Ellie's teenage veins, pounding at her temples, cinching around her chest until it was hard to draw a breath. "I don't want to be friends, then."

Tate flinched, his expression suddenly sad.

Immediately, Ellie wanted to take the words back. Ultimatums worked with Buck. But with Tate... Well, she saw it now. Tate lived and breathed his foster family's code. From what little she'd gleaned about his birth parents, he was lucky to have the Harrison family.

"I'm sorry. I..." She couldn't say more.

The longing had died in Tate's gaze. Hurt replaced it. He took a step away from Ellie. And then another, bumping into a chair. Finally, Tate gave her a brisk nod. And left.

Oh, that had been painful, his leaving. She'd wanted to cry. She'd needed to cry.

Ellie ran to the girls' bathroom and shut herself in a stall, fighting tears, fighting regret, fighting the feeling that she'd made the biggest mistake of her young life. That she was alone. That she'd been alone since her mother had been killed in a car accident when she was almost twelve. That she'd always be alone and needed to be strong the way Dad and Robbie were strong. They never cried. They didn't know what to do with her when she cried. Because they didn't understand her. Not the way Tate did...

But she'd lashed out and he'd walked away.

Gone. Like Mom.

Ellie gave up trying to be strong then and

cried, stifling the sound in the sleeve of her shirt even though no one else was in the bathroom.

And then there'd been a knock on the outer bathroom door.

She'd lifted her head and whispered, "Tate?" The door opened.

"Ellie, are you in there?" It was Buck, sounding tentative and uncertain. "Tate said you were looking for me. He said you were upset. I'm sorry, honey. Can you forgive me?"

Ellie didn't want to. But there it was. The truth. Buck would always be there for her, even when no one else would.

"Yes. I... I'm here." Ellie had dried her tears, come out of hiding and gone back to Buck.

What a mistake that was.

Ellie sighed. The prairie wind kicked up again, blowing the past back where it belonged.

There was no sense admiring Tate's broad shoulders or that hint of a smile. He'd made his choice years ago. Ellie had to respect it.

Still, she felt inadequate all over again.

"Okay, um..." Tate cleared his throat. "At the risk of continuing down the conversational path of weather and ranch animals, my mother has alpaca. They'll be needing shearing this spring. Or sooner." His expression wobbled and then he said firmly, "*Sooner.* She wants them done sooner."

"They'll be a sight easier to shear given how sweet tempered they're rumored to be." Ellie flexed her fingers, feeling the muscles in her hand tightening from overuse. Wielding a hammer wasn't the same as wielding a whisk. "I'm not looking forward to sheep-shearing season. Dad didn't make arrangements for a shearer last fall." She'd discovered her father hadn't done a lot of things in a timely fashion before his stroke. "No one seems available, which means I've got to find someone somewhere to help me shear nearly five hundred sheep." That was a daunting statement. She was woefully out of shape and out of practice. "We've done it before. Just me, Robbie and Dad, but obviously that won't work this time."

It had been a fight to be included in the process then, but they'd needed her and she hadn't let them down.

"About that…" Tate's brow clouded once more. "Maybe there was no one for your dad to book. I heard Lucas Montgomery retired last fall. Could be that's why your dad didn't schedule anyone."

"That makes me feel better." At his questioning glance, she explained, "I'd been thinking Dad was living up here alone and slowly deteriorating without my knowing." Daughters were supposed to keep up-to-date when it came to their parent's health. And Ellie hadn't.

"It's hard to stay in touch with someone in Texas," Tate said in what felt like cautiously chosen words. "If that someone doesn't come home regularly."

"Agree." That was on Ellie. She wouldn't use Buck as an excuse. "But it's especially hard if they're not on social media and don't like to talk on the phone, like my dad or Buck or you."

"Point taken," Tate said without drawing a line in the sand. "If you want help here, Ellie, all you have to do is say the word. Clementine still pulls together for those in need."

"Would that include you?" she wondered aloud, glancing behind her at the precariously leaning sheep shelter because if Tate was going to exclude himself, she didn't want to witness it visually. It would be that much harder to forget.

"Yep. I'm in," he said simply.

His unexpected statement had her whipping around to look at him. From this distance, it was hard to see any subtle hint of expression beyond that dark beard of his.

Tate's horse danced, impatient to be on his way.

Tate settled him with the subtle movements and low-spoken words of a fine horseman. "I don't have much spare time and I can't shear sheep, but I can help you with repairs. Maybe... Wednesday afternoon?"

Ellie was warmed by the sincerity of his offer. But she knew that cowboys couldn't often spare time at the expense of a paycheck. "I can't pay you." She had yet to sit down and analyze the accounts, but she felt certain there wasn't much extra cash on hand, given the state of the place.

She'd have to have a talk with her father about that, too.

"I didn't ask to be paid," Tate said, again without revealing any emotion.

"Thank you, but…you helping me…" How to say this tactfully? "Won't it be…awkward?" Because it was. Now.

Tate gave his horse a pat on the neck. "We haven't talked in years, Ellie. If we were to catch up, it wouldn't be awkward. Probably. I hope, anyway." There was that tentative smile again. Just a flash before it disappeared. "And to be honest, I was wondering if you could help me shear those alpaca I mentioned in return."

"We're bartering?" she gently teased. "Shearing alpaca for help with sheep-shelter repairs? It sounds like a bad bargain…for you."

His horse pawed the ground.

"Easy, Prince." Tate tugged his hat brim down, smiling in a way she'd never seen him smile at her before, in a way that made her heart beat faster. "As I recall, Ellie, you always were good at getting folks motivated to volunteer without much in return but your thanks. You've been gone awhile, but I bet you haven't changed that much."

She felt as if she'd changed a lot but kept that to herself. "Wednesday afternoon, you say? I've got to pick up the girls from school first."

He nodded, tipping his hat. "After you pick the girls up from school. See you then."

He rode off.

A part of her wanted to follow, to revisit those times in her youth when being with Tate made things better.

But Ellie returned to her evaluation of the last shelter. Her stomach growled and her back twinged. She had a lot to do around here and not enough favors in the books to get it all done. But there was Tate's offer of help, his smile and the hug from an old friend to lift her spirits.

At least until a spider dropped onto her shoulder. *"Eeek!"*

CHAPTER FOUR

"TATE, REMIND ME why it is that you only take half days off after working all weekend?" Ryan was sacked out on the couch in the bunkhouse eating one of two ham sandwiches with an open bag of potato chips by his side when Tate came in from riding fence. "Why not take the whole day off? Like me."

"Physical work helps me smooth out the travel kinks." The stiff shoulders. The tense neck. The ache in his lower back. Although today, Tate had volunteered to ride fence because it was the section bordering Ellie's property that was scheduled for review. He hadn't expected to see her, but he'd gotten lucky. And he couldn't seem to stop smiling.

Not that I plan on making a move.

Nope. Tate was just storing up memories for when Ellie left again.

After removing his boots and hanging up his cowboy hat, Tate stole his brother's second ham sandwich, darting off when Ryan tried to retaliate.

"Hey!" Ryan protested, although he didn't get

up. "You got me up early to help Ms. Alpaca, and not only did I *not* get breakfast but now you're stealing my lunch?"

Tate tsked. "You know what Mom says." Mom, not Ms. Alpaca.

"*Don't overeat at lunch,*" they both said together.

No one else was in the large, open bunkhouse to hear their subsequent laughter. The other cowboys were either in town taking advantage of a day off or working somewhere on the ranch.

"She's right about lunch," Tate told his brother. "Too much lunch makes you want to nap." Their foster mother was full of good advice. She also recommended stopping and taking in the emotion of a moment every once in a while to make sure you lived without regrets.

That's what Tate had been doing on his ride back, storing away cherished memories. Like the way Ellie's reddish-brown hair lifted in the breeze, playful and carefree. Or the sound of Ellie's voice when she was nervous about spiders. It got all high and tight, words clipped, like the *clickety-clack* of a roller coaster heading up a big hill. He always knew that some truth was going to drop out afterward.

Tate held those truths about Ellie close to his heart. Because sometimes those truths involved him. Like the fact that she knew he didn't like to talk on the phone and still wasn't on social media.

"You didn't even wash your hands," Ryan lamented.

Tate smiled, taking a bite of ham sandwich. He swallowed, getting down a glass and filling it with water. "I washed my hands in the tack room."

"What's on your work agenda this afternoon?" Ryan asked. "Jo said we could come by for an hour of practice with Prince and Pauper before she picks up her boys from school."

They often brought their horses to her ranch to train. Jo wasn't just a good horse trainer. She was good at coaching Ryan and Tate on how to capitalize on the strengths of their new mounts. And she was Ryan's fiancée.

"Sure. I've got to help Mom in the attic after I eat. Dad said she had some boxes she wanted to go through. And after practice, I need to go into town to pick up the ranch's feed order."

"I have a good feeling about this year," Ryan said happily. "Things are really coming together."

"We're due." And they were working hard for this opportunity. But that didn't stop his head from replaying his mother's voice, *It's safer not to try.*

After eating, Tate went to the main house to find his foster mother. Mary Harrison was just finishing cleaning the refrigerator. Her pallor seemed a little gray.

"What's wrong?" Tate asked, feeling a niggle

of concern as he hung his hat in the nearby mud-room. "You don't look so good. Is all the wedding stuff getting to you?" His older foster brother, Wade, was getting married in less than two weeks to Ronnie Pickett. "Dad said you shouldn't have insisted on catering."

"I like doing the cooking. Especially for one of my own." She tucked her gray hair behind her ears, then straightened, pressing her thumbs into the small of her back. "Besides, who were we going to get to cook? No one caters in town."

"I know someone who could." Ellie.

"Pish. It's too late. I'm coming down the home stretch." Still, she looked haggard, like she could sit down, close her eyes and be asleep in a blink. "I went to look at a pony Friday morning over in Friar's Creek. That unruly devil bit my arm." She gingerly touched her bicep.

"Why are you looking at ponies?"

"Because there's a new round of you boys get-ting married. There'll be babies soon. And a well-behaved, gentle pony is hard to find. So yes, I'm looking about three years before we'll need one." She thrust her nose in the air. "Do you have a problem with that?"

"Only with you being bitten. Sit down. Rest. And forget about ponies and weddings." Tate pulled out a kitchen chair from the table, gestur-ing that she should sit.

"No." Mom shook her head, tugging down the

ends of her pink-checked button-down over her faded blue jeans. "I'm restless is all. It's like I feel a bit muddle-headed. Hay fever or something. I want to tackle my list before the muddle takes hold."

Tate studied her, making note of the pinched, aging features, the pale complexion of winter and the determined look in her eye. Doing physical chores wasn't a great idea. Was it allergies? He didn't know. "Spring *is* coming early this year," Tate allowed. Wildflowers were beginning to bloom in the fields. "What do you need from the attic? Dad said to help you get something down."

"Your father doesn't want me traipsing about up there." She led Tate through the living room to a pull-down ladder in the ceiling of the hallway. "He's afraid that at my age, I'll fall down and break something."

"*Your age?* You're a spring chicken." Tate pulled down the ladder and set the legs firmly in place. "I'll go up. Stay here. You can call out instructions."

"Nonsense. I said your father doesn't want me up there. I didn't say I agreed with him." Contradicting her weary demeanor, she climbed the ladder with sure feet and disappeared into the attic, leaving Tate no choice but to follow.

She and Ellie are both too stubborn for their own good.

Stop thinking about Ellie.

Tate reached the attic and looked around.

Plywood had been laid as a floor in a ten by twenty area beneath the apex of the ranch-style house's roof. Neither Tate nor his mother could stand straight without hitting their heads on the roof joists. Dusty cardboard boxes were stacked in neat rows and labeled in bold letters. *Books. Extra Kitchen. Grandma Layton's China. Taxes. Trophies. Keepsakes.* There were a lot of boxes labeled *Keepsakes.*

"What are we doing up here exactly?" It looked organized to Tate and not overstuffed.

"We're taking all the keepsake boxes down." She opened the flaps on one box, poking around inside before falling into a coughing fit. "Darn dust. These are the things that all you boys came with but eventually decided to put away. Blankets, stuffed animals, photos and such." She coughed some more. It was a deep, worrisome kind of cough.

"If the dust is bothering you…" Tate stopped talking, muted by her withering stare. "All I'm saying is that you can climb down. I'll hand you the boxes. Or we can do this another day." When she was feeling better.

"There will still be dust another day," Mom said in a hoarse voice. She cleared her throat. "You boys are old enough to decide if you want to make peace with these things and keep them or let the items of the past go."

Tate wasn't interested in opening up his box and said so.

Mom hit him with a stern glance. "Do you even remember what's in your box?"

He shook his head. All he remembered was that he'd been given a box way back when.

"I thought so." Mom returned her attention to the contents of the open box. "It's not healthy to gloss over the past. Sometimes you can't move forward if you don't. And by moving forward, I mean with healthy relationships and a positive outlook on life." Her voice still sounded coarse and dust-strained.

"I *am* moving forward. I *do* have a positive outlook on life."

"And relationships?" She coughed and cleared her throat some more, blinking watery eyes. "I've been meaning to do this for a long time. Putting it off, more like. Because like you, I don't necessarily want to open old wounds I helped you boys try to heal. But I feel this urgency." She smoothed a hand over her throat. "Maybe it's Wade getting married or Chandler getting divorced. Maybe it's the hot flashes or the hip that's giving me problems. But it's got to be done." She coughed some more. "This box is Chandler's. Put it on the shelf in the mudroom for when he comes to dinner next."

She had directions for all the boxes, including Tate's and Ryan's.

But Tate didn't look inside his. He had no intention of doing so.

Ever.

"Mom, THERE ARE more cowgirls our age here at school than in Texas," Della said happily, clicking her seat belt when she got in the truck after school.

"And cowboys." Lulu plopped into the opposite back seat from her sister, fastening her seat belt over her purple dress with equal ease. "They just don't always wear their cowboy hats."

"You've been going to this school for two weeks and you're just now noticing this?" Smiling, Ellie pulled away from the school pickup line.

"Yes, ma'am." Della waved at a young cowgirl walking home.

"'Cuz it took awhile to learn kids' names." Lulu smiled at Ellie in the rearview mirror, twirling a reddish-brown curl around one finger. "Did you miss us, Mom?"

"She looks too dirty to have missed us," Della noted, still glowing. "Did you save any work for us? I hope not. I want to ride today."

"Don't I always save you work?" Although perhaps that wouldn't be the case on Wednesday when Tate helped her. Instead of taking the turn out of town, Ellie headed toward the feed store. "But we've got to run errands first. Maybe pick up valentines for the school party next week." With any luck, they'd have some at the feed store.

"Yay!" Lulu wasn't much for ranch work. "Can we buy something at the store?"

"Valentines, like I said."

"I don't care if we buy something or not. I want to ride. I've got to practice my rodeo skills." Della sounded excited. "Kids here rodeo."

"I saw a flyer last week for a girls' softball team." It was sponsored by the local bank. "You like playing softball."

"No softball. I want to do barrels," Lulu piped up. "Most girls do barrels."

"No softball or barrels. I want to rope and ride sheep." There went Della, always the tough girl. "All the boys are riding sheep at the junior rodeos. When they get older, they're gonna ride bulls. And I—"

"You're not riding bulls." Ellie shuddered at the thought.

"That's what a boy said to me," Della confessed, adding in a mulish voice, *"You're not riding bulls."*

"It was Crockett," Lulu supplied sympathetically. "He never has a kind word for nobody."

Well, that just riled Ellie. "He sounds like what Gigi would call a pill. We'll see about sheep riding, Della. Maybe with one of our rams first." Perhaps Bess would know how it was done since she coached the high school rodeo team.

"Yay!" Della cried as Ellie turned into the feed store parking lot, which was rapidly filling up with trucks she recognized from the school pickup line.

"Don't get too excited, Della. I said we'll see." Ellie pulled into a wide slot. "I need to figure out how you're supposed to ride sheep to make sure you're safe."

"Were you safe when you roped and tied calves?" Della said with faux innocence.

Touché.

"I was careful, doing all I could to be safe. Accidents can happen anywhere." Ellie put the truck into Park and turned to face the girls. "You remember how bad my face looked after that calf kicked me?"

The girls nodded, gazes not quite meeting Ellie's. They'd been shaken to see the damage. Lulu had cried.

Lulu faced her sister. "Are you sure you wanna ride bulls? Mom said it hurt something awful."

"I'll wear a helmet and a face mask, like when I was a catcher in softball," Della promised. "*Please.*"

"We'll see. Now, come on. I need to order some lumber." And buy valentines. Maybe there'd be an extra one she could write an apology to Tate on.

Stop and think, Ellie. You aren't even sure you're staying.

They trundled into the feed store, which was

crowded. One side of the store was devoted to boots, hats and ranch clothes displayed in racks, on hooks and in shelving on the walls. The other side of the store had tall aisles filled with goods to keep pets and stock healthy and fed, along with tack, tools and lots of miscellaneous items that you never thought you needed until you saw it.

Like valentines!

"Girls, you each need a box of those." Ellie pointed to the display and left them pondering choices. She wove through the shoppers, heading toward the sales counter at the back.

"Tate, I haven't seen you in ages." A pretty cowgirl holding the hand of a tiny cowboy beamed up at Tate, whose back was to Ellie. "Where've you been? I was thinking we should get a drink sometime soon."

"I've been busy, CeeCee. Sorry, but I need to get a new headstall." He pointed toward an aisle behind CeeCee and her son.

Two other women had turned at the sound of Tate's voice and closed in. He'd always been a favorite of the female population of Clementine. No pondering why. Tate was attractive and went out of his way to be nice. And now, years later, dusty and dirty from a day's work, that beard covering nearly half his handsome face and shielding his expression, he was still a catch. Why hadn't some woman reeled him in?

The women who swarmed around him wore

spotless blue jeans and makeup. Not to mention their hair wasn't in a wind-blown tangle that a cowboy hat did little to hide.

Pride reared its ugly head. Ellie put her head down, tugged her hat brim low and proceeded to the counter. She placed her lumber order when her turn came, resigning herself to the wait when the clerk couldn't immediately authorize charging the supplies to the ranch account without her manager's approval.

But even at the back of the store, Ellie could hear women accosting her former friend.

"Tate, have you been ghosting me?" A woman sounded incredulous, as if this was an impossibility. "We had a few dates, and then you dropped off the face of the earth."

"I need to get a new phone," Tate said in a voice filled with apology. "My horse stepped on mine, and I haven't been able to pick up a new one yet."

That sounded like a whopper of a lie.

"Hey, Tate." This time, a man's voice called out a greeting. "Can we count on you to play on our softball team this spring?"

"Gee, Gunner, I don't know. Maybe as an alternate?" That sounded as if he didn't want to commit but was being polite.

"I'll put you down," the man said without mentioning what Tate's role would be.

Ellie sighed, noticing a business card by the

register advertising sheep shearing. She tucked it into her pocket.

"Tate!" another man called out. "We were just talking about you at The Buckboard this weekend. We're going to an Oklahoma City Thunder game and knew you'd want to come."

"Uh...text me the date?"

That definitely wasn't a yes. But the other guy took it as one.

"Will do! Maybe you can drive."

"Sure."

Did Tate ever turn anyone down?

Before Ellie could answer that question, the twins ran up to her, each carrying a box of valentines and a snack. "Please, Mom," they said together.

Ellie rolled her eyes but nodded. She was lucky they hadn't come forward with a new pair of boots or something equally pricey.

"There's Crockett." Lulu pointed out Della's nemesis over by a display of candy.

A small cowboy with pinched features that conveyed unhappiness looked up at the sound of his name.

Della stuck her tongue out.

Ellie moved in front of Della, blocking her line of sight to Crockett. "That's not nice."

"Sorry, Mom," Della mumbled, not looking one ounce remorseful.

Lulu inched her way in between Ellie and her

twin. "Mom, can we get milkshakes if we promise to be good?" With her back to Ellie, Lulu smoothed Della's hair beneath her cowboy hat, probably sending her a signal of some kind. The twins were often communicating without a word.

"That's a maybe on the milkshakes," Ellie said in a resigned voice, looking around for the store clerk. A line was forming behind her.

"Tate Oakley, as I live and breathe." Another woman cooed, if one could coo in a heavy voice. "It's like one of those rare bird sightings my grandpa gets so happy about. Say you're going to The Buckboard this weekend. We haven't danced in weeks."

"It's rodeo season, Lottie. Sorry, but I won't be having many weekends free." Tate didn't sound at all put out by another interruption. How on earth did he keep his attention focused on selecting a headstall?

But more importantly, was this how he went through life? Accosted by men and women wanting his company, dates and dances? Vulnerable because he had no personal boundaries?

"Tate!" Another woman cried, her nasally voice possibly indicating allergies.

Ellie decided another eye roll was required. At herself, not Tate or his many admirers. In the back of her mind, she'd had this fantasy that Tate was here in Clementine pining for her *friend-ship*. Yes, friendship. She wouldn't allow herself to think of it any other way. But the reality was that Tate seemed to be the most sought-after man in town. He darn sure wasn't lonely or pining for her company.

"Give the guys ten minutes to get your order ready," Izzy Adams told Ellie when she'd returned and rung her up. Her white-blond hair hung straight down her back. "I went ahead and charged your ranch account. My manager said it was okay since your father's been ill."

"Thank you." Ellie handed the girls their snacks and turned, nearly running into a brick wall behind her.

A brick wall that turned out to be Tate.

"We've got to stop meeting like this, sunshine," he said, steadying her. "Me bumping into you. You bumping into me."

A fancy-looking cowgirl behind him huffed, giving Ellie a dirty look.

"I'll get my footing soon," Ellie assured him.

"I'm sure you will." Tate brushed something from her cheek. "In the meantime, leave the hard stuff until Wednesday."

Blushing, she promised no such thing.

Della stuck her tongue out at Crockett once more.

"Della," Lulu gasped. "*Milkshakes.*"

"He did it first," Della insisted, although she apologized to the boy under the weight of Ellie's stare.

Meanwhile, Tate had turned toward Della's adversary. "Crockett. You've got to be nice to people."

"You know him?" Ellie asked, surprised.

"Yeah. He's Rochelle Vavre's." Tate nodded toward the fancy-looking cowgirl who'd given Ellie a dirty look. Who was still giving her a dirty look. "Great kid. Testing the limits with the newbies is all."

Della's chin was jutted out as if she was finding it hard to leash that tongue of hers.

Ellie drew her close and moved away from Tate, toward the door. "See you Wednesday, Tate."

Two other cowgirls in line watched them leave, muttering to each other.

"Mom, why were those ladies staring at you?" Lulu asked, glancing back.

"And whispering." Della still had a dark look on her face.

"It's nothing," Ellie assured them, hurrying out the exit. "Just a case of mistaken identity."

Those cowgirls thought she had designs on dating Tate. They didn't know she'd blown that chance years ago.

"LET'S TALK ABOUT Wade and Ronnie's wedding," Mom said at family dinner that night at the Done Roamin' Ranch. She still looked drained of energy. But she hadn't coughed. Not once. "Who doesn't have a date?"

Griff and Chandler lowered their heads over their plates of fried chicken and okra. Others followed suit.

Belatedly, Tate did the same.

"I'm so happy that I'm engaged," Ryan said in a sappy voice. He elbowed Zane, who sat next to him. "I bet Mom hired Ronnie to find you dates." Ronnie, the bride and local matchmaker.

Everyone at the table groaned. Everyone but Ryan, Mom and Dad.

"I can't believe you men haven't taken care of this already." Mary Harrison was going to keep trying to see them all settled, even if the dozen men gathered round the table weren't ready. "I'll have to check the RSVP list for single women coming without a plus-one."

"There's nothing wrong with the best man going solo," Griff said quickly. "I've got to sit with the maid of honor most of the night anyway."

Tate had a hard time holding his tongue. Bess, the maid of honor, was a woman who held a grudge against Griff for being a no-show at prom. No way could that be considered a date.

"And I'll be coming back from the junior rodeo we're supplying stock to," Chandler said in that businesslike voice of his. He was among the first and oldest of the former fosters. "I'll hardly have time to shower, much less pick up a date. In fact, if things run long, I might not even make it."

Mom had been scooping up the last of the okra

to give to Dad. She let the serving spoon clatter back into the bowl. "The whole reason Wade and Ronnie chose to have their wedding on a Sunday night was so our family could all be there. Together."

"No dates required, I bet," Tate murmured, even if he did want one. Ellie. No sense denying it to himself. The memory of Ellie blushing when she'd run into him at the feed store returned. She looked so pretty with that color he put in her cheeks. It would be a pleasure dancing with her, to flirt a little and maybe steal a kiss or two. To create a memory before she left again.

"Look at Tate's smile," Griff said, always one to stir up trouble, especially if it put the attention somewhere other than himself. "I bet Tate's thinking of asking Ellie Rowland."

Tate tossed a piece of okra across the table at him.

Griff deftly caught it and popped it in his mouth, chewing around a big grin.

Meanwhile, Ryan was frowning, most likely because he feared Ellie would mess with Tate's head and that would negatively impact Tate's performance in competitions.

"We should invite Buck to the wedding," Dad said, entering the conversation for the first time. "Saw his cousin Pete in town. He mentioned Buck was coming up to visit his daughters the same weekend."

"Let's not invite trouble," Ryan said before Tate could, flicking a glance Tate's way.

"Buck made mistakes." Dad picked up the serving spoon and put the last of the okra on his plate. "We all know that the aftermath of mistakes is what tears family apart." This was a common reference to their foster pasts.

"I'm not bringing a date to the wedding," Tate said firmly instead of arguing. "You can drop the subject."

"Makes no matter to me if you do." Dad stabbed okra with his fork. "Bring Ellie, if she'll be okay with her ex possibly being there, or invite any of those other women you date."

Ryan scoffed. "I vote for the other women."

"Which one?" Griff asked.

"Anyone but Ellie. We're trying to accomplish something this year," Ryan said in a somber voice. "We need to be even-keeled. Winning is serious business."

"Don't remind me," Tate muttered. But talk of Ellie reminded Tate of something. He turned to Chandler. "Can I take Wednesday afternoon off?"

"Of course," Chandler and Dad said at the same time. Dad had recently retired from running the rodeo-stock operation, but old habits died hard.

"Why?" Chandler asked, grabbing the last biscuit before Zane could.

"I'm going to help someone fix a shed." Or several. Sheep sheds, that is. But his family didn't need to know that.

Except Ryan seemed to be reading Tate's mind because he shook his head.

Tate ignored him.

"Always nice of you to help the community," Dad said, working on making his okra disappear.

"Makes us proud," Mom added.

Chandler gave Tate his blessing and then turned the discussion toward stock choice for the junior rodeo. They never wanted to send the most energetic roughstock for kids and teens to ride, and they'd recently purchased bulls and broncs that were too big and ornery for kids.

Once that was settled and plates were cleared, talk turned to who'd done well at the last rodeo. Wade had won the bronc-riding competition.

"And the ropers we've sponsored this year are off to a good start," Dad said with pride. "I hope everyone congratulated Ryan and Tate."

"I did." Griff talked over some of the other guys giving late congratulations. "They're gonna make the D Double R famous if they keep this up."

The air in the room suddenly felt thick and stifling to Tate. They'd only won one rodeo event. There was plenty of rodeo ahead. Plenty of opportunities to fail. After all, they'd never qualified for the postseason before.

It's easier not to try...

The season stretched out before Tate with depressing clarity. Months of competitions, months of family dinners, months of carrying the weight of expectations.

Mom scooted her chair back. "Tate, it's your week to help with the dishes."

The rest of the cowboys streamed out of the kitchen. Dad headed for the living room, his remote and favorite chair.

Tate took to the task of rinsing the dishes and handing them to Mom to load in the dishwasher. "You should have taken a nap today, Mom."

"Everybody has an off day now and then." Mom scoffed, albeit weakly. She looked wilted. "Why do you seize up like a possum playing dead whenever anyone talks about you winning?"

Tate sucked in a breath. "Are you saying I'm scared?" Could she tell? Could Ryan?

Mom eased him around, forcing him to look her in the eye. "What are you scared of?"

"Nothing." His voice sounded strained. Tate tried again. "I'm just very much aware of the trust you and Dad put in us. I don't want to cause a rift in the family—you know, have some of the guys look down on us because we were a bad investment for you." He finished rinsing a plate and handed it to her.

Mom dropped it. The plate hit the linoleum and broke, shattering into pieces, big and small. "Shoot. How did that happen?"

"Sit down." Tate guided her into a chair. "Please."

"Everything all right out there?" Dad called from the living room.

"*Yes*," Tate and Mom replied in unison.

"You're not fine." Tate got her a glass of water.

"Like you've never had a bad day. I've got a lot on my mind with the wedding and…" She fanned herself with one hand.

"You're distracted and worn out," Tate finished for her. "Take a rest while I clean this up."

"You make me feel as if I'm not needed." But she didn't get up.

Tate hugged her. "I'll always need you."

"Maybe you shouldn't. Need us so much, I mean. We won't always be around. You should be thinking about making a family of your own, relying on your wife for emotional support."

"How did we get back to me finding a date for the wedding?" Tate teased, retrieving the broom and dust pan as a way to end that conversation.

And it was a testament to Mom's weariness that she let him.

After the floor was swept, the dishes were done and Mom was safely ensconced on the living room couch, Tate headed for the barn to check on Prince.

"How are you doin', fella?" Tate entered the gelding's stall.

Prince extended his nose and playfully gummed Tate's shirt sleeve.

"Why do you do that?" Tate gently brushed the gelding's nose away and made a note to ask Jo at their next practice session. She'd raised and trained Prince. She'd know.

Thwarted, Prince stuck out his tongue.

"You're too classy and expensive to make funny faces, bud." But that seemed to be what Prince loved the most, getting into a human's personal space and interacting in any way he could. Nudging, nibbling, sticking out his tongue. "Della and Lulu would like you."

Footsteps sounded in the breezeway. Prince poked his head over the stall door to take a look-see.

"That there is a fine horse." Dad rested his arms on top of Prince's stall door. He wore a wide-brimmed white cowboy hat and a relaxed smile. Retirement suited him.

Not that Tate was fooled. After meals, talks or conversations in the barn were when Dad broached the touchy subjects. There was a reason Dad had sought Tate out. Only time would tell what that reason was.

"Is Mom okay?" Tate took a small carrot from his pocket and fed it to Prince, who quickly made it disappear.

"She's losing sleep over this wedding." Dad rubbed the white stubble on his chin. "I've never seen her like this. She's got me worried."

"Me, too."

Prince tried to nibble Tate's hat brim.

Dad *cluck-clucked* softly to attract Prince's attention, offering up his jacket sleeve for the gelding's exploration. "This horse has a lot of nervous energy. Best put some distractions in his stall."

"I will."

"According to your mother, you're stressed and in need of a distraction, too," Dad said slowly as Prince continued to gum his sleeve. "You know, I won't love you any differently if you don't win. Sponsorships are advertising. Nothing more." Dad reached over the stall door and patted Tate's shoulder. "And if you can't wrap your head around that, remember the money you've given to your biological mother. She's never paid you back. And you've never asked her to. Yet you love her just the same."

That may have been true, but there was something about his foster family paying for a sponsorship that struck Tate differently.

Prince shook his head and stuck out his tongue because no one was paying attention to him.

"Prince says you're talking too much, Dad." Tate ran a hand over Prince's back, much the way one would pet a dog. "Are you excited about Wade's wedding?"

"Are you purposefully changing the subject?" At Tate's nod, Dad gave him his trademark easy smile. "I'm excited now that I got your mother's approval to wear a western tie instead of her strangling me with a silk bow tie."

"And she said we can all wear boots with our suits." The dress code had been last month's battle. This month, apparently, it was a wedding date.

Dad cleared his throat. "We should talk about Buck."

"No need." Tate nodded briskly.

But Dad was going to broach the subject anyway. "You always were sweet on Ellie. And it proved what kind of man you are that you didn't interfere between Buck and Ellie in school. I'm proud of you for that."

A horse nickered somewhere.

Prince nudged Dad out of the way, hanging his head over the stall door to see what was happening.

"What is it I always say is the most important thing in life?" Dad asked.

That was easy. "Family."

Prince backed up, delicately took excess material in Tate's sleeve in his teeth and gave it a tug as if to say, *Good job.*

"Family," Dad repeated. "We want what's good for one another."

Tate nodded.

That, in a nutshell, was how the Harrisons had been so successful as foster parents to dozens of teenage boys over the years. Every kid fostered here was family, not just for their term on the ranch, but forever. It was a bond. A brotherhood. For some, like Ryan and Tate, it was the only loving, dependable family they'd ever known.

CHAPTER FIVE

"Is that Robbie?" Ellie's father perked up at the sound of a vehicle coming down the drive after an early lunch on Wednesday.

"It might be the delivery man. I ordered you a copper bracelet for strength." Gigi walked to the front window to look, pulling aside the heavy gold-colored drapes behind the blue velvet couch Ellie's mother had loved so much she'd covered it in plastic. Not that it was covered now.

"More woo-woo?" Dad smiled.

"More woo-woo," Ellie confirmed. She sat in the wooden rocking chair in the corner of the living room, mending loose buttons on one of her father's shirts. She was feeling a bit of déjà vu. The rocker was where her mother used to sit and do the mending.

Mom had lovingly nagged Dad from this chair, too. *Take off those boots! Watch what you're eating. Grab a jacket before you head out.*

Ellie had done her share of nagging these past few weeks as well. *I can pay the bills for you,*

Dad. The doctor didn't clear you for work, Dad. Don't get up, Dad. I'll grab it for you.

"Well, I'll be darned." Gigi walked to the door, colorful skirt swishing, bracelets jangling. She tossed her thick mane of white hair over her shoulders. "It's not for me. It's that *friend* of yours, Ellie."

"Tate?" Ellie folded the shirt with hands that suddenly trembled. She smoothed her hair and joined her grandmother at the door. "I've got it. Tate offered to help me mend some sheep shelters." But he was early. Hours early. And she was suddenly nervous. Like *this is a date* nervous.

But it wasn't a date. It was a favor from a friend. One she was going to repay in kind.

"You fixed…sheep shelters yesterday," Dad said, slurring his *s*'s. He'd been going to all kinds of therapy since the stroke, but progress was slow.

"I couldn't do all the repairs by myself." Although she'd tried. And she had the bruises to show for it, not to mention the heebie-jeebies from startling a tarantula out of a gopher hole she'd stumbled into after a smaller spider dropped on her shoulder.

"I told you…to wait…for Robbie," Dad said, fully on repeat. "I'm afraid you're…working too hard, honey."

Ellie sighed, touching the scar on her lip, struck by the thought that she'd never be enough in her father's eyes. She shouldn't waffle about staying. She should be talking to Dad about selling and retiring. But because she expected that conversation to be upsetting, she'd wait to have it when Robbie finally showed up.

Ellie joined Gigi at the open door.

Tate got out of his truck and took to the front walk. He had a confident stride, black boots striking pavement. Today his straw hat had a curled brim, allowing his shaggy, nearly black hair to be center stage. His dark beard made him look different, more mature. But his eyes were the same warm brown.

I could watch him walk all day, coming or going.

Ellie pressed her lips together, stifling the thought. She wasn't going to be one of those women who trotted after him at the feed store.

"I know I'm early, but my dad always says it's better to be early than late." Tate tipped his hat to the two door greeters, smiling as if there was no place he'd rather be. "Plus I finished all my work ahead of schedule."

"Might be that I was wrong about you," Gigi said, giving Tate a considering look. "Might be you let the wrong gal get away." She elbowed Ellie, who shushed her as they backed into the foyer to make room for Tate to enter. "Would you like a cookie?"

"Depends on the cookie, I suppose." Tate's smile became more modulated.

"True enough." Gigi nodded. "Ellie likes macadamia nut. I'm a snickerdoodle gal myself. And you…"

For whatever reason, Tate didn't play that game.

Gigi tsked. "I should have known. You're a plain sugar cookie."

Tate chuckled. "Why would you say that?"

"'Cause nobody can find fault with a sugar cookie." Gigi's bangles filled the air with sound. "I've heard about you. You're the nice Oakley."

"So some say." Tate stopped on their welcome mat to wipe his boots before entering. "You still didn't tell me what kind of cookie you had to offer."

"I was trying to decide what kind of cookie to make while you're helping Ellie. And I've decided. It's sugar." Gigi gave a brisk nod and made for the kitchen, humming as her colorful skirt swung about her ankles and bare feet.

"I tend to ignore her," Ellie told Tate, realizing belatedly that she had a hole in her sock. She tried to discreetly move one foot behind the other.

"We all…ignore her," Dad called from the living room. "Introduce me…to your beau, Elizabeth."

"*My friend*, you mean." Ellie only let Tate in as far as the foyer, where he removed his hat while she grabbed her boots. "Dad, you remember Tate Oakley from my high school years."

"You a… Done Roamin' Ranch boy?" Despite half his face and body being out of alignment, Dad could still look austere when he wanted.

"Yes, sir." Tate nodded, unfazed by Dad's appearance. "Nearly twenty years now."

"Don't remember you." Dad waved a hand. "There were so many… Couldn't keep you… straight."

"*Dad.*" That was uncalled for.

"There were a lot of us." Tate grinned. "Always someone new, as I recall."

"Mary and Frank…no longer foster… I hear." Dad was suitably put off the negative track by Tate's good nature.

"No, sir. But the bunkhouse is often filled with their success stories, me included."

Dad nodded. He was seated in his recliner with the footrest extended. He reached down for the handle. "I should…head out with you. Haven't been…for a few weeks."

"No, Dad." Ellie held up a hand. "You haven't been cleared by the doctor for work."

"What do doctors know?" Dad put his footrest down and sat up slowly, leaning and looking like he was having a dizzy spell, about to tumble to the peach-colored carpet.

Ellie rushed forward to right him.

"How long have you been running this ranch,

sir?" Tate asked, casual-like, as if he hadn't just witnessed her father's weakness on full display.

"All my life." Dad's chest puffed out with pride. He tapped it. "Third-generation rancher."

"And how many vacations have you taken over the years?" Tate asked politely.

"Just my honeymoon with my Irene." Dad's eyes welled with tears. He scowled. He'd always hated any kind of emotional display.

"Seems like you're due for a vacation, then." Tate settled his hat on his head and nodded to Ellie before opening the front door. "We'll let you know if we need an extra pair of hands."

"Thank you," Ellie said when she'd shut the door behind her. She jingled the ranch-truck keys, much the way Gigi did her bangles. "You helped me avoid an argument back there."

Tate nodded briskly. "Your father is a proud man. And he's got the right to be, having kept the place going for so long."

She let it rest at that.

Tate's gaze roamed the property. Did he see the warped boards on the ancient barn? The split wooden fence posts? Did he register the ranch's air of neglect and despair the way Ellie did?

"What do we need in the way of tools?" he asked.

"I put the tools and supplies in the back of the truck this morning."

Their boots crunched on gravel as they walked

to where the red ranch truck was parked next to a pile of old tires. The air was crisp, not too chilly. The sun caught the dark ends of Tate's hair, making the fringe beneath his cowboy hat look blue, making Ellie want to reach out and touch it.

She clenched the truck keys in her fist. "This is feeling awkward." Not that it was his fault.

"It won't soon enough," Tate reassured her. "I promise, sunshine."

That made her smile. "Pinkie swear?"

He held out his hand, pinkie extended.

They shook on it.

This. This was friendship. Nicknames and pinkie swears. She'd been divorced for so long that the impact of Tate's handsomeness had been landing outside her friend zone. But now… Now they were back on track.

They climbed in the cab. Ellie did the usual ritual to get the red truck started—pump the gas twice, say a silent prayer and turn the key. Thankfully, she didn't flood the engine. The old gal sputtered to life. She opened the window a crack, worked through the gears to find Reverse, backed out and then headed toward the pasture gate, shifting to Second.

"I don't think we've ever ridden in a car together," Tate noted.

"Nope." Odd, that.

He leaned forward as they passed the barn. "Are those your horses?"

"Mine and the girls'." Dad didn't keep horses. Nothing but sheep for him.

"We haven't ridden horses together either."

"You have a good memory."

"Sometimes that's more of a curse than a blessing." Before she could comment, Tate hopped out because they'd reached the gate to the road between their main pastures. He opened it for her and then closed it when she'd driven through. And then he hopped back in and stretched his arm across the bench seat, hand near her shoulder. "Driving a manual transmission is an art form. You're good at it."

"Didn't you have stick-shift vehicles on your ranch?" She shifted and shifted again, picking up speed since the shelters in the worst shape were farthest from the house. They bounced along the dirt road.

"We had one truck that had a manual transmission. It was the oldest truck on the property and had more dents, rust and dings than you could count. Dad said one manual shift on the ranch with boys learning to drive was all his blood pressure could handle."

She laughed—as she supposed she was meant to because he said, "Not so awkward now, is it?"

"Nope."

"Never doubt a pinkie promise, sunshine."

Ellie laughed again.

This time, the ensuing silence didn't seem so uncomfortable.

"Look at that wool on that barbed wire." Tate pointed at a fence post. "Why is it that sheep always seem to rub up against fencing? You don't see cattle or horses do that as much."

"If you wore a thick wool coat twenty-four seven, you'd get itchy, too."

"Point taken."

The point…

The point was that they'd been blown back in time to a place filled with easy banter. But it wasn't the friendly place Tate had promised the other day. Not by a long shot. His fingers were close to her shoulder. His smile felt made just for her. The air in the cab felt charged with something Ellie hadn't thought of in a long time—the excitement of attraction.

Don't get carried away, Ellie. Friends. Friends. Friends.

She couldn't repeat that mantra often enough because if she breathed long and slow, she could smell a hint of Tate's cologne along with the aroma of horse and hay. The scents of a working cowboy. Buck had always smelled of gasoline and motor oil. On that measuring stick, she preferred the aroma of cowboys.

But the comparison made her think.

"Do I smell like a sheep ranch?" she asked, sniffing her shoulder. She'd spent a good chunk of the morning cleaning the barn. But all she smelled was fabric softener.

"No sheep smell here." Tate didn't even lean over to take a whiff. "You smell like fresh air and sunshine. I guess you didn't make barbecue today. That's what you smelled like at the rodeo."

"Eau de brown sugar plus or minus a thing or two." She smiled, inviting him to smile along. "I guess that's my new weekend perfume."

"And it smells good enough to eat." Tate fidgeted in his seat, as if uncomfortable, until he added in a thick, low voice, "And that's what my dad would call an inappropriate remark. No offense."

"None taken. Let me shift back into neutral territory by saying that I like seeing wool on fencing. It's something I associate with Clementine and home. If only I had a restaurant in town to cook for, I'd be in heaven. The steakhouse in town is more of a beans-and-baked-potato kind of place." Not her preferred style of cooking at all.

"Do you miss it? Being a fancy chef, I mean."

She felt his inquisitive stare and frowned. "I suppose a part of me misses the fast pace of a big kitchen and the satisfaction of making beautiful food. But it's a nice change being home and just cooking for family. And at the barbecue booth. But that's just temporary, something to keep my culinary brain challenged." Until Dad got better and she decided where to settle.

Tate was silent.

They reached one of the shelters needing a support beam replaced. She shut off the truck near the gate. It gave up with a shuddering wheeze, something that made them each chuckle. But it wasn't a carefree sort of laugh. The awkwardness was returning.

They got out. The afternoon couldn't decide if it was still winter or not. Out here, the breeze was stronger, chillier, more bracing.

Just what I need to blow away attraction.

"Here's the plan." She hitched up her jeans. "First, we need to remove the aluminum on the roof," Ellie explained, slipping into management mode as she lowered the tailgate and then slid out a heavy beam. Together, they heaved it over the pasture fence. "Then we prop up anything needing the failing beam's support. Then we remove and replace the beam and put the roof panels back on." She checked the batteries for the screw and nail guns. "Overly simplified, of course."

"*Overly simplified.* That's new." Tate chuckled. And then he smiled at her. "You used to be overly detailed. Remember the time you explained to me how to staple notices on the bulletin board? Open the stapler… Lay it flat against the bulletin board… And—"

"I was never that bad. Was I?" That would explain why she was a pain in the butt to her workers in the kitchen though.

His chuckle grew into a full-throated laugh. "Oh, you were that bad." He grinned. And that grin… It should have felt more familiar. More… more friendly. That grin wasn't friendly. That grin…

Her heart *ka-thumped*.

Darn beard.

Ellie shook her head, trying to collect herself. Failing. "Wow. It's hard to recognize that smile of yours under all that facial hair." Impulsively, she moved closer and placed her palms on his bearded cheeks, applying pressure upward, broadening his whiskered smile until it resembled the expression he used to give her in high school. "But there it is. My favorite smile." Meanwhile, that beard… It was thick and dark and silkier than she'd expected. She stroked it with her fingertips.

Tate expelled a breath in a rush, the way one did when searching for control, like when you'd unexpectedly burned a finger on a hot pan or…

When a woman unexpectedly touched a man.

"Sorry." Ellie popped her hands off him but held them inches from his face because they'd always moved easily in and out of each other's personal space and…

I want to see what he's holding back.

"We're friends," Ellie said with the utmost care. "And adults. That was uncalled for. Practically a violation of the friendly pinkie swear." But her hands were still held midair.

Tate drew a deep breath and took hold of her hands, bringing them to rest between his over his heart. "I'll have to report you to the head of the friendship committee." His gaze was a warm brown with a shade of longing.

Longing? That's got to be my imagination.

But neither one of them moved to give the other space the way friends should. And neither one let go.

With their hat brims shading the sun, it felt as if they were sheltered in privacy in a place where secrets could be shared and vulnerabilities voiced.

So, instead of freeing her hands and stepping back, Ellie asked in a whisper, "How've you been?"

Tate stared at her intently, taking his time to answer. And then he smiled, just a hint, as if testing the water between them. "Well, I haven't dissected any frogs or had to estimate when a train carrying apples would arrive at the station after three stops of varying lengths."

Ellie held back her disappointment that he'd made a joke of her question. "I didn't ask you to identify a frog's reproductive system or solve for X," she gently chastised. "I asked how you've been. People were accosting you in the feed store, desperate for the pleasure of your company." He was nice, but not that nice. And handsome but not that handsome. "It's not like you're royalty or heir to a fortune. All that attention has got to wear thin."

"*You're* worried about *me*?" Those thick, dark brows lowered in confusion.

She squeezed his hands, trying to reassure him. "Yes. It's not normal that women and so-called friends chase you around town. Isn't it exhausting?"

"I..." Tate looked lost.

"You can't like it." Or maybe he did because he continued to stare at her as if she'd just said his horse had sprouted wings.

"I don't," Tate admitted, shoulders sagging a little. "Not that I hold that against anyone. It's good to have friends and a community that embraces me."

"Oh, Tate." Was belonging still so important to him?

He stiffened. "Is that pity in your eyes?"

"No. It's me lamenting you still being so driven to please everybody but yourself." She gave his hands another squeeze because his expression had turned fierce, as if pity was something he didn't want from anyone. "Do you know one of the benefits of being married? It gives you a sort of invisibility. People respect the fact that you aren't single and free for dates or nights out on the town. Invitations dwindle." Sometimes too much. Until Ellie had no longer felt like part of a couple. She and Buck had each had their own lives and social circles—his at the base, hers at the restaurant, on the rodeo circuit and with a few other school moms.

That's what was wrong with us, Ellie realized. She and Buck had no longer been a couple, no longer two people working to keep their love alive.

"You're saying I should get married?" Tate's expression hadn't changed. It was still closed off.

"Yes." She refused to be put off by the wall he was trying to erect between them. Besides, if she did, she'd dwell too much on the mistakes she'd made in her marriage. "I can't understand why you're still single. You're handsome, smart, funny and kind. I can't emphasize the *nice* part enough." Unlike Buck, he'd never have put her in a traditional marital box. He'd never have been threatened by her becoming a chef. "You're nice."

"Heaven forbid I grow out of the *nice Oakley* label," Tate muttered.

"Exactly. You're employed and datable, other than that beard. So I ask you, why aren't you married?"

WHY AREN'T YOU MARRIED?

Tate pressed his lips together against the obvious answer.

Because you married Buck.

He couldn't say that.

How had this conversation turned so personal so quickly?

Not that Tate minded Ellie keeping hold of his hands. Her skin was soft and the smell of wild-flowers drifted to him.

Not that Tate minded being near enough to kiss Ellie. It felt nice being this close, familiar and new at the same time.

Not that he minded…

Well… Tate couldn't think of anything else he didn't mind because he very much minded the fact that Ellie wanted to get personal and he had to keep her at arm's length, literally and figuratively.

"You're overthinking, I bet." Ellie freed one hand and gently poked his chest. "Or you don't know the reason. Or maybe…you don't want to tell me because someone broke your heart?"

Yes. You.

He'd never been good at doing or saying what he wanted to with Ellie. Not completely.

"Oh, my goodness. Was it Nia Plevins? You always had an on-again, off-again thing for her." Ellie was on a roll. "I bet she bought a really nice car and offered to give you a lift. And then before you knew it, she had you standing at the altar and… Were you jilted?"

"No." Tate couldn't seem to get more than that one word out.

Somehow, someway, he had to put a halt to this conversation.

A bird swooped past, chirping nonstop. It landed

near a gopher hole and began pecking about, searching for worms, grubs, bugs or…

"Is that a spider?" Tate asked, nodding toward the bird.

"Where?" Ellie leaped back, glancing furtively around.

"Made you look." Tate grabbed the toolbox and hustled for the gate. "Now, move. We're burning daylight."

"YOU'RE HANDY, ELLIE."

"Thanks." Ellie smiled at him from atop the ladder, basking in Tate's praise.

She would have basked in his praise more if he hadn't run from her questions about hot tickets and marriage. She hadn't hounded him about not answering, the way she might have when they were teens, because she didn't want to seem like one of those women in the feed store. And she didn't want to probe what felt like a gaping wound from his childhood—his need to be everyone's good friend.

Including mine.

Ellie climbed down from the ladder, battery-powered nail gun in one hand. "I can't take credit for knowing *how* to do this. I looked that up on the internet." Which, frankly, didn't always turn out as well as it had today. "But don't tell my dad about the internet. He'd consider it a sign of weakness." Her feet landed on solid ground, and she turned.

Tate tipped his cowboy hat back and studied her like they'd never stopped being good friends. "I'm happy to bear witness to you proving your father wrong. Like I said, you're handy."

Ellie blushed, searching for something to say, finally coming up with, "You should see me with a butcher knife."

Tate's laughter rang across the pasture. Several sheep lifted their heads, looking their way.

Ellie should have put the nail gun down, but she was nervous and needed something in her hands. "Are you laughing at the image of me being in a horror movie, looking deranged and coming at someone with a stabbing knife motion?" At his nod, she said, "I'm a chef. Should I have said *frying pan*?"

Tate shook his head, laughing harder.

"Too destructive?" When he nodded, Ellie tried again. "*Meat tenderizer*? *Soup ladle*?"

He waved her off. "Quit while you're ahead. I get the idea. You're handy in the pasture and handy in the kitchen. Why weren't you handy with tools in high school?"

It was her turn to laugh. "Who says I wasn't? You were always there to do it for me."

Tate sobered. "Really? You didn't need me?"

"I wouldn't go that far. Everybody needs help,

and I'm no different. Although a stint as a military wife made me more independent."

"How so?" Those swoon-worthy thick eyebrows quirked.

"Military partners have to be able to fix things themselves. If I got nothing else from my marriage, it was getting rid of that first impulse to cry for help when something went wrong. Even when Buck wasn't deployed elsewhere, it was faster to fix it on my own." Ellie bit her lip, wishing she hadn't said anything even vaguely related to Buck because Tate's smile was long gone. But now that the barn door was open, she found it hard to think of or say anything else. "Do you ever… Do you ever hear from Buck?"

"Nope." Tate shrugged, looking away. "Not since you two left town."

"He's coming up to visit the girls soon. You'll have a chance to catch up."

Tate was oddly silent, not looking her in the eye. In fact, he stared at the nail gun and seemed like he was about to hold up his hands and retreat to the *barely know ya* zone.

"I should have realized something was wrong with our marriage sooner," Ellie rushed on to say, apparently unable to stop herself. "All the signs were there, of course, I just didn't see them. And then… And then… And then the girls. I had to think of my girls." Her hands seemed to have a life of their own now, moving to emphasize syllables, syllables that made up words that tumbled from her mouth. "None of that is on you."

"You don't have to tell me, Ellie." Tate took a step back.

And she should have read his body language and taken her own step off the topic. But she'd kept things inside for too long, and this was Tate, her former confidante. "I want you to know my side. Not that I want you to *take* a side, I guess. I mean, back then, I wanted you to take sides and you wouldn't—not even to go out with me. You wanted to keep things friendly with both Buck and me. Which is fine. Right, even." She couldn't seem to shut up or stop moving, pacing and gesturing. All her pent-up frustration had apparently been waiting for this outlet. One she hadn't known she'd needed. "If you want me to stop, just say so, and I'll try harder to hold it all in."

"Ellie…" Tate moved awkwardly, as if he'd stumbled in a gopher hole and was slow to recover.

She shook her head, still a ball of energy and fire. "It's just that things hadn't been right for a long time, and I did nothing about it, not until two of his girlfriends showed up on my doorstep when I didn't exactly expect company and…" Ellie blinked suddenly tear-filled eyes at him. "I wish I could stop talking. Why can't I stop talking?"

"*Ellie*." Tate took the nail gun from her and set

it down. And then he took her hands. "When I first came to the Done Roamin' Ranch, my foster mother told me something that has always stuck with me. When people aren't happy, either because of a situation they're in or because something not so happy happened to them in the past, keeping that locked inside will only fester. You have to let it out to free up the happiness."

"I am happy. Now." Or at least the path was cleared for her to be happy. Someday.

Someday? Shoot. Was she doing this divorce thing all wrong?

"Do you need to be heard? Do you need me to fix something? Do you…" Tate's voice dropped an octave, and he looked pained. "Do you need a hug?"

Oh, yes. Oh, yes, please.

If only Tate looked like it was something he'd happily give her.

Ellie drew a deep breath, collecting her thoughts and shoving attraction back where it belonged. "You used to say that to me whenever I caught Buck doing something he wasn't supposed to."

Tate would listen. Then he'd hug her, a friendly side hug. But he'd leave the fixing out of it, calling himself Switzerland, a neutral body in the conflict that was Ellie and Buck.

"What do you need, Ellie?" Tate asked in the here and now.

Her throat ached and her mouth opened, and

more than anything, she wanted to tell Tate everything. Every painful wound Buck had caused. Every doubt he'd created. But whatever she chose to tell him couldn't put him in the middle between herself and Buck. It wasn't fair to treat him like her own Switzerland the way she used to.

So, instead of blabbing nonstop with whatever came to mind, she organized her thoughts while staring at her boots and asked in a soft voice, "Can you listen?"

She'd save the hug request for later.

"Of course." He barely moved. Not to put distance between them. Not even to drop her hands.

It had been years since she'd had this much male hand holding in one day. His hands felt good around hers, even though they both wore work gloves.

"Well...um... That day his significant others showed up..." Ellie wet her lips, hoping he didn't notice her scar. "I felt like I'd been swindled. I'd put all my faith in that man, and...looking back...it was a bad bargain to begin with." She closed her eyes, focusing on the warmth of the sun and Tate's fingers curled around hers. "Before I walked down the aisle, Dad asked me if I was sure I wanted to marry Buck. Daisy, my maid of honor, asked me, too. And Gigi. She asked three times. That should have been a sign." Ellie shook her head. "But I was afraid of being alone. Nothing was right at home after my mom died. Robbie was gone. Dad was different and didn't seem to want me around." Grieving, she supposed in hindsight. "Buck was going to leave. Lots of my friends were leaving, too, getting married, going to college. And you…"

Tate said nothing. And that beard… She couldn't read him.

So her mouth kept motoring: "I never should have said we couldn't be friends if you wouldn't date me. I never should have put my faith in first love either. I should have turned my back on Buck when I caught him lying back then." About inconsequential things, like whether or not he'd done his homework. "Or when he was pregaming before prom and neglected to pick me up." She and Bess had driven together, dateless. "I should have dumped him for good then and there. But I didn't. I kept on telling myself he was the one."

Ellie shook her head. She'd been such a fool thinking he'd change if they left Clementine, as he'd promised. She'd been gullible and naive to believe he wanted to change. "You know what I learned from all this?" She didn't give Tate a chance to answer. "First love is the worst. Nobody should ever marry their first love. That should be your learner's permit for relationships. Temporary love with training wheels. Practice only. Not finders keepers." Because she'd been the weeping loser.

"You can't regulate love, Ellie." Tate sounded as if he'd have liked that power himself. "And you sure can't tell your heart who to love and who not to love."

"More'ms the pity," she mumbled. "I feel like such a failure."

"Don't feel that way. Life, love, adulting, surviving…" Tate's gaze caught and held hers. "There's no rule book for any of it. And if there's no rule book, you can't judge yourself a failure at something." The depth of his words and the warmth in his eyes said he understood her. Completely. It was as if they were back in the science lab where he'd listen to her babble about something and then give her a side hug.

She missed those days.

She missed *him*.

"I'm sorry Buck hurt you," Tate said. And he was. He was sincere. It was all in his eyes. That sincerity. That caring.

She felt it in her very bones—or rather the clasp of Tate's hands on hers. They stood altar close. And there was no place she'd rather be. But that didn't mean it was okay to dump on him. "*I'm sorry.* That's what you tell me every time you listen to my tales of woe. *I'm sorry.* But I'm the one who should apologize for bending your ear, same as always."

"That's what friends are for, sunshine." There

was no smile in his voice or on the lips nestled inside that thick beard.

She shook her head, trying to smile, feeling like she was ready for Tate's hug. And not a side hug this time. But he wasn't offering. And she… maybe she wasn't done being heard.

She bit her lip.

"Something else is bothering you," Tate guessed.

Ellie nodded. "Where do I go from here? My dad needs me, but this ranch… From what I can tell, it's not going to support four of us. Not anymore. Dad had mentioned a second mortgage." Worry tried to tangle her up inside. "Gigi wants me to open a restaurant here. She doesn't understand that I can't do that anymore, even if I wanted to." Buck would use it against her in a custody fight.

Don't think about Buck.

Ellie shook Tate's hands the way she snapped the reins when she wanted to gallop.

And Ellie wanted to gallop, to run toward another job as a chef and a firm decision about her future.

"There are no easy answers. And I certainly can't tell you what to do." Tate's frown was new. Or maybe it was the fact that his beard accentuated that frown.

"The logical answer is for me to prepare the ranch for sale. Dad can't run it on his own, and sheep don't pay enough to warrant the investment needed to update everything." It would be near impossible to make him see reason though. "If he sold, we could pack up and move to Sedona to be near Gigi. Or go back to Texas." Although that held no appeal. Besides, she wouldn't have taken the horses if she wanted to go back.

Tate's thick, dark brows drew down.

"I've said too much, haven't I?" Too much, if his expression was any indication. "But you know. What's said in the sheep shelter, stays in the sheep shelter. Right?"

Tate's chin came forward, the way it did when he disagreed with someone. "Ellie…"

"No. I'm not your project, Tate. I know how you get." Ellie bit her lip. "When someone tells you they lack something, you go the extra mile to help them get it. Was that why you listened to me all those years ago? Because you knew I needed to be heard?" And her girlfriends had grown weary of her on-again, off-again romance with Buck. "Or was it because I included you in everything?"

"No. We were friends. No strings."

"Past tense." Sorrow knotted within her. "That's on me."

"I didn't mean…" Tate's frown deepened. "It's present tense, Ellie."

"Is it?" Ellie tugged at him and he stepped forward.

Except she'd brought him too close.

And now, as she stared up at him, she was consumed with the impulse to kiss him.

TATE WANTED TO kiss Ellie.

They stood close, boot toes almost touching, the way couples did when lips were about to lock. She'd spilled more than a decade's worth of truths, revealing some of the challenges she'd gone through and some she still faced, the most pressing of which was finding a place where she could be happy. The fact that she'd mentioned faraway locales made Tate want to hold on to her tighter.

And speaking of tighter...

Tate wanted to bring Ellie close and kiss her. But some of the things she'd said about their friendship had him hesitating. She didn't realize he'd fallen in love with her. That he'd been the shoulder she leaned on for entirely selfish reasons—to be near her. Not to belong or be nice.

Ellie squeezed his hands. The wind lifted the ends of her reddish-brown hair. The sun highlighted every freckle on her pretty face. And that face... It was still tilted up to his. Her lips were delicately parted. And her lips...

They were pink and full and perfect...

Hang on.

Tate gently took her chin in his hand and brushed his thumb over the small scar on her right upper lip. "What's this?"

"I caught a calf's hoof during my last tie-down roping competition." Ellie's cheeks turned a deep red. Unshed tears glistened in her eyes. "It's embarrassing and…and upsetting. Even now, I cringe when I think about how torn up I was. It took all the joy out of rodeo for me. Anyway, while my face was a puffy, colorful mess, that's when Buck's other women showed up."

"That must have hurt in more ways than one." Tate let his thumb graze over her lip once more, noting her sudden intake of breath. He smiled slowly. "We can compare scars if you like." He had his share. "It might make you feel better."

"This makes me feel better," she whispered, covering his hand on her chin with her own.

Family first. Dad's voice echoed in Tate's head.

Tate wanted to shut it out. He wanted silence. Or the bucolic backdrop of sheep bleating and the wind whispering over prairie grass while he kissed Ellie.

He wanted that almost more than anything.

But in the back of his mind, he kept seeing his biological parents when they'd leave, looking happy to be going on whatever alcohol-fueled trip they had planned, ready to forget for hours or days that they had kids. He kept seeing newly made friends at whatever school he was attending that week being led away from him by their well-meaning parents because he looked unkept and untrustworthy. People left. People he formed attachments to. They always had.

That is, until he'd become one of the Done Roamin' Ranch's family members. Only they stood by him. First, when he needed a roof over his head. And now, with this sponsorship.

Family first.

It was the code. It made sure more people didn't turn their backs on Tate and Ryan.

And here was Ellie, unsure where life was leading her. She wouldn't stay. And he couldn't go with her. He was part of a roping team, part of a family and part of a rodeo company. Everything he loved was here.

Except Ellie.

Tate cleared his throat and, with effort, took a step back. "We should get moving to the next shelter. We have, what?" He tugged his phone from his back pocket, checking the time. "Another hour before school lets out? I know this because occasionally I pick up Chandler's or Wade's kids after school."

"Right." Ellie ducked her head and bent to pick up the nail gun.

Tate scooped it up first, setting the safety in case she started using it again as an extra appendage, one that might shoot nails in places other than wood.

Ellie marched away.

With each step, he felt the distance grow between them. And oh, he didn't like it.

Without thinking, he followed her, extending an olive branch. "Do you think your girls would like to meet my mother's alpacas?"

CHAPTER SIX

DELLA CLIMBED INTO the back seat of Ellie's truck and leaned over to look at Tate, who was sitting in the passenger seat. "Are we having a date?"

"No!" Ellie said as Lulu climbed into the seat behind her. "Mr. Tate helped me with some ranch work. And now he's going to show us his mother's alpacas to see if I can shear them."

"And *then* will we go on a date?" Lulu asked, buckling in as Della did the same.

"No!" Ellie ignored Tate's soft chuckle and drove slowly through the school parking lot toward the exit. "Mr. Tate isn't interested in dating me." How did she know? Because she'd raised up on her toes in a sheep pasture and offered her lips, and he'd left her hanging.

It was high school Valentine's Day all over again.

Embarrassment burned through her veins, not that she could let it show. Oh, no. When Tate offered to show off his mother's alpaca, she'd forced cheer into her voice as she accepted, just to show him that even if he'd thought she'd been open to kissing him that he was mistaken.

Friends. We're just friends.

She ground her teeth to keep her composure, hurt that he'd treated her like he did everyone else in town—a friend he couldn't bear to lose. And she'd been just as bad because she'd accepted to keep up the appearance of their friendship.

And hope he overlooked the way I begged for a kiss.

"I tell you what I *am* interested in," Tate said in a chipper voice that made Ellie want to poke his shoulder once or twice. "Coffee. Or maybe some milkshakes. What do you girls think?"

"Milkshakes!" Lulu cried, thrusting her hands in the air.

"Milkshakes all day long," Della added. "Breakfast, lunch and dinner."

"Milkshakes aren't a recognized food group," Ellie felt compelled to say, checking the road was clear before pulling out of the parking lot.

"But milkshakes sure taste good, don't they, girls?" Oh, Tate was laying it on thick.

And her daughters were eating it up.

"You should date our mom, Mr. Tate." Lulu giggled. "That way we'd always get milkshakes after school."

"Not just when we're good," Della said dreamily. "And if he doesn't want to date you, Mom, you should just skip dating and get married."

Tate gave a shout of laughter.

"Don't start, girls," Ellie warned, fearing that it was too late. They were too much like her when they latched onto a topic—babblers. "Don't start talking about dating, love or marriage. Mr. Tate and I are friends."

"*Friends?*" Della scoffed. "Don't even say that word."

"Why not?" Tate asked, turning in his seat to look at Della.

"Crockett said he was friends with Della today," Lulu reported when Della remained mum. No secret was safe with Lulu.

"Fat chance." Della frumped in her seat, frowning and slumping at the same time. "He still says I can't ride bulls."

"Is that so bad? *I* can't ride bulls." Tate turned back around in his seat and pointed toward the Sugar Freeze, which had a line of cars waiting for its drive-through window. "Milkshakes for everybody. My treat."

"Have you *tried* to ride bulls, Mr. Tate?" Della sounded less frumpy.

"Yep. I rode one last week. Big Stomper Chomper dumped me as soon as the gate opened."

"You must not be very good." But there was awe in Lulu's tone. "You shouldn't ride anymore, Mr. Tate. Or you'll get hurt."

"Not to worry. I bounce." Tate twisted in his seat, tugging his wallet from his pocket.

"You bounce?" Della asked slowly, as if processing Tate's statement. "I could bounce. How do you do that? Do you roll up like a ball?"

"Not exactly. You just let momentum take you instead of throwing out your arms to stop yourself."

"That's not bouncing. That's being thrown," Ellie told him as the Sugar Freeze line inched forward. "Like a rock skipping across the water until it naturally slows down and sinks to the bottom."

"I think I'm a good judge of how I land, sunshine." Tate grinned at Ellie. "I don't skip. I bounce."

Ellie scoffed. "There might be something skipping up here—" she tapped her temple "—especially after all those bad *bounces*. If you're so bad at bull riding, why do you keep trying?"

Tate heaved a very weary, very fake sigh. "If at first you don't succeed, try, try again." But instead of smiling at the cliché, he frowned, seeming to pause and consider the meaning of the words.

"I like your boyfriend, Mom," Della pronounced.

"Let's marry him," Lulu added.

Tate laughed loudly once more.

"Nobody is marrying anybody," Ellie said shakily, feeling as if she was standing on the beach while a wave rolled back out to sea, taking the sand beneath her feet with it. "I don't know where you kids get these ideas."

"From Gigi," Lulu said cheerfully. "She says we have to find you a job or a husband if we want to stay in Clementine."

Tate made a noise suspiciously like a stifled laugh.

Ellie frowned at him. "Don't encourage them."

He held up his hands, fighting a smile. "I didn't."

He did.

The girls were laughing in the back.

The line moved forward again, giving Ellie more time to process Lulu's comment. "You girls never told me you wanted to stay in Clementine." Was there no end to the surprises today? The muscles in Ellie's neck stiffened. She reached a hand back to knead them.

"We didn't want to stay at first because we didn't have any friends." Lulu twirled a lock of reddish-brown hair around her finger. "But now we have friends. Cowboy and cowgirl friends."

"Is that true, Della?" Ellie asked, glancing at her in the rearview mirror. "You want to stay?"

"Yes. I like Gigi and Grandpa and having our horses in the backyard. It's just…" Della's lower lip thrust out. "Crockett don't count as a friend."

"Don't say that about Crockett." Tate swung around in his seat to face Della. "Do you know what my mom says about childhood frenemies?"

Wide eyed, Della shook her head.

"That's your future cowboy valentine."

Della gasped, horrified.

Lulu giggled.

And Ellie? Ellie gave Tate a dirty look for that valentine reference.

"What?" He sat back, looking all innocent, stroking that silky beard. "We were never frenemies."

Ellie frumped.

"Mom's looking at you like you're frenemies now, Mr. Tate," Della said in a superior voice.

"Bet that means they'll be married soon." Lulu high-fived her sister. "And we're staying in Clementine."

Della nodded, annoyance disappearing. "For sure, for sure."

"MILKSHAKES MAKE EVERYTHING BETTER, don't they?" Tate settled back into the front seat of Ellie's truck.

Ellie said nothing. She hadn't said anything since she'd started drinking her strawberry shake. The girls were quiet in the back, too.

"We need to make a left here." Tate pointed to the turn toward the highway out of town.

Ellie frowned. "I thought we were going to see your mother's alpaca."

He didn't like her frowning at him. Or to be considered her frenemy. "We're going to my mom's."

"Not the Done Roamin' Ranch?"

"No. Uh… My *biological* mother has alpaca.

She lives in Friar's Creek. I texted her we were coming," he added, just in case Ellie decided the trip wasn't worth it.

Ellie slowed and took the turn. "You're talking to her, then?"

"Talking to her, yes. Helping her around the house and yard."

"Helping her with…the bills?" Ellie asked softly, casting a tentative glance his way because she knew of a few times he'd given Ms. Alpaca money in high school.

"No. She's got a job. Raising alpaca." She was still working at it, wasn't she? Tate hadn't actually heard what her next steps would be since her business arrangement with her buddy had fallen through. "And she can sell her alpaca wool to a co-op."

Ellie gave him a look that his twin, Ryan, had down pat: *skepticism*.

"What's an alpaca?" Della asked. "Can you ride it?"

"Nope. They're just like sheep. Only taller and cuter." Tate had never thought about describing one before. "Long necks. *Happy to see you* look on their face. They smile."

"Like a giraffe? Giraffes have long necks." Lulu slurped her milkshake. "But they don't smile."

"Ostriches have long necks," Della chimed in.

"How about a flamingo?" Lulu chewed on her straw. "Are alpacas pink?"

"Alpacas aren't a bird." Tate said, keeping his patience in check. "Forget birds."

"Is it bigger than a bread box?" Ellie murmured, teasing him, which was encouraging. For their continued friendship, of course.

"Okay. Let me try again." Tate searched for words. "They're tall...ish. Taller than sheep anyway. But smaller than a horse. Long neck and a face like a...a...goat? A sheep? No. A llama." He looked over his shoulder at the twins. "Is that better?"

"Nope. I'm still confused," Lulu admitted. She handed Tate her empty milkshake cup.

"He's not very good at this." Della sucked her milkshake dry and did the same.

"Mom is really good at twenty questions," Lulu said. "And describing stuff."

"Mom can talk for hours about the taste of chicken." Della rolled her eyes.

"Or how *savory* something is," Lulu added in a dramatic way.

The twins looked at each other and then said in unison, "*Beet salad.*" They made gagging sounds.

"Tastes like dirt," Della said.

"And it gets everything it touches red." Lulu turned up her nose.

Tate stopped looking at the twins and turned his attention to Ellie. "You feed them beets?"

"And liver." Della sounded horrified.

"Fish eggs." Lulu didn't sound like she liked that any better than liver.

"I'm developing their palate." Ellie's nose rose. "Beets and liver are full of vitamins. And caviar—"

"Eww," the twins chorused.

"They love foie gras," Ellie said with superiority.

"I don't even know what that is." Suddenly, Tate felt out of his depth. He was just a cowboy. And Ellie was a fancy chef. "*Foh-goh* what?"

"Foie gras. It's French," Ellie said crisply, not helping at all. "Do I need to turn soon?"

"Foie gras?" Tate shrugged. "Is that grass? It sounds like it's French for something Harry Turner would feed to his hogs."

"I suppose you could do that, and I could cook it." Ellie laughed.

And there she was. The Ellie of old. Not some fancy chef. Not out of his league.

"Uh-oh," Della said. "Cancel the wedding."

"Why?" Tate glanced back at her even as Ellie muttered, "*There is no wedding.*"

"Mom's a foodie," Della said. And when Tate frowned in confusion, she added, "She makes little plates of pretty food with names that are hard to say."

"I like pretty food as much as the next guy." Tate grinned. "Set down a plate of food in front of a hungry cowboy and he won't generally ask what it is."

"I don't know about canceling the wedding, Della." Lulu twirled a lock of hair around her finger with the utmost precision. "Grandpa doesn't like beets either and he loves Mom."

"There is no wedding," Ellie repeated, although softer this time. "And Gigi loves beets. She's a nurse. She knows what's good for you."

"I guess you're right, Lulu." Della shrugged, glancing at her twin. "We don't like beets and Mom still loves us."

"No wedding," Ellie said. "Are we turning soon?"

"Yeah." Tate caught sight of the swayback mare. He pointed out the upcoming road on the left. "After your turn, it's the third house down. The blue one."

"Did you take Gigi's love advice, Mr. Tate?" Lulu asked. "She gave it to you at the rodeo."

"I remember seeing her there." Tate faced forward. "But no, I did not take her advice."

"If you're not a foodie, you're gonna need it," Della told him. "If you want to marry Mom."

"Friends don't need love advice," Ellie said through what looked like gritted teeth. "You guys should stick to selling cookies."

"Maybe," Lulu allowed. "Folks like Gigi's cookies."

"I like her cookies," Della said.

"And foie gras," Ellie muttered.

"ARE THOSE ALPACA?" Lulu asked excitedly from the back seat, leaning over to see through the middle of the windshield. "They're so cute. Can we take one home?"

"No." Ellie got out, feeling out of sorts. She'd never liked the way Tate's biological mother swooped through town and took his savings. And when Ellie had agreed to shear alpaca, she'd thought she was doing it for Tate's foster mother, who was a lovely, soft-hearted woman. "We have enough to do around the ranch with sheep. We hardly have a chance to ride anymore." And their horses were on property, not miles away in a rented pasture.

"But Uncle Robbie is coming back this weekend to help." Lulu slid her hand into Ellie's. With her other hand, she sent her yellow skirt swishing.

Ellie sighed. Her girls always seemed to have an answer for everything.

Tate walked along the side of the house toward the alpaca. There were a half dozen of them, all different colors. They stood at the fence, eagerly watching Tate approach.

Eager? They seemed to be smiling.

After hitching up her blue jeans and pressing her cowboy hat more firmly on her reddish-brown hair, Della took Ellie's other hand. "Aren't they adorable, Mom?"

"They are," Ellie allowed, but she'd heard they

were very expensive, several thousand dollars each. She wondered where Tate's mother had gotten the money for so many.

A compact woman came out of the house to greet them. She had ink-black hair and a friendly smile that didn't quite reach her eyes, not because she seemed unfriendly but because she seemed kind above it all. "You must be Ellie. I'm Donna. Or Ms. Alpaca, which is what my boys have taken to calling me lately."

Ellie introduced her daughters, trying to discreetly evaluate Tate's mother. Donna looked nothing like Ellie expected. She didn't come across as sharp or calculating. She seemed too distant, as if she'd just gotten out of bed and had yet to drink her coffee. "I hear you need a shearer."

"That's right." Tate's mother led them toward the alpaca with unhurried steps.

Della and Lulu ran ahead, unable to wait any longer to meet the alpacas.

There were signs on the property of recent work. A new board next to old ones on a small shelter in the pasture. A pile of thin tree branches in a burn pit. Wire fencing without any layers of rust.

They reached the corner of the house just as Tate let the girls into the enclosure. Lulu burst in and threw her arms around a black alpaca without any caution whatsoever, while Della showed a little more restraint, approaching a caramel-colored alpaca with her hand extended.

I need to teach them how to approach live-stock safely.

"Be careful," Ellie warned, fearing they'd scare the alpaca or get bitten.

"No need. My babies are gentle." Beside her, Donna tucked her hands in her pockets. "Do you take special shearing requests, Ellie?"

"I'm not sure what you mean." Ellie braced herself. She was afraid Donna was going to ask for charity. Ellie didn't know what she'd do if she did. She glanced at Tate, seeking some clue, but he was engrossed with the girls and the alpaca, going so far as to put his straw hat on the black alpaca's head.

"Special cuts, I mean," Donna explained in that slow cadence of hers. "I want to cut my herd's hair like a poodle's." When Ellie didn't say anything—*because yes, she was speechless*—Tate's mother added, "You know, puffs like cuffs at their ankles, a puff tail and a big puffy head. In the French style."

Tate looked as if he was asking the girls a question, although he did so too quietly for Ellie to hear.

"Foie gras," the twins chorused, dissolving into laughter.

"That's French, just like a poodle cut," Donna said.

Ellie and Donna reached the back pasture gate. Ellie still didn't know what to say to Tate's mother. It felt like *Are you kidding me?* was an inappropriate response.

Luckily, Tate had overheard his mother's request. He put his hat back on his head and turned to her. "I thought the point was to harvest as much alpaca wool as possible, Mom. Doesn't that mean no puffs?"

Donna hemmed and hawed a bit, cradling the face of a brown alpaca and kissing its nose. "I'm willing to leave some on for at least a few months. It's the price of my happiness." She smiled to herself.

My dad would harvest every penny of that wool. It brought more per pound than sheep wool.

The black alpaca circled the girls, sniffing at pocket level, perhaps seeking treats. The twins giggled, clearly in love.

"Well, Ellie." Tate's mother turned to her, not quite facing Ellie or looking her in the eyes. "Are you up to the task?"

"I can try. But I've never done anything like that before," Ellie admitted. "My poodle cut might look hideous." Which would be a shame. The alpaca were adorable, rapidly melting Ellie's heart. And she hadn't even interacted with one.

"I have complete confidence in you." Donna nodded, turning her unfocused gaze back to the brown alpaca. "And who knows? You might discover a knack for it. I know several people in the alpaca world who'd pay a pretty penny for a stylish cut."

"How much does an alpaca cost, Ms. Alpaca?" Della asked, hopping after a white alpaca that skipped to the watering trough. "I have money saved."

"Is it in a jelly jar?" Donna chuckled, and it was as if the clouds in her expression seemed to blow away. There was warmth in her gaze. Real emotion in her voice. "My Tate always kept his savings in a jelly jar."

On the other side of the fence, Tate stiffened.

Immediately, Ellie became wary. "Girls, I don't think Donna wants to sell her alpaca."

"I don't."

"We have piggy banks," Lulu said, twirling and sending her yellow bell skirt poofing in the air. The black alpaca tentatively stretched its head over the skirt as if checking to see if Lulu was all right. "Mine is shaped like a sheep, not a pig."

"How much?" Della wasn't about to let the possibility of a purchase go. She hopped back toward the gate. "We could trade you a sheep for one."

Ellie tsked. "Oh, honey, I think these cost as much as a pasture full of sheep."

"We've got those, too." Della hitched up her blue jeans and smiled at Donna.

"I'll stick with my alpaca, honey." The clouds blew back in, obscuring whatever it was that

Donna was feeling. "Tate can bring you to visit anytime."

"He can bring us every day." Lulu stopped spinning, throwing her arms around the black alpaca to help regain her balance. "He's gonna marry our mom."

It took quite some time for Ellie to convince Donna that wasn't true.

An hour after they arrived at Ms. Alpaca's house, Ellie drove them back to Clementine, looking as if she was lost in thought. Tate took a moment to study her.

Ellie was quiet, perhaps thinking about the logistics of shearing alpaca at his mother's property. She needed more than just an outlet for her shearers. She needed a safe place to work, for both her and the alpaca. Tate had made note of her requirements on his phone. A four-point anchoring system so the animals wouldn't shift or run away. Bags for wool and other miscellaneous items.

The twins were quiet in the back, perhaps daydreaming about an alpaca of their own. They'd hugged each alpaca and his mother before leaving, something that pleased Ms. Alpaca to no end.

And Tate? He was quiet and content, too.

Things had gone better than he'd expected at his mother's house. The girls had a blast. Ellie had been uptight at first, a mood he'd attributed to a combination of things—that near kiss, the wedding talk and her suspicion that his biological mother couldn't be trusted. But over the course of their stay, Ellie had begun to loosen up and joke with Ms. Alpaca.

"Is Miss Alpaca going somewhere?" Lulu asked, breaking the silence.

"No." Tate twinged his neck spinning around to look at her, no longer content. "Why do you ask?"

Lulu shrugged, staring out her window. "She had a suitcase in her bedroom."

Tate felt cold. He hadn't looked in her bedroom.

"Lulu, did you snoop when you went to the bathroom?" Ellie asked in a chastising voice.

"No. The bedroom door was open. Both of them." Lulu reached for a long, reddish-brown curl, twirling it around her finger.

That suitcase...

"It was probably just sitting there from her last trip," Tate said, easing back around in his seat and rolling his shoulders to relieve the sudden knot of tension while trying to convince himself that was true.

And failing.

"It was packed the way Mom likes," Lulu said, yawning, drawing Tate's attention again. "Everything was neat and folded."

Ellie caught Tate's gaze before returning her attention to the road. "I'm sure she lacks storage.

That house is really small. Maybe she's using it like a dresser."

Tate's hands felt cold. He rubbed them on his blue jeans.

"Our clothes are in suitcases," Della said in a voice that sounded just as worn out as Lulu's. "And we've been here for weeks."

It made sense. Or it would have if Tate had never seen a suitcase at his mother's house before.

She's leaving.

Tate couldn't believe it. She seemed so vested in staying. The house. All the improvements. The alpaca.

Ellie and the girls kept speculating reasons why his mother's suitcase was packed. But nothing they said stopped the cold from sinking deeper inside Tate.

By the time Ellie parked in her ranch yard, he needed to hop out of the truck, if only to feel the warmth of the sun.

The girls spilled out almost as quickly as he had, running inside as if fully recharged.

"Goodbye," Tate called after them. He glanced at Ellie. "What's their rush?"

"You know how kids are." Ellie shrugged, smiling tentatively as if gauging how much support he needed.

Not wanting her pity, he turned on his boot heel and headed toward the truck. "I need to get going. Family dinner tonight."

"Okay." She walked with him instead of heading toward the house. "The girls probably want to tell Gigi and my father about the alpaca and try to get them interested in buying one. Are you okay?"

Yes. The trip to Friar's Creek had felt a lot like a family outing. He hadn't wanted it to end.

And no. What was he going to do about his mother wanting to leave?

And now...

Ellie was walking beside him to his truck the way couples did before they parted with a kiss goodbye. How he wanted that kiss. And if he wasn't mistaken, she looked like she wanted that kiss, too.

Family first.

Tate had to reassert the boundaries of friendship. But first he had to stop Ellie from looking at him like that. Green eyes wide and filled with warmth. Walking close enough that he could curl his arm around her.

Stopping at his truck fender, Tate lifted his cowboy hat and ran a cold hand through his hair before plopping it back onto his head. "Earlier... when we were talking about Buck in the pasture... I should have told you that folks who come out of foster care have baggage."

"Okay. We're talking about emotional baggage now, not your mother's suitcase." Ellie nodded once, not asking a question. Strands of her reddish-brown hair lifted in the breeze. She pressed down on the crown of her cowboy hat. "Emotional baggage, like the way Buck always seems to be searching for something better."

"Yeah." Tate rubbed his fingers through his beard. "My brother Ryan has spent most of his life trying to protect me, most recently from our biological mother."

"And you? What do you think your emotional baggage is?"

You. He carried memories of Ellie around in his heart.

But he couldn't tell her that. And so Tate opted for a different truth. Why wouldn't he? She'd been telling him truths all day long. "I have a hard time disappointing people I care for."

"I knew that already." She studied his features, moving closer with slow, almost absent-minded steps. "Why?"

"My parents never told us we were..." *Loved.* His throat clogged. He cleared his throat of emotion and tried again. "My parents would leave. I know that sounds simple, but they were my parents, and I didn't want them to go because I never knew when, or if, they were coming back."

"I knew that, too." Somehow Ellie had come in close, moving so that he stood between her and the front of her house. There was understanding in her eyes. "This is why you have the busiest social calendar on the planet. Why you date women who pursue you that you have no interest in marrying. And why you play on softball teams when you don't have time for it."

He shrugged. "I suppose."

"Oh, it makes complete sense to me." Her voice was barely above a whisper, magnetizing him closer so he could hear. "This is why you haven't gotten married. Why you're so nice to everyone. Why you were nice to *me*." Hurt darkened her gaze to a deep forest green. "I was just another string of a long line of females clamoring for your attention. That's why you turned me down on Valentine's Day. It wasn't just your family code. It was because you can't commit to one person, almost the way Buck can't stay true to one person. Except Buck likes to have his options covered."

Tate cleared his throat again. "That's not how it was. Or is."

"No, it's worse. Because I can never be enough for you. You have to save enough to go around." Bumping the brim of her hat up, Ellie rubbed her forehead as if she was working on a hard math problem. "At least with Buck, I thought he was mine. But with you… I'd know you could never be mine completely." Her breath turned ragged, as if this final thought was upsetting.

It was upsetting to Tate, too. "If you were mine, you wouldn't think that, Ellie." She'd know. She'd know how deeply he loved her. He'd prove it to her every day.

She shook her head slowly. "I can't compete with the world, Tate."

"Ellie…" He couldn't think of what to say, primarily because she was talking as if they could be more than friends, and a part of him…a part of him didn't want her to stop, even if she was trying to work out the logic of why they shouldn't be together. Because it was here, in this tiny sliver of time, that he realized she wanted to be proven wrong about him.

She still wants me to be her cowboy valentine.

And Tate wished… He wished with all his heart that he could be hers.

"It's so weird," Ellie was saying. "All this time I thought I misread things between us. That you were looking at me with male interest and appreciation."

I did.

I do.

"But it's just you not wanting to alienate me." She raised her wounded gaze to his. "Isn't it?"

He wanted to tell her no. He wanted to tell her she was wrong.

Instead, Tate's hands, no longer cold, reached for her, settling on her waist. And his arms drew her close, then closer still until her curves snugged against his chest. And his lips…

Well, his lips went the way of his hands and

arms. Doing what his brain had kept him from doing for years. Doing exactly what his heart wanted.

Which was to kiss her.

CHAPTER SEVEN

I'M SO CONFUSED.

Except Ellie wasn't confused. She was kissing Tate. And it was wonderful. Like finding the perfect spice to bring out the flavor of a new recipe.

The kind of dreamy wonderful that made her lose her train of thought and snuggle closer, breathe Tate in, slip her arms around his neck.

And kiss.

There were no worries about where to live. No niggling concern at the back of her mind that Dad might refuse to sell and retire. No pang of regret over quitting her job and uprooting the girls.

There was just the feeling of being in a strong cowboy's arms and being kissed like there was no tomorrow.

Someone…somewhere…opened a door.

"Mom?"

Tate released her and stumbled back, bumping against the door of his truck. Ellie may have imagined it, but it seemed like he was reaching in his pocket for his key fob, too.

"Don't you move," she whispered. "We have to talk." Ellie stepped into view of the front door. "Hey, Lulu. What's up?"

"Grandpa said no to an alpaca and Della went to our room and locked the door." She twirled her hair. "Can you help?"

"With the alpaca or the door?" Tate whispered, never one to miss a punch line.

Ellie shushed him. "I'll be there in a minute, Lulu. Go inside, please." She stepped back in front of Tate, keeping her hands at her sides when what she wanted to do was reach up and stroke his whiskered cheek. "You've got some explaining to do." She needed to hear some reassurance, like the statement he'd made before she'd gotten lost in a what-if scenario about loving him. He'd said something about how she'd know she was enough if they were together. If she was his.

Tate leaned back against the truck and held up his hands. He looked stricken, seriously in pain. "I shouldn't have done that."

She noted Tate didn't apologize. And boy, he was always apologizing for something, even when it wasn't his fault. "This makes no sense. *You* make no sense. You just told me—"

"I shouldn't have done that," he said again. "It goes against the family code. You're with Buck and—"

"I am not with Buck. Or anybody." Frustration rumbled through her veins, making her hands tremble and her mind whirl with snatches of things he'd said to her today.

You can't tell your heart who to love and who not to love.

Life, love, adulting, surviving. There's no rule book for any of it.

We're friends.

Had he said that last bit more than once? She couldn't remember. But it sure felt like he was saying without saying that he had feelings for her. Because he'd been saying those things sprinkled between mentioning that dreaded family code.

"You…" Ellie's index finger landed on Tate's chest and stayed there, right against the blue check of his cotton shirt. "You've had feelings for me all this time."

Tate didn't say yes, and he didn't say no.

Ellie pressed her finger against his chest in rapid succession. More silence. "I'll take that for a yes." Because, come on, he couldn't kiss her like that if he didn't have feelings for her.

Which brought her around to another thought. An unpleasant thought. He wanted everyone to like him. What if he'd only kissed her because she'd sent signals that she wanted to be kissed? And she'd misread him, and he just *liked* her as a friend? He'd said that repeatedly the past few days after all. "Do you kiss all the women you date like that?"

"That—" his hands lowered, finding purchase

on her shoulders "—is none of your business." He gently guided her backward. "I've got to go." He released her and opened his truck door.

"This conversation isn't over," Ellie told him.

He shook his head. "It has to be."

"Because of the code? Or because I'm just like all the other women?"

"Ellie…" he began. But he didn't finish. He got into his truck and drove off.

"HE DIDN'T EVEN take a cookie," Gigi told Ellie while they were making dinner that night. "Did you hear me, Ellie?"

"Yes." After Tate left, Ellie had unlocked the girls' bedroom door, talked to Della and cleaned up for dinner in a daze. She wasn't sure what her family had been saying to her, only that they seemed to be repeating themselves. "Sorry. I have a lot on my mind." Kisses and cowboys.

Gigi tossed salad ingredients into a bowl. "He knew I was making him cookies. I was napping when you came back from the pasture. And you left while I was still asleep. No cookies were eaten—not until the twins appeared. I feel as if I've been stood up. Maybe I misjudged him."

"You wouldn't be the only one." Ellie kept her head down, her own hurt and confusion locked away, and her fingers knuckle-deep in the hamburger she was forming into a meat loaf. "We had to hurry to pick up the girls when we came in this afternoon, and I forgot about the cookies. Then Tate had to get home for dinner at the ranch, that's all. He didn't mean to snub you." Nope. It was Ellie he'd snubbed.

He left me like his house was on fire.

"Did something happen between you two?" Gigi stopped sprinkling croutons onto the salad, faced Ellie and put one hand on her hip. "Did he try something you weren't ready for?"

"I was ready hours earlier," Ellie muttered under her breath, belatedly hoping her grandmother wouldn't hear. "You know, Tate is a gentleman. He has a code."

Gigi's brow wrinkled. "A cowboy code?"

"Sort of." His foster father was a well-respected cowboy and rancher, wasn't he? Was that where the code had come from? "I can't explain it."

So much for Tate's promises that rekindling their friendship wouldn't be awkward.

"Oh, honey." Gigi hugged Ellie. "You've only dated one man. You probably approached your friend the same way you would have done Buck. Every man is different. Your grandfather was a hand holder. But the man I dated before him was a kisser. And boy could he—"

"I get the point." Ellie moved out of the circle of Gigi's arms and washed her hands in the sink. "But it's not like that with Tate."

"He's a bad kisser?" Gigi whispered. "You

know, I hear there are tips for that on the internet and—"

"*La-la-la-la-la-la-la.*" Ellie put her fingers in her ears. "Please. No dating advice while I'm making dinner."

"You're too good a cook for me to distract you. You should text your *friend* and tell him how much you appreciate his friendship." Gigi put the salad in the refrigerator, circling back around to Ellie's side. "Men can get scared. Confused. You know, it's easier to keep their distance if they don't know where they stand."

"We're friends. He made that perfectly clear." *After he kissed my socks off.*

Gigi peered at Ellie's face. "You're disappointed. He hurt you, more than he would have with a crummy kiss."

Ellie caught her breath. Did it show? Was there any use in denying it? No, she decided. "I'll get over it, Gigi. I'll get over him." She had to. "That stupid code of his won't let him date me anyway."

"Well… I'm trying not to defend him, but you have to respect what people believe, Ellie. It's what Tate believes that makes him special to you, even if you disagree with him sometimes." She fluffed Ellie's hair. "You know what they say. *Date him until you hate him.* You don't hate him, do you?"

"No. And… *Date him until you hate him?* Who

says that? It's got to be the dumbest statement ever."

Gigi ignored her. "Or you can back up to square one and be his *friend*. Occasionally moving into his space." Her grandmother moved past Ellie, then she turned, positioning her face just over Ellie's shoulder and smiled a wry smile.

Ellie laughed, gently bumping her grandmother back and turning to face her. "I think I'd be better off baking him cookies."

"Hmm." Gigi took hold of Ellie's shoulders. "Let me tell you something I've learned the hard way. When you want something—*if you want something bad enough*—you won't let one setback put you off. You'll try and try and try again. And in this case, you want Tate. Don't give up after one day together."

It was good advice. But Ellie wanted *uncomplicated*. An uncomplicated man wouldn't find her lacking. She looked Gigi in the eyes. "What if I don't know what a certain man wants in a certain relationship? What if it's different than what I think he wants?"

"You're asking the wrong question. What is it *you* want?" She winked, then moved to put the meat loaf in the preheated oven for Ellie. "Have I told you lately that I love your cooking? Weren't you going to make us some pasta to go along with this?"

What is it that Tate wants with me?

Ellie didn't know. She opened the pantry cupboard to find the pasta, which was easier to locate than what Tate wanted from her long-term. Was it a girlfriend or was it just a friend, a buddy, a pal?

I could ask him.

Ellie grimaced.

It would be less embarrassing to be just friends. If only he hadn't kissed her.

IT WAS STILL Tate's week to help Mom with the dinner dishes. During those times, his presence at the meal was required.

And that was as good an excuse as any to leave Ellie after that dynamite kiss.

Ka-boom!

There went all his boundaries when it came to her. Tate couldn't kiss her again. He had to keep things even-keeled in the family. And as for being friends...

He'd work on hiding his feelings until he had to see her again. If the weather report was correct, it wouldn't warm up enough to shear the alpacas for another few weeks.

Even his luck was bad. He needed months to reestablish the emotional distance between them.

Tate rinsed plates and handed them to his mother to load in the dishwasher. Ryan and Griff had lingered after dinner, waiting on the brownies Mom had just taken out of the oven.

She looked just as wrung out as she had all

week, if not more so. But no matter what her appearance said, she was still full of that vinegary attitude. "Boys, when I took those keepsake boxes down from the attic and gave them to you, I expected you to review the contents and then…"

"And then…" Griff prompted.

"Do something with them." Mom dropped forks and knives into the silverware basket, filling the kitchen with their metallic clatter. "Find closure. End a chapter on your life. Realize how far you've come."

"What if we aren't looking for closure?" Ryan asked, straight-faced. "I'm kind of in my happy place. Employed. Engaged to Jo. Entering the rodeo season with a positive outlook."

Mom snatched the spatula Tate had handed her and shook it at Ryan. "If you don't look for closure on the people and events that brought you to us—*on those wounds from the past*—then sometime, when you least expect it, it's going to be a problem with your life today."

"I see no problem." Tate began putting space between him and his mother. The same way he'd tried to put space between him and Ellie all day. He was more successful now. "I'm fine." If he didn't count worry for his mothers, fear of failure and the broken family code.

"Me, too." Griff scoffed. "I'm as fine as Ryan and Tate, Mom."

Mom sighed. "Griff, you're the least fine of the bunch."

"Ouch." Griff clutched the front of his shirt. "That hurts."

"It's tough love, Griff." Mom loaded the last of the cutlery into the racks and shut the dishwasher. She placed the salt-and-pepper shakers next to the sugar bowl on the counter, faced the three men and didn't hold back. "If I find that you've hidden those boxes away somewhere without looking at them…" She reached for a crumpled dishtowel and began to fold.

"That hardly seems fair." Griff went to stand over the pan of cream-cheese-and-chocolate brownies cooling on the stove. "You're sending boxes to everyone who was ever fostered here, including the dozen or so who no longer live in Clementine. How will you know what they do with their boxes?" He opened a drawer and pulled out a dinner knife, leaning above the brownie tray and taking a deep inhale.

"I plan to call and check on everyone." Mom plucked the knife from Griff's hand. "Don't you dare. The brownies aren't cool enough yet."

"You know I love warm brownies, Mom." Griff took her into his arms and began to dance her around the room.

Mom laughed, but it didn't ease the feeling in Tate's chest that something was wrong with her.

She was quickly winded, looking pale, not pink cheeked.

Tate put a stop to Griff's revelry. "Come on, Mom. Let's get you to the living room. Dad's sports update must be done by now. You can watch your true-crime shows."

"Thank you." She let Tate take her arm, leaning on him heavily. "I know you'll look inside your box."

"You do?" Tate experienced a flash of panic.

"Yep. You never want to let anyone down." She reached the couch and sank down heavily. Dad was snoring softly in his chair, gripping the remote control. "I'm asking you to open your box, Tate. For me. So I won't worry about you."

The last thing he wanted was for her to fret over him. But he hesitated to reassure her.

"Is everything okay?" Tate asked instead, covering her with a tan crocheted afghan.

"Okay with me?" Mom ran a hand through her gray hair, trying to fluff it a little. But it wouldn't fluff. "I'm just tired is all. And it's been nagging me lately, those boxes. As your mother—*your foster mother*—I want to give you every chance to succeed. And facing your past with distance and strength will help you succeed at anything you put your mind to. Roping… Romance…" She smiled wearily. "Promise me you'll look."

"Do I have to promise you by when?" Tate needed time to work up the courage to look inside. His past was shut up as firmly as the flaps of that cardboard box.

"By the wedding," Mom said without missing a beat, adding, "And make sure those two don't cut into my brownies. They can come back later when they're cool."

"Okay." Tate gently removed the remote control from his father's hand and gave it to Mom. He returned to the kitchen and told the other two what their mother had said about the brownies.

And then he went to the mudroom to get his boots and coat because he didn't want to be around when Griff disobeyed Mom.

A few minutes later, he and Ryan went out the door without Griff. They traipsed across the ranch yard.

"Did you look in your box?" Ryan asked.

"Nope." Tate shrugged deeper into his jacket, suddenly remembering what Lulu said about Ms. Alpaca's suitcase. "I don't care to see what's inside."

"Me three." Griff trotted up to them, a brownie in one hand. He took a small bite. "So good."

"She said they weren't cool yet." Ryan slowed, turning to look back at the house. "I don't suppose you brought enough for all three of us."

"Nope." Griff popped the entire brownie into his mouth, smiling triumphantly while he chewed. "If we take the whole pan, the bunkhouse will devour them."

"But if we don't, she'll know it was you," Tate surmised. Because it was always Griff who snuck treats.

"Don't be a hater." Griff brushed his fingers clean on his blue jeans. "A brother always needs a good alibi."

Ryan and Tate gave him some good-natured wallops with their cowboy hats, the way they used to when they were kids. And then the three of them snuck back into the house to steal the tray of brownies.

CHAPTER EIGHT

"TATE, YOU'RE ON fire today." Ryan pulled up next to Tate on Pauper, flicking his rope to release it from a steer's hind feet. "That was a great run."

They'd taken their horses over to the Pierce Ranch for practice Thursday afternoon. Jo had a newer chute system than they had at the Done Roamin' Ranch and cows at the ready, saving Ryan and Tate time since they didn't have to round up roping targets in far flung pastures.

"You're in the zone." Ryan continued, grinning. "Things are going great, right?"

On the contrary, things weren't going so well. Their foster mother still looked ragged around the edges. Their biological mother was planning to leave. Buck was coming soon for the wedding, Tate had kissed Ellie and there was still a voice in his head telling him it was safer not to try to be a roping champion.

But Tate nodded anyway. "Right. Great." He coiled his rope.

"Tate." Jo walked over.

She was a slip of a woman, a tomboy. She wore a wide-brimmed white cowboy hat and had tucked her faded blue jeans into her brown cowboy boots. And someday soon, as soon as she and Ryan set a date, she'd be Tate's sister-in-law.

"Can we talk for a minute?" Jo gestured for Tate to dismount. "Ryan, can you remove the steer's head gear?" She pointed to the cow they'd just roped, who waited patiently in the exit chute.

Tate hopped off, bringing his reins over Prince's head. "What's up, Jo?"

"I'd like to ask you the same question." She leaned around him to look at Ryan, preoccupied with the steer, before continuing in a low voice, "You're tense. I can see it in your throw."

Tate hesitated a bit too long before refuting her observation.

Jo stared him down. "It's okay. For now." She was channeling her best impersonation of a reprimanding but supportive school teacher. "However, you need to clear your mind before you seize up during competition. My brothers meditate and—"

"I'm not trying Pilates or going to yoga, Jo." Tate mashed his cowboy hat onto his head.

Prince nudged his shoulder from behind, as if saying, *Amen.*

Tate turned, scratched Prince behind his ears and took a deep breath. "Sorry, Jo. But I draw the line. Our throwing times were good. I don't need yoga."

Jo looked at Prince. And then at Tate. "I want to nip this in the bud before it becomes a thing."

"What thing?" Ryan led Pauper up to them.

"Lots of *things*," Jo said at the same time that Tate said, "*Nothing.*"

He and Jo had a little stare down.

Jo crossed her arms. "Gentlemen…"

"Uh-oh," Ryan muttered, shuffling his boots in the arena's soft soil.

"First off, Tate's tenser than an upset rattler. Which is fine, if not left to fester." Jo smirked. "But he's determined to fester."

"She suggested yoga," Tate pleaded his case to Ryan, bumping his hat brim up with his knuckles.

"*Meditation,*" Jo corrected, not taking her focus off Tate. "No yoga mats needed. I just want you to sit and breathe and clear your mind."

"I do that before I fall asleep every night," Tate grumbled. Although he hadn't been sleeping well all week. Last night had been especially rough. Kisses like Ellie's weren't supposed to rob a man of shuteye.

"If not meditation, you need to talk to somebody." Jo pointed toward Ryan. "I've found your brother can be a good listener if you give him a chance."

"Thanks, honey." Ryan beamed at his bride-to-be.

Jo's demeanor softened before she turned back to Tate and got serious again. "When you have too many worries, your thoughts get jumbled, then your body gets too tense. Now, you can rely on muscle memory and a steady cow to get some good scores. But eventually, all that jumble in your head is going to cramp your throwing motion and tank your scores."

Her words settled between the three of them, and the only thing Tate could think of was one powerful word: *failure.*

Is it time to give up?

Prince gummed the brim of his hat.

"No," Jo said firmly to the gelding, who immediately pulled his head back and tried to look innocent. She switched targets, jabbing her finger at Tate. "Second, you're letting Prince be too playful. When he's working—*which he is now because he's in the arena*—he can't be messing around. He's an intelligent horse, and at some point, he may discover that playing is more fun than competing. He can play around when he's not saddled. But once that saddle goes on, he should be looking forward to the game of catching cows and *only* catching cows. No other horseplay allowed."

Tate resisted hanging his head or commiserating with Prince by giving him a friendly pat. "I get what you're saying."

"Good." Jo nodded, and then her expression relaxed. She almost smiled. "Prince is a gem, Tate. A smart athlete with a big personality. But you've got to remember that you're the adult in this relationship. Okay?"

Tate nodded. It might have been his imagination, but Prince nodded, too.

And yet Jo wasn't done. "Now, one more run and then I want Tate to spill all his worries to you, Ryan."

"I'm ready to listen, give hugs or solve problems." Ryan removed his hat and took a bow. "All for the good of the team."

Tate made as if he was going to comply.

But he wasn't. Tate was silent all the way home, through dinner and on the ride into town with the boys for a beer.

Much to Ryan's chagrin.

"THURSDAY IS THE new Saturday," Bess told Ellie when they met at The Buckboard after dinner on Thursday night. "At least during rodeo season. Because Saturday is when we usually have time for us."

"And Saturdays are all rodeo for the next six months." Katie raised her glass.

"Here's to rodeo season." Ellie proposed a toast on this, her first girls' night out in Clementine. She and the other women clinked their glasses.

Silently, Ellie added, *And here's to hardening my heart toward men who don't know what they want.*

Because, clearly, that was Tate. He claimed to

want to be her friend. He almost kissed her. Retreated to the friendship zone. And then he did kiss her, only to make a lasting impression and a hasty escape. She was almost glad he'd initiated radio silence today. It had allowed her to stew and apply herself to ranch work with renewed vigor.

If indeed Thursday was the new Saturday, at least the women were dressed for it in their best going-out dresses, glam cowboy boots and only-on-special-occasions cowboy hats.

Ellie was no exception. She wore her best dress, silver boots and a blue felt cowboy hat with a silver-and-turquoise hat band. Her dress was a deep green that brought out the color in her eyes and had a full, long skirt. If she'd been Lulu, she'd have swished her skirt at every opportunity. It was nice to get gussied up and put on makeup, even if it was just her and a handful of cowgirls celebrating "the new Saturday at The Buckboard."

"There aren't a lot of patrons tonight," Ellie noted.

Bess nodded. "Ronnie had to miss this week because of her upcoming wedding and stuff with her family. I heard some cowboys were heading north for a big rodeo this weekend."

"Their loss." Katie pointed to the stage. "I heard they were adding line dancing on Thursdays, just for an hour. And look. There's a DJ."

"I'm glad the crowd is sparse." Ellie took a

handful of popcorn from the bowl. "I haven't danced in ages."

"It's just like riding a bike," Bess assured her.

The Buckboard's front door opened. Several cowboys and cowgirls entered the bar. Some Ellie recognized as old friends. Others she didn't know. It seemed like as soon as the door closed, it opened again almost immediately. Over and over.

"Look at all the people coming in." Katie rubbed her hands together. "Nothing like a last-minute crowd turning up to get this party started."

Bess sipped her beer, but something by the door caught her eye and seemed to cool her enthusiasm.

Ellie glanced toward the door in time to see Tate enter. He followed Ryan and Griff and a few other cowboys Ellie didn't remember.

Tate's gaze found hers.

Butterflies took flight in Ellie's stomach. She reached for the popcorn bowl and spilled it. By the time she'd cleaned up her mess, several women around the bar had their radar locked on Tate. He'd be busy tonight, talking, laughing, dancing.

Ellie took silent inventory.

Definitely jollier than me.

The feeling of not being enough coalesced into a bitter taste at the back of her throat.

She glanced at the DJ, who put on his headphones and turned knobs on his equipment. "Come on, ladies. It's time to start dancing." Ellie didn't want to watch Tate's fan club make their move.

She and Bess were the first on the dance floor.

Ellie caught Bess's arm, suddenly nervous. "You may have to call out the moves because I might not remember the steps."

"I'll do the honors," a familiar male voice said from behind Ellie.

She turned and came face-to-face with Tate. Her pulse picked up.

Ellie's silver cowboy boots added more than an inch to her height. But Tate was still taller than she was, an impressive figure with broad shoulders covered in a black checked shirt and black felt cowboy hat. His dark gaze regarded her in a way that felt guarded.

As it should be.

He'd kissed her thoroughly and then claimed to not know his own mind with regards to whether there'd be any more kissing her. She should tell him to take a walk.

If only Ellie was motivated to do so. Because her hands wanted to reach for Tate and her heart wanted reassurance that his kiss wasn't a fluke.

But her head…

Her head was staging a siege, taking a stand so she didn't become one of the women who trailed after him, eager for a crumb of his attention.

And yet she was reluctant to walk away. She'd always hold a spot in her heart for Tate. He was the nice, upstanding Oakley. A fact proven by him having the wherewithal to face her now after repeated bouts of awkwardness. So, she didn't tell him to get lost.

But just because Ellie was letting him off the hook about that kiss didn't mean that she was going to make it easy on him.

Ellie turned to face the stage, ignoring Bess's wide-eyed look of surprise at Tate's appearance. "That's nice of you to offer to help me with the steps, *friend*."

"Now, *this* is awkward," Tate said from behind her.

"You're the one who said it *wouldn't* be awkward if we talked. And then suddenly, after…" She would not say *kiss*, not with Bess listening. "…you didn't want to talk." She risked a glance at him as the DJ announced a classic: "Cotton Eye Joe." "And now you want to dance, not talk. Huh. I guess you deserve a little awkwardness."

Tate looked as if he carried the weight of the world on his shoulders. They sagged. "Ellie, it's been a long day for me. I'm trying here."

"He really is," Bess cut in, leaning around Ellie to be included in their conversation. "I mean, wow, Ellie. It's unprecedented that Tate would approach a woman."

Unprecedented.

Ellie glanced around. A few cowgirls were forming their own line nearby, gazes trained on

Tate. And instead of allowing them to come to him, Tate had sought out Ellie. Why? Because he was nice? Because he wanted to salvage their friendship? Because he'd had time to think about that kiss and decided he liked where things between them were going?

She liked that last thought.

Careful.

"I just want to forget everything for an hour and dance with you, Ellie," Tate said wearily, stroking his beard. "We can talk after."

"Can't," Bess said, grinning as she bobbed her head to the opening chords of the music. "It's ladies' night out."

Tate frowned. "I thought that's what you and your friends did on Saturday night, Bess."

"Ronnie made a new rule this rodeo season. Thursday is the new Saturday." Bess was enjoying this. Her blue eyes sparkled, and she was swishing her long skirt in time to the music. "Isn't that why you're here? For a night of cutting loose before a weekend of work? Or is there some other reason?" She gave Ellie a pointed look.

Ellie felt a bit trapped—between Bess and Tate, between the lovelorn cowgirls and Tate, between friendship and something more with Tate.

She held out her hands toward Tate and Bess. "Can we just dance? No talking? No drama? No... *unprecedented* moments?"

"Always." Bess laughed and started dancing.

"Whatever you need," Tate assured Ellie as he took to the steps, too.

Well, what Ellie's heart needed was another of Tate's kisses, but since that wasn't what her *friend* needed, Ellie was going to settle for dancing in his company.

The dancing was fun. Ellie clapped and stomped, laughed and hollered. It felt as if she was back in high school with a bevy of good friends having a roaring good time, her life an open road in front of her, free of speed bumps and longer than anticipated detours, like a bad marriage or a custody agreement that hinged on her not working as a chef.

And while they danced, Tate never left her side. Their smiles started tentative, but by the end of the hour, they were grinning at each other.

The music ended amid protests from the folks on the dance floor.

"Thank you for that, Ellie." Tate laid a hand over his heart. "It was just what I needed. Enjoy ladies' night."

Ellie walked slowly back to her booth, watching Tate make his way to Ryan and Griff and then head toward the door, wishing it wasn't ladies' night, wishing she was at a quiet table with Tate.

"That was epic!" Bess glowed. "Tate stayed with you the whole time. No other gal edged between you."

"Did they try?" Ellie hadn't noticed. She'd been enclosed in Tate's bubble.

"Did they try?" Bess burst out laughing. "Just look at all the dark frowns you're getting."

Ellie did. Bess was right. She was on the accusing end of several less-than-happy glances.

Tate had singled her out.

But what did that mean?

"WHAT JUST HAPPENED?" Ryan demanded when he, Tate and Griff were seated in his truck in The Buckboard's parking lot. He was still annoyed that Tate hadn't opened up to him about what was bothering him at roping practice.

"We came. We danced. We left," Griff quipped from the back seat.

"*Griff!*" Ryan chastised. "I'm asking Tate."

"I know." Griff sniffed as if hurt. "Just trying to take the tension down a notch. I don't know what happened to you guys over at Jo's this afternoon, but you've been frowning and snapping at Tate since dinner, Ryan. Lighten up."

Tate declined to explain his brother's mood. He was too busy tucking away the memory of being on the dance floor with Ellie, taking her arm when she turned the wrong way, leaning over to call out the steps and getting a close up look at her sunny smile. For the last hour, he'd forgotten his worries. It had felt glorious. He wasn't ready for Ryan to heap them all back onto him.

"Jo gave us homework," Ryan said hotly, starting the truck.

"Did we enter the wayback machine?" Griff chuckled. "In school, you guys were always more likely to get your homework done on time than I was."

"Not this time. Tate's refusing to do Jo's homework." Ryan backed up and then pulled out of the parking lot.

"Can you just drive us home in silence while I meditate?" Tate sank into his seat and lowered his hat brim as if intent upon seeking sleep.

"Talk, Tate," Ryan said with less ire. "Jo wanted you to talk."

"But first she told me to meditate."

"We're gonna need to stop at the feed store and see if they have some stretchy yoga pants for Tate." Griff sounded like he was enjoying himself. He loved getting under people's skin.

Ryan ignored him to snap at Tate. "You don't want to talk tonight? Fine. We have to drive stock to Tulsa in the morning. And then we have all day to spend together afterward. Plus there's the rodeo on Saturday. Plenty of time to talk. I can wait you out."

"Or you could just let him meditate," Griff teased.

Ryan made a sound that was half growl, half grumble.

"What's the problem with you, Ry?" Griff

asked, suddenly serious. "All Tate did tonight was line dance and not talk to you."

"He danced with Ellie Rowland," Ryan growled. "She's his kryptonite. Always messing with his head."

"Nah. What's the big deal?" Griff shifted in his seat. "They're friends. Always have been."

At that moment, Tate loved Griff enough to do something he never did—single out his favorite foster brother. "I love you, Griff."

"Back at you, buddy," Griff said good-naturedly.

But there was something that Tate loved more than his foster brother, perhaps even more than Ryan. In the past two days, he'd had a glimpse of what loving Ellie could be like—teasing banter, laughter on the dance floor and sizzling kisses.

If only Tate knew how to hold on to her *and* his family code.

CHAPTER NINE

RYAN AND TATE took the top prize in their team roping event on Saturday.

No easy feat since Ryan was clinging to grumpiness like a life preserver in choppy seas.

After their final run, Ryan took a swipe at Tate with his straw cowboy hat. "I'm dying of worry over here. I know you think you just proved something by doing so well, but we're in this for the long term. We should talk."

"I appreciate you," Tate said with a nod. "But I'll talk when I'm ready." And he was nowhere near ready to unburden himself of any of his concerns.

Ryan didn't like it, but he didn't argue. He rode Pauper out of the arena toward the parking lot and the Done Roamin' Ranch's portable horse paddock. Ryan didn't like to ride Pauper while they worked stock in the arena.

Not long after, Ryan returned riding Suzie, his ranch horse.

The afternoon progressed slowly. Tate wondered where Ellie was. Every so often, he caught a whiff of barbecue. Dad had treated them to burgers for lunch, bringing them out to the stock trucks. Tate had no excuse to swing by the food booths. Every so often, he heard a ripple of childish laughter. He wondered if Gigi and the girls were having good luck selling cookies and love fortunes. He hadn't had time for the merchant aisle today.

The rodeo was efficiently run. If someone wasn't competing, there were clowns putting on a show, telling jokes or gathering volunteers for some whacky distraction, like tricycle races and quick games of cornhole.

"We should hire some rodeo clowns with better comedic skills." Astride a fine-looking black gelding, Chandler nodded toward a so-called clown who'd forgotten his punchline.

"Technically, those *barrelmen* are here for safety purposes." Griff waved to a pretty blond cowgirl in the stands. "Like flight attendants on airplanes."

Ryan nudged Griff's shoulder. "See how hard it is to be funny?"

"Hardy-har." Griff nudged him back. But it took a lot to steal Griff's good humor. He went back to grinning good-naturedly almost immediately.

"Blade Stower is about ready to take on Big Stomper Chomper, trying for an eight-second ride." The announcer chuckled into the microphone. "Big Stomper Chomper is a new bull to the Prairie Circuit. In fact, this is his debut ride."

The Done Roamin' Ranch cowhands sat taller in the saddle. The feisty bucker had been purchased two weeks ago. He was the bull that had tossed Tate to the dirt a second or so into his ride attempt.

Where I bounced.

Tate smiled.

The mixed-breed bull had a strong record in the Texas Circuit, but he'd become increasingly too hard for the rodeo-stock company who owned him to handle. Dad and Chandler thought it was worth the risk to take him on. Their stock company had a good track record when it came to safety, and they'd been fairly certain that a little training would make Big Stomper Chomper better behaved.

Close to two weeks of work later and the bull was beginning to get the idea—come out of the chute like he had a bee in his bonnet, rid himself of a rider and then trot kindly toward the nearest exit without trying to stomp any cowboys on the ground or gore any horses in the arena. He was going to put on a good show. Exciting, but potentially dangerous.

Big Stomper Chomper was a mottled white-and-kidney color and large. Larger even than the Done Roamin' Ranch's star bull, Tornado Tom. No one at the ranch had been able to take him for eight seconds. Tate wished the cowboy who'd drawn him good luck.

"Blade's arm is up, and here we go!" The announcer's voice disappeared beneath the roar of the crowd.

Chomper leaped into the arena and kicked out his hind legs almost at the same time. He went rocking and rolling with a vengeance. On the third buck, Blade's head was thrown back so far it struck the bull's back. And then his torso was flung forward with such force that his face landed somewhere near the bull's skull. Blade's shoulders slumped and his legs went slack, his heels no longer scoring the bull's flanks.

"Looks like Blade ran into a spot of trouble," the announcer said in the worst kind of understatement. Blade looked to be seriously hurt, even if he was somehow managing to hold on.

Griff galloped to one side of Chomper. Ryan spurred Suzie to the other. Tate followed, giving the men some space to work just in case the bull decided to change directions. The rodeo clowns were darting about in front of Chomper, trying to slow him down. Griff and Ryan were trying to straighten the bull's path and rescue Blade. Ryan got in close first, able to reach over and free the flank strap from the bull's back end. But before he or Griff could grab hold of Blade, Chomper flexed and twisted mid-buck, like a champion gymnast making a gravity-defying dismount. He tried to kick Ryan and Suzie.

Ryan and Griff had their horses lunging to safety, but Blade was still clinging tight to the rigging. Whatever the bull had knocked out of him, it wasn't his will to compete.

Acting on instinct, Tate cued Prince into Ryan's place, wrapped his right arm around Blade and dragged him off before trying to get away. Chomper lunged for them, catching Blade's legs, Tate's leg and Prince's flank, sending the gelding jolting sideways to safety.

So many things happened so fast.

Chandler and Griff roped the bull's head from opposite sides.

Tate brought Prince to a halt, losing his grip on Blade. Luckily, a rodeo clown grabbed on to him, easing his fall.

Tate bent over as the pain in his leg below the knee grew to a sharp sting. And when he bent over, he registered Prince trembling. Blood dripped down the gelding's right haunch. Tate hopped off and hobbled to inspect the wound just as the rodeo veterinarian appeared by his side.

"Flesh wound," the vet said, placing his fingers at either end of a six-inch gash. "Bring him back, and we'll get him disinfected and stitched up." He walked toward the same chute Big Stomper Chomper had disappeared into.

Tate brought Prince's face in front of his. "You're

going to be okay. I got you." And when Prince buried his face into Tate's chest, Tate naturally held on to him, tossing aside Jo's advice about treating his mount like he was only his employee. "I got you."

But the rest of the roping season?

Tate's heart sank.

"Looks like everything's going to be all right, folks," the announcer said. "Let's give that cowboy and his horse a hero's round of applause."

Thundering applause followed them out of the arena, the kind of applause Ryan and Tate earned from a winning run.

Would Tate ever hear that sound again?

"Is PRINCE GOING to be okay?" Tate asked the vet several minutes later.

"You shouldn't have ridden him in the arena." Ryan paced in the small medical paddock, chaps flapping with each step.

"I didn't plan on doing pickup duty," Tate countered. "Doc? You said it's a flesh wound. What's the recovery time?"

"This is a disaster," Ryan moaned, practically wringing his hands. "We're just starting the season. We're paying top dollar to lease Prince and Pauper every month, and now you've—"

"Don't say it." Tate whirled on his brother, the sickening braid of guilt, anger and frustration whipping out in search of a target. "Don't say that I've ruined things."

"I busted my butt getting us these horses, and you…" Ryan drew a deep breath. "*I* rode Suzie."

The accusation fell between them like an angry door slam, shaking Tate's foundation. What followed was a painful silence.

Silence had defined much of their childhood.

Left behind, Ryan and Tate had waited silently while their parents ate, drank or dined.

They'd wait watching TV, daydreaming or dozing. Going outside to play wasn't allowed. Making noise or a spectacle wasn't allowed. Anything that attracted undue attention to the unsupervised boys wasn't allowed. Dad had rules. Lots of rules. Sometimes rules they didn't even know about.

And when their parents returned, Tate would always be chipper. *How was it? Did you have fun?* Chipper was better received than Ryan's disapproving scowl. Chipper might gety Tate a pat on the head or a promise to buy them doughnuts in the morning.

Ryan had resented Tate's upbeat *welcome back*s. *It's like you're telling them it's okay to leave us.*

It makes them remember us, Tate would argue. *If we're good, maybe they'll change.*

Yes, they. Their biological mother drifting along without making waves. Ryan resented that, too.

Change? Ryan scoffed one time. *You are living in fantasyland.*

Tate was determined to prove him wrong. When

they'd finally been removed from their parents' care, such as it was, he still hadn't admitted defeat. But defeat was surely what he was feeling now.

Tate's mouth felt dry, his heart heavy.

The crowd was applauding something. Nearby, a steer lowed. The announcer's voice was overly cheerful. Someone shouted with laughter.

It was just another day at the rodeo.

Except it wasn't. Tate had made a mistake, one that risked his and Ryan's futures, the same as he had when they were kids.

"Prince will need ten to fourteen days off," the vet said without paying the arguing brothers any mind, as if he was used to cowboys losing their composure when their mounts got injured.

Prince nibbled on Tate's shirt sleeve, as if to say, *You worry too much. I'm okay.*

The gelding wasn't okay. They'd lose two weeks of points on the Prairie Circuit leaderboard if they didn't compete. Or rather, Tate would. Ryan could find a new partner since they were scored separately. But after that hiatus, when Tate returned to the arena Prince might have lost his drive for competition.

The initial injury had been a painful disappointment, but the look in Ryan's eyes and the reality of their situation crashed around Tate, threatening to break him.

"I can ride Suzie or another ranch mount for the next two weeks in competition," Tate spitballed ideas, leaning against Prince. The gelding could eat a hole in his shirt for all he cared, as long as he recovered and retained his drive to compete.

Ryan removed his cowboy hat and ran a hand through his dark hair. "Let me talk to Jo. She might have a horse she wants to sell that you can ride until Prince recovers. It'll be good advertisement for her." He turned to go.

Tate grabbed hold of Ryan and gave him a fierce hug. "Thank you. Thank you for always watching out for me." Despite Tate being his own worst enemy—*their* own worst enemy. "I won't make the mistake of riding Prince in the arena again."

Ryan drew back. "And the other thing?" His voice was husky. "The talking thing?"

Spilling his guts about Ellie, Tate thought he meant. "I know where my priorities lie, Ryan."

Tate took a stilted step back, suddenly realizing how tender his leg was. It throbbed painfully. And there was a rip in his chaps just above his cowboy boots.

"You should get that leg looked at," the vet said without deviating from his stitches.

"I'll be fine. It's just a bruise."

"You can't treat it like it's *just a bruise*." Ryan gave Tate a stern look. "Professional athletes take care of their minds and their bodies. You'll get it looked at. Now."

Tate nodded. How could he refuse?

"I've been waiting for you. For sure, for sure." Gigi smiled at Tate as she handed him a large cookie decorated with hearts and a cupid. She sat behind a table with her blue-and-purple paisley tablecloth. She was dressed as colorfully as always, and her fingers were adorned with similar rings of different styles, stones and colors. "I made you a sugar cookie. I owed you one from earlier in the week."

"Thanks, but… I didn't come for cookies or love advice." Tate tried hard to find his smile, but it felt permanently missing. He rubbed his beard.

"Mr. Tate!" Della came up, set her feet on top of his foot and grabbed his thigh for balance. "You're our favorite customer!"

"Mr. Tate!" Lulu claimed his other leg. She noticed her sister was standing on Tate's foot and did the same. "You smell like horse. You need a bath. But I like your chaps. Look at all this fringe." She finger-combed the leather fringe on his chaps.

"Thanks, little cowgirls." Tate walked behind their cookie table toward an empty chair next to Gigi, ignoring the exacerbated pain caused by two adorable cling-ons. "I came to see your great-grandmother."

"Me?" Gigi preened, tossing her thick white hair over her shoulders. "Let him sit, girls. If we sell out of our cookies, we can go help your mother at the barbecue stand and get a milkshake."

The future sales stars scampered back out into the crowd.

Gigi surveyed him.

Tate imagined he looked a sight. Dirt streaked and sweat soaked. It might only be February, but the sunny day was warm. He swiped at the sweat on his forehead.

Without a word, Gigi took the cookie she'd given him, unwrapped it and handed it back to him with a tinkling of her metal bracelets. "You look like you need some comfort food." And then she dug into a large tote at her feet, producing a small bag made of bright orange tulle and filled with colorful rocks. She rummaged around inside and then handed him a small blue stone. "Tuck it in your pocket."

"It's like a rabbit's foot? A lucky charm?" Tate tested the smooth, cool surface in his palm. "I don't believe in luck."

"It's aquamarine. For balance, courage and peace." Gigi handed him a stone of a different shade of blue. "And this one is Larimar, for healing."

The two stones clacked together in Tate's palm. He didn't feel healed or balanced.

She closed his fingers around the two stones. "Larimar is also good energy to apply toward love, especially when your road has been rocky. You should have seen Ellie these past few days. She alternates between moping and stomping.

She almost burned the pork chops the other night. That's how distracted you've gotten her."

Much as Tate appreciated the share, he'd sought Gigi out for a different reason. "I heard you were a nurse."

She nodded, hands still wrapped around his and those stones. "I was a certified nursing assistant at a doctor's office. Met all kinds of people. Did some good. Caught all kinds of germs."

"Well, I don't think I have any germs..." Tate reclaimed his hand, set the stones on the table next to his cookie and tugged off his right boot. Then he pulled aside his leather chaps and began rolling up his pants leg. "But I was told to have this looked at and the people doc is busy elsewhere." He turned and showed her the reddened, scraped flesh that went from the front of his shin to the back of his calf.

Gigi bent for a closer look, gathering and twisting her long white hair over one shoulder while he told her what had happened.

"You're the cowboy everyone's talking about." She sat up slowly, studying his features. "How's your horse? Heard he was wounded, too."

"Flesh wound. Bed rest. Two weeks." The diagnosis was easier to accept the more often Tate said it out loud. But his throat felt raw, and his heart ached something awful.

Gigi nodded. "I'm no doctor. But I think if you've walked on that leg without unbearable pain then nothing is broken. That's not to say there couldn't be a bone chipped on your tibia. You'd need an X-ray for that."

Tate gingerly pressed around the front of his shin bone, hissing softly through the discomfort. "I don't think anything's broken. And I don't feel anything loose."

"But you'll get it checked out. That's an order, although I'm not licensed to give medical advice." Gigi handed him his cookie once again. "Sit here for a minute and eat. I know how you cowboys get. You run around as if you aren't hurt. You need to prop that up and ice it down for the next twenty-four hours, or the pain will linger and healing will be slow. Be smart."

"Thanks." Tate took a bite of his cookie, thinking that, and a milkshake, would make him feel a whole lot better.

A cookie, a milkshake and Ellie's kiss.

Tate shook his head. He'd rocked the boat enough for one day. Ellie was leaving. It wasn't smart to lose his heart to her. Tate eased his pants leg down, put his chaps back in place and slid his foot into his cowboy boot. All with a minimum of grunting and groaning. Amazing how a little sugar and fussing over could put a person back together inside.

The twins brought a pretty young cowgirl to the table. Gigi told her to stop trying to make the man who loved her into Mr. Right, sold her two cookies and sent her on her way. Tate was content to eat his cookie and stare out over the crowd.

"How's the bull rider you rescued?" Gigi asked, as the twins skipped back into the crowd. "Folks said he passed out."

Tate nodded. "Someone told me he had a concussion. And a similar set of bruises on his legs."

"Great PR for that bull of yours." Their conversation paused as the girls brought up some cowgirls who were willing to buy cookies but passed on love fortunes.

Tate continued to sit with his thoughts, trying to box up the replay of Chomper coming at him and the look on Ryan's face when he'd blamed Tate for ruining everything.

"TATE." ELLIE LED her family up to a long horse trailer with the Done Roamin' Ranch's logo on it. It was parked in the warm glow of a light, which was good considering the sun had set and the rodeo grounds were cast in shadows.

They'd been walking for several minutes through the parking lot, trying to find him among all the other stock vehicles.

Tate closed the back door to the trailer and locked it in place. "Hey, ladies." He turned to face them, avoiding looking at Ellie directly. His face was in shadow beneath his hat brim, his expression muted behind that beard.

Ellie's feet felt his rejection first, coming to an

abrupt stop before she fully registered that Tate didn't want her here. She chalked up his mood to his bad day. She'd heard about it from customers at Curly's BBQ Shack. And then from Gigi. It had to be hard to be the talk of the rodeo.

I won't apologize for coming to see if he's all right.

Ellie lifted her chin.

Ryan came around the front of the truck that the trailer was hitched to. He crossed his arms and leaned against the truck bed.

"That's not much of a welcome," Gigi muttered, bracelets jingling.

Ellie quietly shushed her. She had a purpose in this visit other than seeing for herself that Tate was all right. If only it wasn't already nighttime. She wanted a look at his injury and a better read on how he was handling this setback. Word around the rodeo was that Tate and Ryan hadn't started winning until they'd acquired those mounts. With his horse's injury, folks were predicting an end to their brief winning streak.

But even if Gigi and Ellie were wary of Tate's standoffish demeanor, Ellie's children were not.

"Mr. Tate, where are your chaps?" Della skipped up to him, tucking her thumbs into the waistband of her jeans before taking a stance like a bow-legged cowboy. "Can I try them on? I want to make the fringe flap."

"That sounds like fun." Lulu was hot on the

heels of her sister, swishing her blue cotton skirt. "Can we see your boo-boo?"

"No chaps or boo-boos. Not right now." Tate limped toward Ellie and Gigi, gently sweeping the girls along with hands on their backs.

"You haven't been icing that injury," Gigi noted. "Not good, not good, cowboy."

"There was work to do. I've got ice in the truck." Tate gave a little shrug, still not meeting Ellie's gaze. "We've got to head home. Our stock is tired."

"And your horse has a boo-boo." Lulu swished her skirt a little less. "I don't like owies. Does your horse need a hug?"

"I gave him one earlier," Tate assured her. He stopped a few feet away from Ellie, staring at her boots. His face and jeans were smudged with dirt. His features streaked with defeat.

Nearby, several large truck engines started. Ryan's cell phone pinged. The darkness felt as if it was closing around them, shutting out whatever chance Ellie had of helping Tate.

The twins lingered near him, as if knowing Tate needed folks around him who cared, even if he wasn't quite himself. But for once, they were quiet.

"Do you need a hug?" Ellie asked Tate, not sorry to make the offer despite Ryan's frown deepening. Her *friend* needed some moral support. She didn't think Tate needed someone to listen to his problems. But she did have a solution, if only he'd *listen* to her.

"I'll make do. Thanks." Tate tipped his cowboy hat. "I appreciate you checking on me."

"The other trucks are moving," Ryan said impatiently.

A horse nickered inside the trailer, echoing Ryan's annoyance.

"I feel decidedly like chopped liver," Gigi murmured. "How odd."

Tate inclined his head to her, as if in agreement. "See you around, ladies." He turned toward the truck.

"Wait, I…" Ellie came forward, catching his arm, gaze searching Tate's face, perhaps lingering too long on those lips of his because it didn't feel like they'd ever kiss again. "If you need a competition horse, you can try mine. Goldie loves to compete. She's a good roper."

"Wah-pow!" Della pantomimed throwing a rope. "Mom's that fast when she rides her."

"And she's pretty." Lulu swished her skirt.

"The horse and my granddaughter both," Gigi clarified with a wry laugh.

"But mostly," Ellie said steadily, resisting the urge to move closer to Tate, to reacquaint herself with the thick softness of his beard. "She's a born-and-bred roping athlete." She'd paid a pretty penny for her after she landed her first job as a head chef.

Tate didn't look like he was going to jump on Ellie's offer. And Ryan was still as closed off as a freshly harvested clam.

Unsure of where to go from here, Ellie let Tate's arm go. "I'm sure you have other options. I just thought I'd throw it out there."

And now I'll try to carry my head high as I walk away.

"Come on, girls." Ellie gathered her family. "They need to leave, and we need to get home, too."

"IT'S NOT A bad idea," Tate said when he and Ryan had been on the highway for a few minutes, following the truck caravan that was heading back to the ranch.

"You can't borrow Ellie's horse," Ryan said flatly from behind the wheel, knowing exactly what Tate referred to.

"Why not? Jo said she didn't have any horses I could use." And despite Tate experiencing one of the worst days of his adult life, the more he considered Ellie's offer, the more his spirits lifted. Perhaps aided by the numbness in his calf from the melting ice bag. "This may be just what we need."

What I need.

There were benefits to borrowing Ellie's mount. He'd have an excuse to talk to her, for one, to apologize for kissing and running away, as well as his ornery attitude earlier. Even though she was leaving, he wanted to be friends. She was important to him.

"You know why I'm against it." Ryan's words were punched with annoyance. A mile passed in silence before he said anything else. "You haven't even seen her horse."

It was a weak excuse. Tate took it as an indication his brother's disapproval of the idea was weakening.

Tate cleared his throat. "To be fair, I saw a palomino in one of her corrals," he gently teased, keeping quiet until another mile marker was passed. "So, I have seen her."

"But you haven't ridden her." Ryan removed his cowboy hat and tossed it on the dashboard. "If it was anyone else offering a horse, then maybe... I need to keep you free of anything Ellie-related."

Anything Ellie-related.

It felt as if Tate's life had been revolving around everything Ellie-related since she'd come back. They kept bumping into each other, as if the universe wanted them to overcome obstacles and be together. Tate stuck his hand in his pocket, drawing out the two small blue stones Gigi had given him. He rolled them in his palm, wishing they had the power the old woman claimed. To heal. To smooth a path to love.

A few more miles went by.

"You could be my chaperone when I try her out," Tate offered, tucking the stones back in his pocket.

Ryan sighed. "You're not going to let this go, are you?"

Tate sobered. "I need to make this right somehow. Do you have a better idea?"

"Give me a day, and I will," Ryan promised. "Now, what are we going to do about Wade and Ronnie's wedding gift?"

"The gift seems easy."

"The gift *isn't* easy," Ryan insisted. "They don't need anything. Why don't you look up a list of gift ideas for newlyweds on your phone?"

Tate dutifully reached for his cell phone in the cup holder. "Them not needing anything means we give cash or a gift card. Haven't you heard Mom's gifting rules?" She recited them often enough when holidays or events like this came around.

"You know I don't listen to stuff like that. I just politely nod my head."

Tate opened his phone and noticed he had a text message. He always kept his phone on silent while he was working and had forgotten to turn the sound back on. He clicked on the message app. It was from Ellie.

She still has my number.

Amazing how that one detail warmed him inside. And he hadn't even opened her message.

"Gift cards are lame. Search for wedding gifts for the couple who has everything," Ryan told him.

Tate dutifully typed in a search for wedding gifts. But he didn't review the results. He was too curious about Ellie's message.

He glanced at his brother. "I don't think Ellie is my kryptonite."

How could she be? Tate loved Ellie. He'd loved Ellie for most of his life. She was kind and thoughtful, stubborn and driven to succeed; she made him laugh and think and hope. With Prince injured, Tate should have been buried beneath the weight of impending failure career-wise. But her offer...

It wasn't just that she'd offered a solution to his problem. He felt much of the weight of expectation lighten, as if it was bearable to compete now that she helped carry the load. This was what love was supposed to be like. This was the love he wanted.

He also wanted to read Ellie's message, wanted to answer back but didn't want Tate any the wiser.

Ryan turned on the radio. "Tell me if you find something original to give them."

"Nope. We're giving them cash or a gift card, per Mom's rules." Tate gave into impulse, opened his phone anyway and read Ellie's message.

Goldie's bloodlines.

There was a picture of the mare's pedigree. Names that Tate recognized because they were horses of known roping champions. Ellie's horse came from quality stock.

Photos of Goldie in action.

There was a picture of Ellie riding the palomino at full gallop, twirling her lariat as she chased down a calf. And the look in Ellie's eyes... Intense, fully engaged, determined.

The same look that was in the mare's eyes.

It made sense that Ellie would choose a top-of-the-line horse, one of the same temperament as the woman herself.

Tate returned his phone to the cup holder, smiling. He didn't plan on sharing Ellie's message with Ryan until his brother confessed they had no alternative.

But the day had been rough. And Ryan... He always meant well. Here was something Tate could do to make it up to Ryan.

Tate turned off the truck's radio. "I'm ready to tackle some of my homework now. *Jo's* homework," he clarified, waiting for Ryan's nod to continue. "I was at Ms. Alpaca's house on Wednesday. She has a packed suitcase in her bedroom, according to Ellie's daughter."

Ryan bit off a curse. "This is what's been stuck in your craw?"

"Among other things." Ellie. Mom's health. The fear of failure.

"You can't make her stick around," Ryan said bitterly, adjusting his grip on the steering wheel.

"She has to want to stay," Tate agreed, thinking of both Ms. Alpaca and Ellie.

Ryan blew out a long breath. "I admit…reluctantly…that the fact that I know where Ms. Alpaca is and that she's sober is a comfort to me."

This was new. Ryan had never confessed to anything close to caring about their biological mother before.

"But I'm not going to fall apart if she leaves tomorrow." Ryan spared Tate a glance. "And neither are you."

Tate nodded, not quite believing it.

"If she disappears or falls off the wagon, it's not on you, Tate. You can't save her." Ryan cleared his throat, as if the topic got to him emotionally. "When you're old and looking back on your life, you can be proud of the way you tried to help her. You're a good person, Tate. Truly, the nicest Oakley—although Jo would argue with me on that point." Ryan grinned at the mention of his fiancée. It wasn't a long-held grin though. In fact, in a blink, he was back to full-on serious mode. "Ms. Alpaca gave up her right to make you feel guilty or sad or regretful a long time ago."

Tate nodded, and this time, he felt he could almost shift his thinking. Because he wasn't alone in his conflicted feelings toward Ms. Alpaca. And that made him feel better somehow.

CHAPTER TEN

"LOOK, MISS MARY. LOOK!" Lulu ran up to Mary Harrison after church on Sunday with a bouquet of wildflowers. "We bought you flowers."

"And chocolate." Della ran up next, with Ellie not far behind them.

Both girls wore their church dresses and matching blue coats. Della wore a pair of white leggings under her dress. Lulu had chosen bright orange tights. Both girls wore their pink cowboy boots and their hair in a simple ponytail, although Lulu's was high and perky on top of her head and Della preferred hers at the base of her neck.

"What's this?" Tate's foster mother bent to receive her gifts and hugs from the girls. "It's not Valentine's Day yet."

"Someone told me you weren't feeling up to par," Ellie explained, giving her mother's friend a hug. They'd seen Mary after church every Sunday, but this Sunday she looked unwell. Her skin was pale, her gray hair limp, and there were circles under her eyes. She held one arm across her waist, as if it was broken and in a sling. "I thought you could use a pick-me-up, what with Wade and Ronnie's wedding so close."

"Just seeing this pair brings joy to my heart." Mary sniffed the wildflowers. "It's so nice seeing you back in town. You need to stop by the ranch."

"We've been busy. When things settle down, we'll make sure to visit." Ellie looked over those leaving the service, looking for Tate. She didn't see him.

Before she could ask how he was doing, Mary's husband came out of the church, setting his wide-brimmed, white cowboy hat on his head and joining them. He greeted Ellie and then fussed over the twins, complimenting their dresses and hair.

A little girl on the church steps called to Lulu. She scampered over to join her friend.

"Mister Frank, have you ever ridden a bull?" Della smiled like an angel without an agenda. But of course, she had one.

However, Ellie let her little dynamo investigate her interest in extreme sports. Better to have her make up her own mind.

"'Course I've ridden a bull." Frank chuckled. He had the kind of smile that inspired trust. "What kind of rodeo stockman would I be if I didn't take a turn on my own roughstock?"

Della frowned a little. "And have you ridden a sheep, Mister Frank?"

Frank hesitated, gaze cutting to Ellie before

going back to her daughter, suddenly seemingly aware that Della wasn't just making polite conversation. "Why yes. Yes, I did. When I was a boy."

Della turned to Ellie and pointed at Frank. "He knows how to ride a sheep. He can teach me how to do it without getting hurt." And then she faced Frank, and said sweetly, "*Please.*"

"Oh, how can you refuse that face?" Mary slipped her arm through Frank's, using her bouquet to tap him lightly on the chest.

"Here's the thing," Frank said plainly, addressing Della. "All you need to ride a sheep is a chute and a strong grip on their wool."

"And a helmet," Ellie slipped in.

"And a helmet," Frank amended. "You should look for a clinic like our boy, Chandler, runs. Or just try it at home. Now's the perfect time to give it a go before you shear all those sheep of yours."

Della clasped her hands together under her chin. "The perfect time to ride sheep," she crooned to Ellie.

"I don't have to do it, do I?" Lulu returned in time to catch this last bit of conversation.

The glow of near victory still radiated on Della's face. "Can we try when we get home, Mom?"

"We have a helmet. And we have a pasture full of rams," Ellie admitted. "But what we don't have is a chute like at the rodeo for you to climb on one."

Della frowned. "We have a chute leading to the shearing shed."

"Yes, but the shed has a concrete floor. If you fell off, you wouldn't bounce like Mr. Tate."

Frank chuckled. "Tate doesn't bounce. He gets flung."

"My sentiments exactly." Ellie smiled. But now that Tate was part of the discussion, she saw her opening and took it. "Did Tate seek medical treatment today? Or is he going to tough it out after being gored by that bull?"

"Tate's hoping to see Doc tomorrow." Mary's brow furrowed with concern. "Today he's on bed rest. Leg propped in the air and iced. But we all know that he won't stay there. He'll be checking that horse of his."

"How a man treats his horse says a lot about him," Frank said gruffly.

"It does indeed," Ellie agreed.

"Can we talk about sheep?" Della bounced on her toes excitedly. "Mister Frank, you're the only one who said I could ride one."

"I said we'd see." Ellie stroked a hand over Della's ponytail.

"I tell you what, Della." Frank adjusted the brim of his hat. "If your mother can bring a ram or two over to the Done Roamin' Ranch, you can use our chute to ride."

"That is awesome." Della spun around, floating on a cloud of happiness. "Thank you, Mister Frank."

"What do you think, Mom?" Lulu took Ellie's hand. "Will Della bounce like Mister Tate? Or get flung?"

"I'll bounce," Della said smugly. "Just you wait and see."

"WHO ARE THOSE flowers from, Mom?" Tate asked as he sat down to dinner on Sunday night, having limped over to the main house.

Other cowboys were streaming in, complimenting Mom on what smelled like a delicious pot roast.

"Ellie's girls gave them to me after church." Mom set a basket of cornbread rolls on the table. There was more color in her cheeks today, but he noticed she was favoring the arm where the pony had bitten her. "And if that makes some of you feel guilty because you didn't make it to church today or you haven't given me flowers in a long time, then good."

"I was on bed rest and tending to my injured horse," Tate said, beating most others to the excuse punch.

"Ah, yes. That poor horse." Mom gave Tate a teasing smile that implied she was purposefully ignoring Tate's injury. Her sympathy tended to end when one of her boys got out of bed. "How is Prince?"

"Good." Prince didn't seem at all bothered by his wound or Tate putting salve on his stitches. Tate was hopeful that his horse wouldn't have any emotional scars from the accident. As for Tate, he had a glorious raised bruise that circled half his calf, but the broken skin was scabbing over and he only experienced pain when he walked.

They all settled in for Dad to say grace.

"Speaking of our newest bull," Dad said when prayers were over. "Should we pull Chomper from the next few events and train him a bit more?"

"Yes," Tate blurted without thinking. "Pull him."

The cowboys at the table frowned, even Dad and Ryan.

"I might have said differently if Chomper hadn't tried to seriously injure everyone and everything around him," Tate qualified. He didn't like the vibe he was getting from the family.

"We should keep him on the circuit." Chandler chose a cornbread roll before passing the basket along to Zane. "Everyone was talking about him and his unusual bucking pattern. If he can be more of a gentleman after a ride, he might make the list of bulls that get asked to go to the post-season." Because only the most devilish of bulls were recruited during championship season, and the contracts for such an appearance were extremely lucrative.

"Sorry, Tate, but I agree with Chandler." Griff

dished himself a large helping of fried green beans. "Chomper caught his rider off-guard this time. He might not have been so frenzied if he'd thrown that cowboy clean off."

"Blade was determined to stay on, wasn't he?" Ryan chuckled. "Now, if it had been Cord Malone..."

Everyone except Tate and his parents laughed at poor Cord's expense. The young cowboy was determined to make a name for himself as a bull rider, but sadly he just didn't have a knack for it.

"He's out there trying," Tate said defensively, feeling like the odd man out on this Chomper issue. "Other guys might have quit by now." Cord didn't seem to have anyone watching his back.

Mom nodded, frowning at the others. "You boys wouldn't laugh at this Cord fella if he was one of your brothers."

"Oh, yes, we would," Griff crowed.

"What did you say his last name was?" Mom shook her fork in Griff's direction. "I'm going to get in touch with that poor boy and offer him a job here. I bet he could use someone rooting in his corner, just like you boys had."

That shut them up. Even Chandler, who was in charge of hiring and firing, said nothing.

Griff cleared his throat. "Cord Malone took that bull-riding course over at the Burns Ranch, Mom. Maybe something will stick this season."

"Maybe he won't draw Chomper or Tornado Tom," Zane said, half under his breath.

A few of the guys chuckled, quickly covering their laughter with coughs at Mom's chastising look.

"One or two of you who competed in bull riding can take him under your wing." It wasn't posed as a question. It was a command. Mom took a bite of pot roast and gave Zane and Griff a meaningful look. "We're here on this earth to help each other, you know."

Again, the table fell silent but for the sound of utensils on plates.

"Did you put something in Prince's stall to keep him occupied?" Dad asked Tate.

He nodded. "We hung a jolly ball in the corner and left a traffic cone outside his stall door."

The others began to offer suggestions.

"What are you going to do for a mount at next weekend's rodeo?" Chandler wondered aloud.

Tate looked at Ryan. They hadn't discussed Ellie's offer any further. In fact, they'd avoided the topic completely today.

"We have a lead on a horse we can borrow." Ryan dropped his gaze to his green beans. "What's on the wedding agenda this week, Mom? You don't need us until Wednesday, right?" His question was clearly a ploy to change the subject before someone could ask whose horse they might borrow.

"The rehearsal is Wednesday night at the church, with dinner immediately after. Remember that the rehearsal got moved back to six thirty." She pointed at all of them in turn with her fork. "Some of you are in the rehearsal, and the rest are required to be at the dinner. None of you be late. You know how I hate cooking for a crowd that don't show up on time."

Everyone reassured her they would be prompt.

After dinner, Ryan fell into step with Tate as they crossed the ranch yard to the bunkhouse. Tate moved slowly.

"We should check out Goldie," Ryan said in a carefully neutral voice.

It didn't escape Tate that Ryan hadn't mentioned Ellie's name. Other cowboys walked in front of and behind them, close enough to overhear.

"I can reach out and arrange something," Tate said, working hard to harness his excitement. "Maybe have her bring Goldie to Jo's?"

Ryan nodded. "During our midweek practice time. It's Wednesday this week."

Tate nodded. And somehow he managed to keep the smile he was feeling contained.

"WHOA. LOOK AT how fancy this place is." Della got out of the truck on Wednesday afternoon and took stock of the Pierce Ranch. She hitched up her blue jeans and strode toward the first of two barns like she owned the place.

"Wait for me." Lulu ran after her, one hand on her head to keep her cowboy hat on. Because she'd heard they were going to a horse ranch, she'd worn blue jeans. "I see some boys from school over there."

Since she'd heard Jo had two boys, Ellie let the girls go, assuming they'd be all right for a few minutes while she unloaded Goldie from the trailer. She took a moment to glance around the ranch. It had two large arenas, one covered, with a set of metal bleachers in between them. The wide breezeways in both barns allowed her to look through to the pastures beyond.

This is how my family's ranch should be.

Buildings built to last, not ones that were barely standing. A well-thought-out arrangement rather than buildings, pastures and pens put wherever there was room. But setting up the ranch right so it could go on for another hundred years would require capital for construction. Did she have enough?

Do I want to spend it on the ranch and not a restaurant?

Goldie nickered in the horse trailer.

"Coming, girl." Ellie opened the back and lowered the ramp. Then she went in, unclipped Goldie's lead rope and backed her out. "Good girl."

Goldie was a bright yellow palomino with a white mane. The sun glinted off her coat. She pranced sideways once she was free of the trailer, taking a good look at her surroundings. She was a prancer, just like Lulu was a skirt swisher.

"I know it's new, baby. But you're going to have fun here, I promise." Ellie patted her neck.

"There's no fun in competition roping." Tate approached, having come from the house behind them on the lane. He wore his working cowboy attire—straw cowboy hat, red checked shirt beneath a jean jacket, faded blue jeans and scuffed cowboy boots. And he didn't limp. "It's all work and no play as soon as the roping saddle goes on."

Ellie frowned. "I disagree with that. Roping is fun. Like a puzzle you only have seconds to solve." She smiled at Tate, a tentative smile that looked for agreement. "I loved competing until I got hurt and lost my nerve. Don't you love it?"

He came up to greet Goldie, gaze roaming appreciatively over her lines. "I do. Most times." He ran his hand over her back, from her withers to her haunches, then down one leg, picking up her hoof when she dutifully shifted her weight for him.

"Most times?" Ellie was perplexed. "When are the times you don't enjoy roping?"

"Frankly…" Tate set Goldie's hoof down and faced Ellie, tipping the brim of his cowboy hat up. "Ryan's determination to win the past few seasons and the addition of sponsors this year have stolen the fun I used to have when I was younger.

Although I admit that I've never enjoyed competition as much as I have practice."

Ellie processed what he was saying, taking note of the traces of burnout. "Any professional athlete has to juggle a love for their sport with a desire to get paid."

"I didn't set out to be a professional athlete." Tate moved closer to Ellie, warm gaze on her face. He covered her hand on the lead rope. "I did it because Ryan wanted me to. When I was a kid and imagined my future, I didn't picture me receiving trophies and cash prizes. I pictured a ranch, a wife and a passel of precocious kids."

My kids are precocious.

Ellie wasn't brave enough to say the words. She was too unnerved by Tate's hand over hers. Was he going to kiss her again? Or explain the reason behind his kiss last week? Or apologize for his mood after the rodeo on Saturday?

He said nothing. And that beard… She couldn't decipher his expression.

Ellie wet her lips, trying to say something intelligent, something helpful, something that would get him talking. "Goldie doesn't care for awards or accolades. She just wants to trap that calf as quickly as she can. She loves that part of it. And once time is called and you loosen that rope to set the calf free, she prances like a princess. That's love of the sport. Maybe you should let Ryan worry about your win record and just learn how to prance."

Tate gave a shout of laughter and took the lead rope from Ellie. "Did you bring Goldie's bridle? My saddle is in the tack room."

"She uses a hackamore. She has a sensitive mouth." Ellie hurried to the truck to retrieve it. "I've never used a bit on her."

"She's sensitive *and* she prances?" Tate shook his head. "Ryan won't like to hear that. He'll think she's not good enough to win on."

"Once you give her a try, you'll put up with her quirks. You and Ryan both." She walked beside him into the first barn and held Goldie while Tate put his roping saddle on her.

Goldie kept looking back at Tate while he worked, curious about him. It gave Ellie a chance to watch him, too. Tate saddled Goldie with confidence. She wished he'd show some confidence in their relationship. Maybe then she'd know where they stood—in the friendship zone or the something-more zone. There were no answers forthcoming.

They walked together out to the uncovered arena, which was farther back on the property.

It hadn't rained in weeks, and the Oklahoma dirt was dry and cracking beneath their feet. A breeze kicked up, swirling dust around their ankles.

Ellie held on to her hat, palm on the crown as

the wind tried to lift it from her head. "I should warn you that Goldie hasn't been ridden much this month. I've been busy with the ranch."

"You mean she needs spring breaking?" Tate grinned at Ellie, stroking a reassuring hand over the mare's neck. "Never apologize for a horse that kicks up her heels because she hasn't been ridden for a while. That makes a cowboy more excited to climb aboard, not less."

Ellie hoped he'd still have that attitude after her mare tested his skill against her winter freedom. She hoped Goldie would help Tate rediscover his joy in competition. And she hoped Goldie would help him win in the coming weeks.

"She's got a look in her eye that I like." Jo greeted them at the arena gate, holding it open. As Tate and Goldie passed, Jo gave Ellie a smile. "Nice to see you again, Ellie. How've you been?" They'd been in the same grade in school, friendly but not close. Jo had been too busy at her family ranch to join in many extracurricular activities.

While Ellie and Jo exchanged pleasantries, childish giggles from the cattle chute drew Ellie's attention.

Her girls were standing on the rails and smiling to beat the band. And nearby a pair of boys were doing the same.

Ellie gestured toward the kids. "My twins are going on ten. Yours?"

"A year older. Max told me the girls are a year behind them in school." Jo gazed at her boys fondly.

There was another round of childish giggles.

Ellie was pleased to see the girls fitting in. "Are your boys as prone to finding trouble as my girls?"

Jo grinned. "Yep. We'll have to set up a date to go riding. Our kids seem to be hitting it off."

"I'd like that. But our availability might depend upon Goldie and Tate's rodeo schedules." She nodded toward the pair just as Tate swung into the saddle.

Goldie pranced sideways, kicking her heels in the air slightly, making Tate laugh. After a bit more bucking, prancing and head tossing, Goldie settled down.

"You and I should talk about breeding Goldie." Jo closed the gate. "I like her spunk. If she's got the drive to compete you say she does, I have a few studs here that might make us both some good money."

"Hold that thought." Ellie felt a rush of relief that her horse had already begun to pass Jo's reputedly high standards. "The show's about to start."

CHAPTER ELEVEN

"MISTER TATE, are you sure you can ride Goldie?" That was Lulu. She sat on the cattle chute fence near the box Tate was trying to back Goldie into. "I think Mom rides her better."

"She's just testing me out, honey." And without a bit in her mouth, Goldie was demanding all Tate's skill as a rider. Legs, hands, voice, even the shifting of his weight. He was using it all to put her through her paces and get her to trust that he was a good boss.

"She's smaller than Prince," Ryan noted, unhelpfully. "And twitchier."

"Prince is a luxury sedan with hidden horse-power. Goldie feels like a little sports car with lots of *get up and go* off the line." Tate didn't care about the mare's size. In roping, the more compact a horse, the faster they were able to get out of the gate and pivot if things went wrong, like crowding a steer who didn't run straight. "Any words of advice, Jo? Ellie?"

"Nope," Ellie said.

"Nope," Jo echoed. "Let's just see what Goldie has under her hood." She stood in front of the chute and turned to the kids. "Max and Dean, don't show off. Girls, there's no straddling a cattle chute fence. That's how accidents happen. Are we clear?"

"For sure, for sure." Della gave her a thumbs-up.

"Both hands on the rails, girls," Ellie called from her seat on the railing near Tate.

"Yes, ma'am," the girls chorused.

Tate readied his rope. "I'm good when you are, Ry."

"Pauper and I have been waiting for the past five minutes," Ryan quipped. "You give the nod to go. No pressure."

No pressure.

Tate sought Ellie's gaze. She'd urged him to have fun. Fun required no pressure, or, at least, manageable pressure.

Manageable pressure.

Tate hadn't thought of his stress in those terms before. He hadn't even thought those two words went together. But they could if Ryan had his back and Ellie stood at his side.

"Boys, are you ready to release and time?" Tate asked Jo's kids.

"Yes, sir," they chorused.

"We're ready," Tate said. And surprisingly, he and Goldie were ready. She'd settled in the box after taking a gander at the steer in the chute.

But the mare hadn't relaxed. Her head was

high, and her weight was balanced on all four legs. She knew what came next—an all-out run.

"Go fast, Mister Tate." That was Lulu, wishing him luck.

"Get that cow so we can have milkshakes later," Della added.

Tate didn't have time to answer either one of them.

The cattle chute opened.

He held Goldie back until the steer's rear hips left the chute.

And then they were leaping forward.

Time decelerated for Tate. The world moved in slow motion.

Tate was swinging his rope, feeling the short rhythm of Goldie moving into a gallop beneath him and the steer running ahead. He didn't think about winning or challenges or puzzles. He felt his opportunity coming. The convergence of a target about to present itself as his rope wound around and behind and...

Tate threw. He cued Goldie to slow, to pivot, to swing the steer around and present its rear hooves to Ryan.

His twin threw, catching both legs.

In no time, both ropes were taut and the Oakleys were facing each other from either side of the steer. Time blinked back to real speed.

"Nice." That was Jo, always stingy with her praise.

Tate and Ryan loosened their ropes. Or Tate tried to. Goldie was prancing, just as Ellie had predicted she would.

Laughter filled the air. His. Joy filled Tate's heart. Practically to bursting.

His gaze sought Ellie's. She beamed with pride.

Things were beginning to turn for Tate. Not a huge change, to be sure. But he felt it nonetheless. There was a thrill in roping that he'd been missing the past year or so. Professionally, he could see the season schedule laid out in front of him, rather than looking at it through the glasses of dread. There would be happiness and fun. He and Ellie…they'd find a way to be together. They'd explore the possibility of a future at her pace.

It wouldn't be easy.

But Tate looked around, taking stock of Ellie and the girls. And he knew whatever obstacles they faced, they'd be worth the effort to overcome.

"WE NEED TO get motoring," Ryan told Tate as he led Pauper to their horse trailer. "Mom is going to be upset if we don't get to the wedding rehearsal on time."

"I know." Tate clicked on his phone and turned on the sound while following Ellie leading Goldie to her trailer. "We're moving now. We'll get there on time." By his reckoning, they had another hour and a half.

The horses had been cooled down, unsaddled and groomed, the cattle returned to their pasture. But one thing hadn't been tackled—a talk with Ellie.

"You win a milkshake, Mister Tate." Della trotted next to him, trying to keep pace with his long stride. "You did good."

"Better than your mom when she rides Goldie?" Tate teased.

Della pretended to think about it for two seconds. "No. She ropes cows all by herself." She laughed.

Tate laughed along with her.

Lulu skipped past. "I'm going to marry Max someday." One of Jo's twin boys.

"We're not talking about weddings." Ellie had the sharp hearing of every mother. "You're nine."

"A girl can dream." Lulu stopped skipping and pouted.

Tate's phone pinged with a text message. He tugged it out of his pocket. The message was from Ms. Alpaca.

Enjoy the wedding. I'll see you around.

He stopped walking. Held his breath. Felt cold inside. *The packed suitcase.*

His mother never texted him messages like this.

Tate was aware of the world around him. Goldie's hooves striking the trailer bottom. Ellie's soft, encouraging voice. Ryan closing the Done Roamin' Ranch's horse trailer. Jo telling the boys to go inside and wash up for the dinner their grandmother was making.

Just another normal day for a cowboy.

I'll see you around.

The packed suitcase.

Tate called his biological mother. She didn't answer.

He hadn't expected her to. Once she left, she didn't look back. She went dark communications-wise, as silent as someone in witness protection.

"Ryan." Tate turned around, gaze seeking his brother. "We need to go to Friar's Creek."

Ryan shook his head. "Another alpaca emergency? We have to be cleaned up and at the church by six thirty."

"I got a text message." Seven words from a mother who always sent much shorter texts: alpaca emergency, kitchen repair, coffee a.m. "She's leaving."

"She said that? In a text?" Ryan met him halfway across the ranch yard. "She never says goodbye."

Tate's mind was racing as he showed Ryan the message. "She thinks we're already at the rehearsal. I mentioned it to her the other day. The time got changed, remember? Moved back. We have to go."

"Tate, she could be gone already." Ryan tipped

his hat back. "We could be going on a wild-goose chase. We'll be late for the rehearsal."

Tate stared at his brother, saying nothing. His twin would know what Tate was thinking. He'd know that Tate couldn't attend a wedding rehearsal, couldn't smile and make nice if he didn't know what was going on with their biological mother.

It was silly on the face of it.

Tate knew their mother didn't love either of them the way she should. He knew he should be more like Ryan when it came to her erratic behavior. But his gut was in knots. He had to know if she was gone. And if she hadn't left yet, he needed to know why she was leaving.

Tate continued to stare at his twin.

Under his scrutiny, Ryan looked to the sky and then back to Tate. "We're going to Friar's Creek, horse and all." Ryan turned toward his truck. "Let's roll."

Tate took a step forward before remembering Ellie and the girls. He spun back around to say goodbye. "I can't thank you enough for today," he said to Ellie. And then he thought better about leaving so quickly. He rushed up to Ellie, took her into his arms and kissed her soundly.

"You gave me more than a horse," he whispered when their kiss was through. "I needed you—not just to listen but to be you."

I love you, Ellie.

Those last words stuck in his throat.

But he hoped the words were written in his gaze because he had no time for declarations or for quiet, romantic moments.

Ryan had started the truck. They had to leave.

"Ellie…" Tate almost asked her to come along, but he suspected this was something he and Ryan had to do on their own. "Can you move your truck?"

JO HELPED ELLIE move to a spot in the ranch yard that allowed Ryan and Tate to leave but meant she'd have to make some careful turns to get out with her horse trailer.

Maneuvering made all while Ellie juggled the questions and comments from her hyper little girls.

"Now I know why you loaned Mister Tate your horse." Della was loud, even for Della. "You love him."

"We're going to get married again." Lulu clapped her hands. "I want to walk down the aisle, too."

Ellie took directions from Jo in the side mirror, then turned her wheel and eased the rig back. No matter what she did, it felt as if little progress was being made. "There's not going to be a wedding."

"You kissed him!" they cried in unison.

Ellie pressed the brake too hard. "Can I have quiet, please?" She was worried about Tate and stressed about backing out. "I promise to answer all your questions when we get out of this ranch yard."

The girls stopped talking.

Ellie wondered if she'd be able to answer their questions. Tate's kiss had been unexpected. When he'd approached her, she'd thought he was going to claim a hug for support. But that kiss implied... That long look he'd given her...

He couldn't love her. They'd barely spoken after either kiss.

And she didn't have the mental space to think about Tate or answers to relationship questions. Her truck and trailer were now perpendicular to the driveway. She was trapped between two other trucks.

Jo tapped on her window, and when Ellie rolled it down, she said, "May I?"

"Please do." Ellie hopped out and came around to sit in the passenger seat. "If there's anything I hate, it's backing a trailer out of a tight space."

"Did you see our mom kiss Mister Tate?" Della asked Jo.

"I did." Jo turned the wheel and began to back up with more skill than Ellie had ever seen. "I was surprised."

"Me, too." Ellie grabbed her phone from the cup holder, calculating that the Oakleys had left five or ten minutes earlier. "I'm worried about them. When do you think we can call to check in?"

Jo finished backing up and pulled forward a

few feet, either engrossed in her task or considering Ellie's question. She turned the wheel the opposite way and backed up again. "I don't think we should call yet."

"Really?" Ellie really wanted to make sure Tate was all right. And to do that, she needed to hear his voice.

"I think we should drive over to Friar's Creek." Jo put the truck into Drive and turned the wheel hard the other way before inching forward and barely squeaking past a blue truck. She eased Ellie's truck onto the ranch's driveway to the applause of Della and Lulu. And then Jo took her phone out of her back pocket and called her grandmother to say she'd be late for dinner.

CHAPTER TWELVE

RYAN AND TATE pulled into their mother's driveway just as her car was backing out.

Ryan—being Ryan—blocked her in.

"You're my favorite brother," Tate told him before getting out.

"Technically I'm your only brother." Ryan followed him until they both stood at their mother's car door.

Ms. Alpaca glanced up at them in confusion. And then she turned off her car and got out. "Hello." Her nose was red and her eyes were bloodshot, as if she'd been crying.

Or drinking.

Tate hated himself for the disloyal thought.

"I think the word you're searching for is *goodbye*," Ryan said in a surprisingly neutral voice.

Tate was grateful that Ryan said anything. He was having trouble finding words. Any words.

"Yes," their mother answered in a choking voice. "*Goodbye.*"

It was as if she'd spoken the one thing that

unlocked Tate's vocabulary. "You were running away? Just like that? Taking off and leaving us to pick up the pieces while not knowing if you were dead or alive?"

"Well, I…" She sniffed, looking more present than she had in months.

"Did you stop and think about our feelings?" Tate demanded because he was having a hard time holding on to his composure. Too many emotions were running rampant inside of him.

"Easy now." Ryan touched Tate's shoulder before turning back to their mother. "Tate didn't mean to shout."

Was I shouting?

Tate hadn't thought so. But there was a roaring in his ears, so who was he to tell?

"We've helped you get set up here, M-*Mom*," Ryan said in a gruff voice, stumbling over her name. "We wanted you to be happy in Friar's Creek. If you weren't happy, you should have told us. Are you lonely? Do you miss Dad?"

"Well, I…" Again, she sniffed. But this time a tear tracked down her cheek, too.

Everything inside of Tate retracted, like a turtle drawing back into its shell. He hadn't meant to make her cry. He didn't think Ryan had either.

"Why would you want me to stay? I'm *Ms. Alpaca* to you. Not *Mom*."

Tate exchanged a glance with Ryan. He didn't know how to answer. He just knew a relationship with their biological mother was looking impossible. Because… Because…

One of the alpacas trilled, echoing Tate's worries.

And then the answers came, the words Tate needed. "It's true that we don't know how to address you," Tate said. "Or how to act with you. But that's because we haven't spent enough time together. We're family by blood. That means we have to try, try, try again until we figure it out. And wherever we end up is where we're meant to be."

"Well said," Ryan murmured in an even tone he used with spooked livestock. "Were you just going to drive off and leave your alpaca?"

Their mother recoiled. And it was like a blow to Tate's heart. Because it was as if she loved those animals more than she loved her own children.

She doesn't love us.

Maybe she never had. Maybe she never would.

But while Tate reeled back, Ryan moved closer to the woman who'd given them life. "Sheila is going to be heartbroken."

More tears spilled onto her cheeks. "You boys… you don't understand."

Tate stepped closer and took one of her hands. "Help us understand, Mom."

After a moment's hesitation, Ryan took her other hand.

Their mother drew a shuddering breath. "I can't do it," she wailed. And then she drew them close and hugged them.

Tate couldn't remember the last time they'd hugged.

They stood like that for a long time.

Tate looked over her head toward the alpaca. The entire herd was standing at the fence, watching. If his mother hadn't been hugging them, he might have assumed she was crying because she was leaving her alpaca behind.

When they all took a breath and a step back, Mom wiped her eyes. "After last Christmas... after all the time we spent together as a family when I came to visit...the pressure got to me." She swallowed thickly. "I was terrified that I'd disappoint you again. And that just made me...made me want a drink that much more." She wiped at her nose. "I checked myself into a program in Tulsa. No phones. No contact with the outside world."

Tate rubbed at his chest, encouraged by her confession, no matter how painful it was to hear. "You need to tell us when we pressure you."

Ryan nodded. "Sorry about that."

"I know." She reached for their hands. And it was so out of character that Tate sucked in a shuddering breath. "I'm trying to say that I can be sober. But...but not when you're around." There was honesty in her gaze. Honesty, no clouds or remoteness. And yet there was pain, too. "I'm the worst mother ever."

Neither one of them argued that statement.

"What you're saying…" Tate had to force the words around the lump in his throat. He needed clarification. "What you're saying is that you can't live near us or have us in your life on the regular *and* be sober."

"That's right. I was sober before I came here." She nodded, voice growing stronger. "I wanted to make things right between us. And I tried." She paused, chewing on her lip. "I tried so hard…" She dissolved into tears again.

Another round of hugging ensued.

The idea was debilitating. Tate had been so careful to be cheerfully helpful, shoving the hurt of the past in a remote corner of his brain. And for what? To be told his very presence was an attack on her sobriety?

Breathe.

He did. And he thought of Ellie. Imagined her hand in his. She'd tell him not to take any of this personally. She'd tell him to take the high road.

Almost immediately, he felt better.

His mother scrubbed at her face as she stepped back toward her car, glancing inside as if she wished she was already gone. "I know that I have no right to love you."

The Oakley men looked at one another and didn't disagree.

"But I do love you. I do care." She was crying again but determined to talk through it this time. "It's just that I can't *be* a mother to you. The pressure to try again just makes me want to drink."

It's safer not to try than to fail.

Hadn't she been saying that the entire time she'd been back? And hadn't Tate adopted that attitude when it came to competing? It had taken Ellie to reinstate the fun in roping.

"You're leaving to stay sober." The fact was finally sinking in, settling with less of a personal sting. Some people weren't cut out to be parents. He'd learned that lesson at the Done Roamin' Ranch. "Why didn't you tell us sooner? We could have talked through this."

"Or we could have given you a better send-off," Ryan said gently. "Bought you a cake. Given you flowers. With a card that wished Ms. Alpaca well." Ryan cast Tate a significant glance. *Not Mom*, he meant.

"We could have arranged for the alpaca to go with you," Tate added.

Her features crumpled once more. "I can't take them with me."

"I thought they made you happy?" Tate glanced over to the herd, taking note of their perpetually happy demeanors.

"They bring me so much joy. But they rely on me." She wiped her tears on her jacket sleeves. "And that makes me—"

"*Want to drink*," they all said together.

How incredibly sad. And Tate was ill-equipped to say anything that might make her feel better because, despite everything she'd said, he didn't want her to leave.

"Does taking off without warning make you feel better?" Ryan asked, perhaps with less empathy than before. He'd always had a shorter fuse when it came to their parents. And rightly so.

Their mother nodded. "I'm no good at goodbyes."

True.

Another truck with a horse trailer pulled up. Jo and Ellie got out. Della and Lulu tumbled out after them.

"Oh." Mom valiantly wiped her tears and tried to smile.

The girls called out greetings as they ran past, heading for the alpaca pasture.

Ellie walked toward Tate, compassion in her eyes. She had windblown hair and her clothes were streaked with dirt and horse slobber, but she'd never looked more beautiful to him.

She walked over to his mother and gave her a hug. "I'm told you're leaving. This must be so hard for you."

Mom shed more tears. She really wasn't made for long goodbyes.

Ellie hugged Tate next and whispered, "Tell me what you need."

"Just you," he whispered back. *Forever.*

Given Jo and Ryan were exchanging a similar embrace, he imagined they were having a similar whispered conversation.

But together, while the girls romped in the pasture with the alpaca, the two couples learned that Ryan and Tate's mother hadn't paid rent since she'd returned from rehab because she hadn't been working. She'd received a letter recently from her landlord claiming that she had thirty days to pay all the back rent as well as next month's rent. It had been the last straw for her.

She refused Tate's offer to pay her rent, much to Ryan's visible relief, a reaction that earned him a scowl.

"Do you have a destination in mind, Donna?" Jo asked kindly. By this time, they'd moved to the back porch, circling the wagons, so to speak. "A friend you can stay with?"

Mom nodded. "My sponsor lives in Oklahoma City. She told me I always have a room with her there. She has a job for me. I'll be able to pay the back rent to the landlord, a little at a time. She's expecting me tonight."

"And the alpaca?" Ellie asked ever so gently. "Are they paid for?"

Tate and Ryan exchanged shocked looks.

"No." It was kind of amazing that Mom still had any tears left, but the waterworks began anew. "I made an arrangement in December to make payments on the herd."

"Are you behind on those payments, too?" Ryan asked, not as delicately as Ellie had.

She nodded, eyes pleading for forgiveness. "I put money down. Tate's money he gave me last year." She sucked in a breath. "You're disappointed in me. I knew you would be when you found out."

"I'll take them," Ellie said briskly and without hesitation. She looked around at four incredulous expressions. "They'd fit right in at the sheep ranch. And Donna can visit them any time."

"Oh, but…" Mom's voice sank to a whisper. "I owe a lot of money."

"I can imagine. They're pricey." Ellie gave Tate's hand a reassuring squeeze. "I have some money saved. And I've been trying to think of ways to make the family ranch more profitable." She patted his mother's shoulder. "It'll be all right."

"Oh. I… Thank you. I knew from the moment Tate mentioned you that you were a trustworthy soul." Mom blew her nose with a crumpled tissue. "I have no right to ask, but…" She grimaced toward Ellie. "Could you…"

"I'll give them a French-poodle cut. I promise." Ellie patted her shoulder again. "Tate will send you pictures."

"Thank you. Oh, thank you." Mom rose to her feet and hugged Ellie, hugged her tight, like she meant it. And then she hugged the rest of them—not politely, the way she had with Tate these past few months, but with feeling.

One step forward, two steps back, Tate thought.

"I'll pay you for your share," Ellie told Tate unexpectedly. "The down payment Donna referenced. I know you need that money for your horse."

Tate frowned. "You don't have to. We can…"

"Share custody?" She shook her head. "No-no-no. It's cleaner this way."

Cleaner? As in cleaner when they broke up? Or if they never got together?

"Tate." Ryan shot to his feet, flashing everyone his phone screen. "Look at the time. The rehearsal."

"It's all right." Jo held up her cell phone, yin to Ryan's yang. "I texted Ronnie earlier. She's going to be a difficult bride and arrive late. The way I figure it, we have just enough time to say farewell to Donna, load the alpaca in the horse trailers and drop you two off at the church."

"Oh. My boys found the perfect partners." Mom started crying again.

"I CAN'T BELIEVE we're taking the alpaca home," Della said from her seat on the way back to Clementine, repeatedly tossing her cowboy hat at the ceiling. "This is great."

Ellie hoped so. She'd committed a big chunk

of money to them. She glanced at Tate in the passenger seat, but he was silent.

"I can't believe we're getting alpaca *and* a wedding." Lulu kicked the back of Ellie's seat.

"Can we have no more wedding talk today?" Ellie returned her eyes to the road.

Tate had been quiet since Ellie had offered to purchase Donna's herd. She might have assumed he was grieving over Donna's departure if he hadn't been sulking beside her.

Well, *sulking* might be a strong word. Tate was quiet, but there was an air of annoyance about him, tension in the way he set his shoulders, a stiffness in the way his hands rested on his thighs.

"Why can't we talk about weddings?" Lulu stopped kicking Ellie's seat.

"There's a lot to be decided. We need to figure out where to put the alpaca. Sometimes it's best to focus on one thing before you move on to another." Or in this case, avoid boxing Tate into a corner with talk of weddings when he hadn't even asked her out.

"Mom, the alpaca have to go in the pasture outside our front door." Della dramatically tossed her hat to the floorboards. "I want to see them from our bedroom."

"That's the rams' pasture." They had to be kept as far away from the ewes as possible. "We can't put the alpacas in there. I don't know if they'll be safe."

"This is harder than I thought." Della stared out her window, much the way Tate was staring out his window.

Except Tate gave the impression that he'd like to be anywhere else but in Ellie's truck.

He'd kissed her goodbye at the Pierce Ranch and looked at her with what felt like love in his eyes. The same look she'd received upon arrival at his mother's house. And then...a wall came down just as it had the first time he'd kissed her.

"I'm going to miss Goldie." Lulu sounded sad.

"Me, too," Ellie said.

They'd put Goldie in Ryan and Tate's horse trailer. After the rehearsal, they'd go to the Done Roamin' Ranch. The alpacas had been loaded into Ellie's four-horse trailer, which was a snug fit.

They approached the outskirts of Clementine. Ellie followed Ryan's rig, slowing as the speed limit reduced.

The reference to snug fits led Ellie to another thought. "I suppose we can put your horses in with the rams, girls. The alpacas can stay in the horse paddock for now." The horses were large enough to handle any annoyed ram.

"You've got that empty pasture by your barn." It was the first time Tate had spoken the entire ride.

Ellie shook her head, much as she didn't want to rain on Tate's parade now that he was talking again. "That's the pasture we'll put the sheep to be sheared in. It's our rotation pasture."

"We could put them in the backyard," Lulu suggested. "That way we could give them carrots from the kitchen."

"There are shrubs back there that might make them sick," Ellie said firmly. "In fact, there are shrubs in the front that might make them sick." She wasn't sure of anything at this point. She turned right after Ryan did.

Tate shifted in his seat to face Ellie. "You don't have to pay me back for the alpaca. I gave my mother that money. I'm not hard up for it. As it is, I should be paying you for use of your horse."

"I didn't ask for payment." Ellie spared him a glance. "Is that why you're upset?"

"I don't want money for the alpacas. Consider that a fee for you loaning me Goldie. You said you wanted to open up a restaurant someday."

"And you're trying to own a competition horse outright." That was the scuttlebutt, after all. "One dream isn't more important than the other."

"It is. To me," Tate said quietly. "You should come first."

It was all making sense now. This wasn't an argument about money. "Why do you always think other people's needs come before yours? When are you going to put yourself first?"

Whether it was the tone of the adults or the excitement from the day catching up to them, the twins had fallen silent in the back seat.

"Tate, opening a restaurant is one of many dreams I *used to* have. Not all dreams come true or last. Nor are they meant to." Ellie pulled up behind Ryan's horse trailer in front of the church.

"Dreams are important. Your dreams should all come true, Ellie." Tate turned to face the girls. "Take good care of those alpacas."

They earnestly promised to do so.

"Hey." Ellie caught his arm when he would have opened the door. "Are…are you okay?" *You*, not *we*.

"I…" He shook his head. "This is all new to me. I need to go." He hopped out, closing the door firmly without slamming it.

"Is Mister Tate calling off the wedding?" Lulu asked.

"There was never a wedding," Ellie said automatically.

"He seemed mad," Della added.

"I think he and I just need to sit down and have a talk." But with Ronnie's wedding this week and a competition looming, it didn't seem likely anytime soon.

CHAPTER THIRTEEN

"YOU LOOK LIKE something the cat dragged in." Their foster mother met Tate and Ryan at the church door.

Tate glanced out in time to see Ellie drive away. She'd accused him of putting her needs before his own. That was what love was all about, wasn't it?

"Working cowboys." Mom huffed and waggled a finger at them. Her face was bright red, as if she'd taken too many emotional laps around the church waiting for them. "You're lucky Ronnie is running late. Something about a broken heel on her shoe."

Mom herded them toward the church proper just as Jo and Ronnie came in behind them.

"We're here," Ronnie said, looking like an unworried bride. She hurried on into the church.

"The bride always operates on her own schedule." Jo took hold of Ryan's arm and marched after Ronnie.

Tate escorted Mom down the aisle.

The minister waved them toward the altar. "Ah, the bride is here. Now we can start."

"Everything okay, honey?" Mom moved with slow, deliberate steps. "Griff said you had an emergency at your mother's place."

"She left." Tate removed his cowboy hat, the gears in his head turning to his biological mother. "Growing up, did we ever make you want to drink? You had ten or more boys at a time."

"I never wanted to drink." Mom moved with slow, deliberate steps. "But I prayed a lot. I still pray for you all. I pray you'll be happy and loved. Safe and settled." She patted his arm. "How's that leg of yours?"

"Colorful." Tate smiled at Mom, sending up a prayer that her physical struggles were only due to a little added stress and a little less sleep. He'd never be able to thank her enough for choosing to be his mother and showing him what family should look like.

Dad waved to them, love in his eyes.

"I like how Dad always puts you first." Tate couldn't understand why Ellie hadn't wanted him to do that with her.

Mom chuckled softly. "Your father *mostly* puts me first. And I try to do the same. You can't neglect your own needs and dreams for someone else. If you do, you'll never be happy. Now, no more talk. We're slowing down the show."

Was Ellie right?

Tate helped his mother to a seat in the front pew, went to stand with the other groomsmen in the vestibule and pretended to listen to the preacher's instructions about how and when to take their places on the altar. But Tate didn't remember a word that was said during the rehearsal. He was rehashing things that Ellie had said to him about never saying no. And things Ryan had said to him about chasing a life he deserved.

Woodenly, Tate followed Griff to the altar, stood there quietly while a few words were spoken and then followed Griff to the center of the dais when the *I do*'s were recited, took the arm of Allison Burns, one of Ronnie's good friends, and walked out.

After walking through the ceremony a third time, his mother piped up as Wade and Ronnie strolled past her. "Where do the dates sit?"

Everyone in the wedding party stopped moving toward the door.

"I mean at the wedding reception." Mom turned to look at Ronnie. "Where do the dates of the groomsmen sit?"

Next to her, Dad was speechless.

Griff chuckled. "Always thinkin', aren't you, Mom?"

That broke the tension. People laughed.

Dad whispered into Mom's ear. She waved him off.

Tate came down the altar steps. He held out his hands to her. "Can I help you up?"

"You're all trying to distract me. It's a valid question." She grasped his hands and let him aid her to her feet. "There are all these new traditions. I just thought I'd ask about the plus-ones of the wedding party. Is there a special table for their dates? Or…" She blinked up at Tate, cheeks pink, gaze a bit distant. "Why does anyone other than the bride and groom need to sit at the head table?"

"Mary?" Dad got to his feet, concern etching his brow. "Are you feeling okay?"

"I'm fine," Mary said in a breathless voice. "I just feel…like time is running out."

And then she crumpled.

"ALL THIS FUSS," Mom said into an oxygen mask while laying on an ambulance's stretcher near the church altar. Her words were muffled. "It's just low blood sugar."

"I think I'm the doctor here, Mary," Doc Nabidian told her in that levelheaded tone of voice Tate imagined he used whether someone had passed a sports physical for school or was dying. He'd been at his clinic a few blocks over when Mom collapsed. "You've got a fever and an infected abrasion." He gestured to the red, swollen spot on her arm where the pony had bitten her. It was as big as a golf ball and had been covered by the sleeve of her dress. "We're going to take you to the hospital and run some tests."

"Nonsense." Mom made as if to sit up before realizing she had a strap across her waist. She turned teary eyes toward Dad. "Frank. Tell them how many times I've been bitten before. These things always swell up and then heal in their own time."

"If you'd have told me," Griff said with a teasing glance, "I'd have rubbed dirt on it for you the way Dad used to tell us to rub dirt on our scrapes and bruises when we were kids."

"And it probably would have helped," Mom raised her voice over the ensuing laughter. "But I'm cooking dinner tonight. I don't have time to be taken to the hospital."

"Honey," Dad's eyes weren't so dry either. "We're doing what Doc says. You want to be healthy for the wedding, don't you?"

"We'll make do, Mary," Ronnie promised.

Not that Mom seemed to hear. "I didn't even fall. You and Tate caught me, honey." She flopped back onto the stretcher, causing a stir from her caregivers. "It's not fair."

"Am I missing something?" Tate asked Griff. "What is she talking about? *She didn't even fall?*"

"It's something Grandma Harrison used to say. Don't you remember?" Griff pitched his voice in a bad imitation of their foster grandmother: "After sixty, one fall and one bone break is all you need to lose your independence."

"Mom's not that old."

"Dude, she's gonna be seventy next year." Griff scoffed. "I know you've been busy practicing to be a world-champion roper, but she worries about dying all the time lately. Why do you think she wanted to hand out those boxes?"

"I thought it was because of this nostalgic kick she's been on lately…"

"Is that what she told you?" Griff scoffed. And then scoffed some more.

"Ronnie, where's your mother? Can she cook for me tonight?" Mom removed her oxygen mask, causing another stir from the medical team. "It's not even cooking." This last she probably added because it was known far and wide that Ronnie's mother didn't cook much or well. She'd hosted Wade and Ronnie's engagement party, and that had been a culinary disaster. "The brisket and chicken are ready for the tacos. I can make you a list of what to do before I go to the hospital."

"No, Mary. You can't," the doctor said firmly.

Mom frowned. "Now, Doc—"

"I know someone who might be able to step in," Tate said in his usual role as Switzerland. "A real, honest-to-goodness professional chef." And when folks looked at him blankly, Tate added, "Ellie Rowland."

Ryan rolled his eyes.

"That's perfect," Mom said in a muffled voice since her oxygen mask was back on. "Get me her number and I'll call her."

"Sure," Tate said, although he had no intention of doing so.

There was a pall over the wedding party as Mom was wheeled out of the church and loaded into the ambulance.

"Griff, I need you to drive your father to the hospital," Doc Nabidian said in a way that allowed for no argument. "The rest of you try not to worry. I'll probably have Mary stay overnight for tests. Enjoy your dinner."

"If you call Ellie, Ryan's gonna have his boxers in a bunch," Griff predicted.

Tate called her anyway.

"THANKS FOR COMING over on such short notice." Tate met Ellie in the ranch yard, looking nervous. "This is the third time you've rescued me today. First Goldie, then my mother's alpaca and now the rehearsal dinner." And yet, despite his thanks, he wasn't looking at her with love the way that he was earlier.

And why would he have love on his mind? Tate was probably reeling from his biological mother leaving and his foster mother collapsing.

She groaned inwardly and hopped out of her truck. "Right. That's me. Clementine's resident superhero." She reached back for a pair of Crocs, her chef's jacket and her set of knives. "I'm going to address the elephant in the ranch yard. We aren't on the same wavelength, and we haven't been since we…since we almost kissed." Yes, that was right. It wasn't any kiss that had messed up their friendship. It was her being attracted to Tate in the first place. "We're better friends than anything more."

They stood staring at each other. The moon was rising behind Tate, just a sliver of a moon in a pinkening sunset. A bird in a tree above them chattered a reprimand. A coyote howled in the distance.

Gigi would have said those were all signs that caution was required. Ellie took it to mean that it wasn't a cautionary yellow light they were facing but a full-on red stop.

"We should talk?" He voiced it as a question.

Ellie stewed a little. But only a little. "I don't have time. Dinner must be served to Mary's standards." She pushed past him toward the main house. "Mary called me from the hospital, which is a good sign. She was very clear about everything." At least, until the nurse made her hang up the phone. "The chicken and brisket are cooked, but nothing else has been done."

Tate matched her stride, walking so close that they bumped shoulders. "We can talk while you prep. I'm helpful in the kitchen. Besides, the rest of the wedding party stopped at The Buckboard for a round of drinks. We have time. Maybe thirty minutes."

"That can go by in a blink of an eye or seem like an eternity." Ellie suspected it would depend upon what Tate had to say.

They hurried up the stairs and into a mudroom where they shed their hats, boots and jackets. And then Ellie put on her Crocs and chef's jacket and entered the kitchen, smoothing a hand over her neat braid as she took in the room with a professional eye.

Immediately, her mood improved.

The kitchen was large and designed to cook for a crowd. The cabinets were oak. The countertops were white quartz. The stove had six gas burners. The refrigerator could have been found in a busy restaurant it was that large. Tate showed her the spice cupboard. It was well stocked. Mary had taken out all the bowls, serving trays, serving utensils, plates, glasses and silverware. Everything was marked with what she intended. A pretty bowl decorated with lemons had a note that read Guacamole. A matching smaller bowl had a note that read Mild Salsa.

Mary could have run a kitchen at any five-star restaurant. She was that organized.

"About that talk… I'm not much good at sharing my feelings," Tate admitted. He lingered at the end of the counter, out of Ellie's way as she made an inventory of things and formed a plan in her head.

She tried not to look at him. If she looked at Tate, she'd fall prey to all that vulnerable handsomeness. The tender gleam in his eyes. Plus he had hat hair and stood in his socks. It felt intimate, like home.

Now wasn't the time for feelings.

"Take a moment, I need to get things moving." Ellie removed the briskets from the Dutch ovens and the chickens from the pressure cookers, delegating the pulling apart and cutting to Tate with one of her knives. She poured the juice from each into separate warming trays on the kitchen table, which she then turned on, readying them for the meat and chicken. Then she prepared guacamole and a variety of salsas and arranged all taco toppings into pretty bowls that Mary had set aside and labeled. All without anything substantial being said between them.

"Your mother is a gem in the kitchen. I'd cook for her anytime."

"Anytime?" Tate slid bite-sized chunks of chicken into a warmer. He'd already filled a tray with brisket. "Remember there's a wedding reception Sunday."

"Anytime. She made this so easy. It's been a joy completing her meal plan." Ellie couldn't remember when she was happier cooking. She began frying tortillas, intending to delicately crisp them and add flavor. "As much as I want to run the family ranch, I'm afraid fixing fence and sheep shelters isn't my passion."

"Not to mention your joy—or lack thereof—for the upcoming sheep-shearing season."

"Yes. Don't remind me." Ellie sighed. "I'm used to running a kitchen and estimating how many hours for service. I did the math. Five hundred sheep to shear. I could probably do four, maybe five, an hour. Five an hour would be one hundred hours of shearing. If I work ten-hour days, that's ten days of work." The tortillas were sizzling. She flipped them. "Have I mentioned how I hate math?"

"Not lately. But I recall that you were good at it in school despite loathing it." He smiled softly when she tried to deny it. "Come on, be honest. You were."

And there it was. An opening. *Be honest.*

"Well, if I'm going to be honest, have I mentioned that I'm not a fan of your beard?" Ellie reached up to gently tug his whiskers. "It hides half of your expression."

Tate caught her hand, holding it to his bearded cheek. "That's the point."

Ellie frowned. "Why would you want to hide anything? Do you have a scar behind all that stubble?" He'd referenced something about scars back when he'd noticed the scar on her lip.

"No. It's gotten harder lately to keep up the pretense of the nice Oakley." His words were somber, resentful, even. "I'm a product of my own PR."

"Of being nice?"

He nodded. "If I'm not smiling around town, people ask me what's wrong."

"All those women on your dating carousel… The guys in your social circle…" Ellie was beginning to catch on. "They want you to be cheerful. Twenty-four seven."

He nodded once more.

"That has to be a hardship. No one's happy every minute of every day. You don't have to smile for me," she assured him. "You can be yourself."

"I'd expect you to understand," he said gruffly.

"Because we're friends?" She held her breath.

He blew one out. "Because we're more than friends."

Those were the words she'd been waiting to hear from him. And yet they didn't bring her joy. Why not?

Because he didn't look happy about it.

"Maybe that's the problem." Ellie realized her palm was still resting on his face. She tried to ease her hand away, but he held on to it, bringing her hand, her arm and Ellie herself close to his chest.

"I want to risk things for you, Ellie. I want to trust that this will be something real." His gaze drifted toward the kitchen table and the wall beyond it. That wall had a large bulletin board. And on it were pictures of what looked like every foster who had ever found a home at the Done Roamin' Ranch. "But to do that, I have to move slowly, even when my heart says to move fast, because folks don't make a habit of staying in my life, not even the ones who are supposed to."

"Like your parents." *Like me.*

"Yes." His gaze returned to hers, dark and full of guarded love.

He doesn't trust me to stick by him.

Ellie was worried about the opposite—him discovering that she wasn't the right woman for him. They were stuck. She thought she might cry. "Loving someone isn't a guarantee that things will work out." Her love hadn't been enough for Buck. Who's to say it would be enough for Tate?

The smell of burning tortillas had her spinning away. "Now isn't the time for this conversation." She dumped the ruined tortillas in the trash.

"If not now, then when?" Tate's voice was low and strained. "Things change, Ellie. Words are left unspoken or misunderstood. Feelings get all bent out of shape. Suitcases get packed. And then what's left is…a big hole." In his heart, she thought he meant.

A vehicle door slammed outside. Voices lifted, announcing the arrival of the wedding party.

"I can't give you promises, Tate." Ellie dropped tortillas into the sizzling pan. "Raising alpacas might not save my family's ranch. Dad might get better and ask us to move out."

"And you might decide you love cooking more than raising sheep." He glanced away.

People began streaming into the house through the mudroom and front door. There was laughter and joyful voices.

"Maybe we aren't ready for anything more," Ellie said softly. *Maybe we never will be.*

Tate frowned.

Ryan entered the kitchen, pausing to take a bead on the mood in the room, if his probing glances were any indication. "Thanks for coming, Ellie," he said after too long of a pause.

"Any word about Mom?" Tate asked his brother, reaching for his cell phone. "I've been busy helping Ellie get ready."

"No. I'll call Dad. You try Mom or Griff." Ryan moved into the living room.

Ronnie entered the kitchen. She had a personality that was larger than life, and it suited her to a tee. She had thick dark lustrous hair that fell halfway down her back. She'd always worn bright colors and large prints, even in school. Tonight's dress was a bold rose print. Her red cowboy boots matched the color of her lipstick.

"You're an angel, Ellie." Ronnie hugged her enthusiastically. "I can't thank you enough. My mother invited everyone on her side of the family to the rehearsal. And Wade's mother invited all the old foster boys. Otherwise we'd have had a quiet dinner at a restaurant."

"No medical updates," Tate said to no one in particular. "But Mom is cranky and requesting a picture of the food before anyone touches anything."

Six or seven people took out their cell phones and starting snapping shots.

Ellie touched Ronnie's arm. "I hear you might need a backup caterer for this weekend."

"Yes. I love you, Ellie." Ronnie hugged Ellie again, even more enthusiastically this time. "I didn't want to ask."

"Friends can ask. Always. Besides, you're the bride. You shouldn't worry about anything." Ellie went back to the stove. "More guests are arriving. Go. I need to get back to the tortillas."

Before Ronnie went anywhere, Wade joined her. "Everything looks great, Ellie."

"Wade, did you hear?" Ronnie wrapped her arms around her fiancé's neck, clearly adoring him. "Ellie can handle the wedding reception if your mother can't. Everything is going to be all right. Ellie's organizational skills are better than mine."

"I told you not to worry." Wade spun Ronnie around. And then he came over to hug Ellie. "We'd owe you. Whatever you need. Just call."

"Oh, I don't need—"

"She needs help sheep shearing," Tate cut her

off. "Rounding up the different herds, moving them through the shearing shed, returning them to their pastures."

"Like we do during branding season." Wade nodded.

"Near enough." Tate stared at Ellie, daring her to contradict her need for help.

She wasn't that proud. Ellie mouthed her silent thanks.

Wade shrugged. "I've always wanted to learn how to shear sheep."

"How funny." Ryan began making himself a plate. "Tate has always wanted to learn how to shear alpaca."

LATER, AFTER THE main meal had been eaten, toasts made and dessert served, Ronnie came over to Ryan and Tate, who were picking up dishes in the living room and loading them into a plastic tub Mom kept for just that purpose.

"Boys." Ronnie picked up a pair of empty coffee mugs and put them in the tub. "What did your mother mean when she asked about where dates were going to be seated? Most of you groomsmen don't have dates."

"She's been hounding us to get dates." Tate balanced plates on his arm.

"Those of us who don't have a steady girl, that is," Ryan quipped, moving to a corner table with a stack of dirty plates.

"Being the date of a member of the wedding party is the worst." Ronnie tapped a hand over her heart. "I speak as the voice of experience. You have no special place in the church. You have to wait for all the pictures to be taken. You don't sit with the family or at the head table. It's only after the dancing starts that it's any fun."

Tate nodded, catching on. "That's why Mom asked where they'd sit. She probably realized that if we *did* get dates, they wouldn't be successful unless we could sit with them at the reception."

"Like any of your dates are successful, Tate." Ronnie teased, although there was a hint of seriousness, too. "You don't seem to even date anyone more than twice. You're a serial dater. Commitment phobic. A confirmed bachelor."

"That's not true," Tate protested, thinking about Ellie. He'd love to be committed to her and have everyone in his family be happy for them. But every time he thought about the future, he worried that Ellie's life was destined to be lived elsewhere.

"Tate has a longstanding thing for Ellie Rowland." Ryan had an annoying way of joining the conversation when Tate would have preferred he stay silent. Ryan filled the tub with plates and silverware. "That's why he never got serious with anyone. They can't measure up to Ellie."

"Ahh." Ronnie sobered, nodding slowly. "I

can help you with that. Remember me? Rancher matchmaker?"

"No thanks." Tate cleared his throat. "Now, if you'll excuse me, I need to check on the woman who saved dinner."

"Flowers are a great thank-you gift," Ronnie called after him.

Tate found Ellie where he'd left her when she'd made him a plate and shooed him out of the kitchen. She stood near the kitchen table, condensing food into one warming tray, looking like the professional chef that she was with her hair in a neat braid and her white, unsullied jacket.

"How's it going out there? Do you think everyone got enough to eat?" She glanced at the remains, which could probably feed five cowboys. Four if they were really hungry. "Or should I pack it up for someone to take?"

"They've moved on to the alcohol end of the evening. If you put it in containers, I can take it to the bunkhouse, and it'll get eaten."

"Okay, containers it is." She went to the corner of the kitchen where Mom had a stack of containers beneath a dish towel and a note that said Leftovers.

While she worked, Tate took care of the dishes.

"How much does it take to start a restaurant?" he wondered out loud.

"A lot. Especially if it's a fine-dining restaurant." There was a wistfulness in her tone, giving

Tate the impression that she hadn't completely set aside her dream.

"Don't pay me for the alpacas, Ellie. You should keep your money and your dreams."

Ellie came up behind him, rested her hands on his shoulders and kissed his cheek. "It's sweet of you to want me to make my dreams come true, but the truth is that being a head chef or running a restaurant is a strain on one's personal life. In fact, a chef has no life. The girls didn't see me five days a week. And for that, I'm forever regretful. That dream is checked as done. It doesn't make me or those I love happy." She kissed his cheek again. "Darn whiskers. Did you even feel that?"

"No." He spun on his heel and wrapped his arms around her, scruffy beard and all. "Let's try this a different way." And then he kissed her.

And he would have kept on kissing her if someone hadn't entered the kitchen and cleared their throat.

"I guess you don't need my help after all." Ronnie deposited a collection of champagne flutes on the table, then hustled off, leaving her full-throated laugh in her wake.

Ellie framed Tate's face with her hands. "What am I going to do with you?"

"Well…" Tate stared into those green eyes, wishing he'd had a so-called normal home life and could dive into a relationship with her head-first. "Move forward with me. Slowly. And eventually we'll get to where we're meant to be."

CHAPTER FOURTEEN

THE KITCHEN WAS empty and the stove cold when Tate and Ryan showed up the next morning at the main house an hour before breakfast, intent upon feeding the crew.

Tate missed Ellie and his foster mother's presence, too. Family was important to them both. They'd appreciate him organizing things this morning, rallying the troops after a day of so much turmoil. But the flip side of that was the absence of his biological mother, not from this place, but from a place he'd created in his dreams. Tate had realized last night that longing for a perfect family that included his biological mother wasn't a dream that made him happy anymore. And, as Ellie had said, dreams should make you and those you love happy. He'd tried. It would take more than a day to set aside that dream about his family.

"We don't have to do this." Ryan stood in the middle of the kitchen, looking out of his element. "Do we?"

"Yeah, we do." Tate checked the fridge for supplies. "Imagine how Mom's spirits will be lifted by a picture of her boys having breakfast together." He handed Ryan a carton of eggs. "A breakfast we made ourselves."

"I always burn the eggs." Ryan set the carton on the counter near the stove.

"Make pancakes." Tate handed him a gallon of milk.

"I always burn the pancakes." Ryan set the milk on the counter.

Tate rolled his eyes and handed his twin a package of bacon. "Put on your chef's hat, brother. Most people like some char on their bacon."

Ryan frowned but didn't set the bacon aside. "I should have been the one to go with Dad, not Griff."

Tate shook his head, searching in a lower cupboard for the right frying pan for eggs. "Griff never went into a situation with a serious bone in his body. When things get grim, you want him there to lighten the mood." Doc Nabidian knew what he was doing when he gave that order.

"I suppose." Ryan used the kitchen scissors to open the package of bacon. "Any word from Ms. Alpaca?"

"You mean our other mother? Yeah. She sent me a text last night when she arrived."

Two words: Here safe.

"I'm trying, Tate." Ryan looked pained.

"I know. And I appreciate it." Tate found the

high-sided frying pan. "It's going to take time for me to let her go. And speaking of time and trying…" He set the frying pan on the front burner and then placed a hand on Ryan's shoulder. "We need to encourage everyone to open their keepsake boxes. Mom would love that."

"Wow. You're acting like this blood infection Mom has is serious. I mean, I know it is, but she's going to be fine…right?" Standing in front of an open low cupboard full of appliances, Ryan ran a hand through his hair, looking lost. "Can I wait to open my box until after the rodeo this weekend?"

"Ry…"

"Think about this." Ryan got out the griddle which was what Mom used to fry bacon for a crowd and make pancakes on. "This is going to be one of those things that gets in our heads."

Afraid of the same thing, Tate wrapped his brother in a fierce hug but said, "What happened to no pressure? No worries?"

"Those boxes have been out of sight and out of mind for years." Ryan held onto Tate. "When you add it to *Mom* leaving and *Mom* being in the hospital… There's only so much hard news I can take. I'm already fighting the urge to crawl back into bed."

Tate held his brother at arm's length. "I have one more bit of hard news."

Ryan grimaced. "What's that?"

"You're not getting out of burning that bacon."

"THIS IS YOUR IDEA?" Ellie's father flipped down the seat on his walker and sat on it, facing the paddock.

The sun was out, and the girls were at school. It was Dad's first chance to take a close look at the alpacas. It was also the first time he'd crossed the ranch yard since his stroke.

"You think these will increase profits?" Dad gestured toward the alpacas, frowning. "Feels like woo-woo."

"It's a start," Ellie said, not without a good dose of trepidation because it was an expensive start.

"They're adorable." Gigi moved past Dad, lifting the hem of her long orange ombre skirt to move closer.

The alpacas perked up at her appearance, perhaps drawn to the tinkling of her bell earrings and the jangle of her bracelets.

"We should ask Robbie," Dad grumped.

Ellie had had enough mentions of her brother as the ranch savior to last her a lifetime.

"Their fleece sells for two hundred times more per ounce than sheep wool." Ellie had done her research last night after returning from the Done Roamin' Ranch. She'd been struck with buyer's remorse. A few online searches and she'd felt better about both the alpacas and Tate. If this venture worked, she could see herself staying in Clementine. That would be the reassurance Tate needed to fully launch a relationship with her.

"I like those numbers, Ellie." Gigi pet Sheila, the black alpaca. "Are all alpacas this friendly? My blood pressure is dropping already. Get yourself up here, Mr. Cranky Pants, and see for yourself."

"Livestock aren't pets." Dad hunched his shoulders and crossed his arms.

"If I was a licensed therapist, we could do alpaca therapy," Gigi went on, paying him no mind. "I bet people would pay a fortune for it. They'd leave feeling happy and refreshed."

"You have no license." Dad's voice sounded how it had back in the day when he'd told Ellie the hour of her curfew. "And you," he continued, pointing at Ellie. "You're a chef."

"True. I did some cheffing last night." It had been fun and somewhat hopeful.

Ellie could love Tate Oakley. She was certain of it. Not because of his occasional kisses—which were excellent—but because he didn't try to portray himself as perfect, the way Buck had. And he didn't seem intimidated by her success, the way Buck had. He was kind to his parents and her girls. And he appreciated Goldie despite her flaws and foibles. Come to think of it, he appreciated Ellie despite her flaws and foibles.

"How much?" Dad interrupted her thoughts, thumping his hand on a walker handle in that cantankerous way of his. "*Per animal*."

Ellie had been hoping he wouldn't ask, not because it cancelled out the profit, but because they were so very expensive up front. Her father hadn't spent a penny upgrading his house or the vehicles since she'd gotten married.

"How. Much?" he repeated stubbornly.

"Ten times the cost of a high-quality ewe," Ellie admitted.

"*Ten times?*" Dad choked out the words. "That's too much!"

"Not when it brings in two hundred times the profit in wool." Gigi turned to give her son-in-law a knowing shrug. "Even I can do the math. It's a good deal. For sure, for sure." She returned her attention to the alpaca, softly murmuring baby talk.

But Dad was silent, and Ellie suddenly doubted her business acumen. He'd been running this place for decades. What did he know that she didn't?

"It's too much." Dad's chest was heaving as if he was having trouble breathing.

"Dad." Ellie rushed to his side. "Are you okay?"

Gigi turned, staring at him with the trained eye of a medical professional.

He brushed Ellie's hand away, shaking his head. "Listen to me."

"Okay." Ellie inched back.

"Go be a chef."

Ellie shook her head, tears stinging the back of her throat.

"Robbie will come. You'll have to go." Her father levered himself to his feet, turned in slow increments, slapped the seat down and made his way back to the house with his walker. "This ranch doesn't run on cuteness and woo-woo."

"Did you hear how well he was speaking?" Gigi chuckled. "I bet it was due to the alpacas."

"Yes, but…not the way you're thinking." Ellie watched him go, knowing he wouldn't want her hovering at his side. "Was I wrong about the alpacas?"

"No. Come pet one," Gigi said. "You'll feel better."

"Yeah, but none of my problems will be solved."

ELLIE BROUGHT THE girls by the hospital after school to visit Mary. They carried a bouquet of flowers and a piece of carrot cake they'd picked up at Betty's Bakery. Ellie knew that carrot cake was Mary's favorite.

"Is she dying?" Della asked, uncommonly quiet in the hospital corridor. "Dying scares me."

"It scares everybody, honey," Ellie reassured her. "But no. She's not dying."

"Are they going to put bandages on Miss Mary and poke her with a needle?" Lulu asked, worrying her lower lip with her teeth. "That's what happened to Crockett's grandma."

"Crockett?" Ellie paused at a junction in the corridor, checking signs for room 212 before leading them to the right. "I thought you weren't friends with Crockett?"

"We're not friends *with him*. But he keeps saying he's friends *with us*." Della looked particularly down about this.

"He follows Della everywhere," Lulu added. "It makes her angry."

"Because of what Mister Tate said about frenemies," Della grumbled.

They reached another crossroad. Clementine's hospital wasn't that big. *Where is that room?*

"That's it, Della." Lulu raised a finger in the air to indicate an aha moment. "We should tell him what *frenemies* means. Then he'll go back to being your enemy."

Della dropped the small box with the cake slice. Luckily, it landed right side up and remained closed. "Don't tell him anything, Lulu Rowland Jones."

"Because you like him?" Lulu asked, unfazed by her sister's outburst.

Ellie spotted their destination to the left and lengthened her stride.

"I don't know, Lulu." Della was back to speaking in hushed tones. "And when a person doesn't know, you can't go blabbing every little thing."

"Huh." Lulu sounded like this piece of information required further thinking.

Ellie led them into Mary's room, putting a cheerful smile on her face and hoping the girls would do the same.

Mary's room was filled with bouquets of flowers, balloons, cards and cowboys. The flowers, balloons and cards were chipper. The cowboys looked somber. They held their hats and stood solemnly, staring at Mary, who looked small and frail in that hospital bed.

"Mom, you said she wasn't dying," Della whispered in her loudest whisper, which sounded like a shout in the quiet room.

Ellie gently shushed her, taking the flowers and cake and setting them on the bedside table.

"I'm not dying." Mary's eyes cracked open. "I was pretending to be asleep because these boys of mine have been planning my funeral. Prematurely."

Lulu took a step forward, reaching through the guard rails for Mary's hand. "Why would they do that?"

"I have no idea." Mary reached for the bed remote with her other hand. "Do I look like I'm dyin' to you?"

"No, ma'am." Lulu shook her head.

Mary adjusted the bed so she slowly came into a sitting position, which sparked the girls out of their funk. They demanded a ride on the magical bed.

While they were occupied, Ellie gathered the cowboys and shooed them out the door. "No one likes being hovered over. Go find yourself a pretty nurse to take to the wedding on Sunday."

That comment wasn't well received.

Ellie closed the door on them anyway.

"Thank you for last night, Ellie. And for this respite." Sitting up, Mary looked better than she had at church on Sunday. "Those boys have experienced so much loss that they don't deal well with even the idea that someone else they love is going to leave them."

Her words had Ellie thinking about Tate and wondering how he was coping with Donna's departure. Did he need a hug? Or a sweet, understanding kiss?

"Did something go wrong last night?" Mary asked. "Is there something you need to tell me?"

"No," Ellie hastened to reassure her. "I had so much fun stepping in."

Della and Lulu nearly fell off the bed.

Mary distracted the girls by telling them to draw a picture on her hospital white board.

"I don't think they're supposed to do that," Ellie said, although without any warning. The white board was where the nurses wrote down her vitals, pain level and goals for the day. Someone had scribbled *oncologist* in barely legible font, although considering that was a cancer doctor maybe they hadn't wanted it to be legible. "But I suppose if it lifts your spirits, it's fine."

Mary smiled and nodded, oddly at a loss for words.

Ellie scrambled for a safer topic. "Did you hear we've adopted Donna Oakley's alpacas?"

"We're drawing Miss Mary a picture of our alpaca herd," Lulu said without turning around.

"I did hear something about that…" Mary caught Ellie's gaze. "When I was told she left my boys again. Bad timing on my part to get sick when they need me."

"If it's any comfort, Ryan and Tate seemed more at peace with it this time." Ellie hoped that was still true.

"That's because she didn't slip away." Mary shook her head. "That came out on the wrong side of charitable. Some things aren't meant to be for some people. I wasn't meant to be a lion tamer. And Donna… I guess she wasn't meant to be… an alpaca farmer." She smiled a little.

A laugh escaped Ellie's throat. "I'm sorry. I thought you were going to say something else."

A cowboy peeked in, a concerned expression on his face.

"Oh, my boys," Mary lamented, although she was smiling. "You should probably head out. I believe Chandler was holding a rodeo clinic tonight for kids. It's a warm-up to the junior rodeo this weekend."

"Will there be sheep riding?" Della spun around, brightening.

"Yep. It's called mutton bustin'," Mary told her. "And it's safe, so long as you follow the rules. Your mama shouldn't be too worried about you getting hurt."

"Oh, I promise. Can we go, Mom?" Della tugged on Ellie's arm. "*Puh-lease?*"

"If you don't let her," Lulu said, "we'll never hear the end of it."

Lulu was right. How could Ellie refuse?

CHAPTER FIFTEEN

"THERE'S CROCKETT," Della said sourly.

"Best behavior," Ellie reminded her as they walked up to the arena at the Done Roamin' Ranch.

They'd had to park at the far end of the ranch yard because there were so many people and vehicles.

"There's Mister Tate." Lulu skipped toward him, swinging her skirt to and fro.

Tate turned at the sound of his name, tipping his straw cowboy hat, acknowledging Ellie and the girls with a smile and a nod. He'd been leaning on the arena railing near Crockett and his mother. He pushed away from it and walked toward them.

Della sprinted ahead of her sister. "Mister Tate! Can I ride a sheep?"

"You're too old, Della." Little Crockett had a know-it-all expression and a tone tart enough to turn up Della's nose. He trotted after Tate.

"You're right, Crockett. But never fear, Della.

When I first came to live at the Done Roamin'
Ranch I was the same, so my dad started me on a
calf." Tate laid a hand on Della's shoulder. "Come
on, honey. Let's get you a ride."

Della smirked at her frenemy.

Ellie and Lulu moved to the railing.

There were dozens of parents and onlook-
ers gathered around the arena and dozens more
kids, old and young, mingling about. In the arena,
Chandler led a group of ranch cowboys in in-
structing kids on how to ride sheep. And just like
Crocket had pointed out, the little cowpokes were
very young.

Tate entered the arena with Della, talking and
pointing things out to her. They came to stand
next to Ryan, who was holding a sheep with one
hand on either side of its head. Griff held the
sheep by the haunches.

A cowboy who couldn't have been more than
five years old climbed on a sheep facing backward. He was wearing a helmet and safety vest.
He laid across the sheep's back, sinking his fingers into a thick layer of fleece.

"Three, two, one." Ryan let go and got out of
the way.

The sheep took off with its backward rider,
who didn't manage to hang on more than ten feet
or so.

Whoops and applause filled the air.

Tate and Della laughed together. And then Della nodded vigorously.

Ellie could just imagine what her little dynamo was saying: I can do that, Mister Tate. Her heart pounded with a mother's fear for her child.

"I see why you're gonna marry Mister Tate." Lulu swished her skirt. "It's because he loves us, too."

"Say what?" Crockett did a double take Lulu's way.

"Mister Tate is marrying my mama."

Ellie looked from Crockett to his mother. Rochelle, she thought her name was.

Rochelle made no apologies or explanations for Crockett's behavior. She exuded entitlement. She looked Ellie up and down from behind her sunglasses. "So, you're Tate's latest girl."

Ellie considered denying it but didn't.

"How many dates have you had?" Rochelle asked with a toss of her head. "You know, he's got a two-date limit."

Ellie shrugged, not willing to admit that she hadn't had any dates. Working on the ranch and helping his mother out didn't count.

"I'm determined to break the record and get a third date." Staring into the arena, Rochelle smiled to herself.

I don't want to be one of the women who competes for Tate's affection.

Ellie didn't want to deal with Rochelle's hostility either. Or get into a game of He Likes Me Best with her.

"Hey, Mom…" Lulu stuck her head between the rails. "Wasn't Della going to ride a sheep?"

"Yes, honey. She's probably going to have to wait her turn."

"She's getting on a bull." Lulu pointed across the arena.

"It's a calf," Crockett said knowingly. "Look how small it is."

Ellie looked all right. Della was wearing a helmet and crash vest and sitting atop a calf in a chute that was twice the size of the sheep in the arena.

"Did you ride a calf, Crockett?" Lulu asked, an unusually sharp edge to her voice.

"My mom doesn't let me rodeo." Crockett had his mother's superior tone—misplaced, the same as her.

Lulu stomped a boot.

"So why are you here?" Crockett stomped his foot right back. "I told you. Mister Tate is marrying my mom."

The chute opened.

Ellie held her breath.

"THAT'S IT, DELLA." Tate followed close behind her as she rode the calf. And maybe the little sparkplug thought his words meant it was time to let go because suddenly, she lost her grip on the gently bucking gray calf and tumbled to the ground.

Only to have the calf's back hoof come down on her wrist. Della screamed, rolling into a tight ball.

The crowd gasped, then quieted.

"Della!" Ellie cried, running toward the gate.

Tate reached Della and scooped her into his arms. "Go ahead and cry, baby girl. You got stepped on."

"It hurts," Della sobbed, cradling her right wrist. "It hurts so bad."

"Della!" Ellie cried, sprinting toward them.

"I've got her," Tate told her. "Let's take her to the tack room." That's where all hurt cowboys were taken. It was private in case they cried.

Ellie reached them. "Tell me where it hurts."

"Here." Della held up her right wrist, supported by her left hand. Her wrist was an angry red and not shaped the way it should have been.

"We've got splints in the tack room." Tate purposefully spoke in a calm, controlled voice, hoping to communicate that Ellie shouldn't panic. "She's going to be okay."

Ellie's eyes looked watery, but she swallowed thickly and nodded.

"I'll call Doc Nabidian," Rochelle said from behind Ellie. She worked as a nurse in his office part-time.

The three of them got Della settled in the tack

room with a splint, a glass of water and a Popsicle from the freezer. Tate doled out Popsicles to Lulu and Crockett, too. They shared a bench near the door.

Ellie had Della in her lap and was rocking her slowly. Rochelle went out to wait for Doc to arrive.

And Tate decided it was time to address the elephant in the room. "I should have gotten your permission for Della to ride that calf. I'm sorry, Ellie."

"Don't be mad at him, Mom." Della paused, eating her orange Popsicle to glance at Ellie over her shoulder.

Ellie sighed. "I'm a ranch kid. I grew up taking risks around animals. If Della hadn't ridden that calf today, she would have found a way to ride one another time."

"True." Della leaned back against Ellie. "I love you, Mom."

"I love you, too."

Tate laid a hand on Ellie's shoulder. "Am I forgiven?"

"Yes." But Ellie drew her arms tighter around Della and didn't meet Tate's gaze.

"Della, you were so brave," Lulu told her twin, catching a drip on her Popsicle before it fell onto her skirt.

"Didn't last long though," Crockett said in that

glass-half-empty way of his. He took a bite of Popsicle.

Lulu leaned over and got in that little cowboy's face. "At least she tried it, unlike you."

"That's true," Crockett allowed, tipping back his cowboy hat. "Della can say she rode a bull, but I can't." He sent his mama a sorrowful look.

"You're not riding a bull. Or playing football. Or climbing tall trees." Rochelle entered the tack room with Doc Nabidian behind her. "We see enough broken bones at the office. I don't need to treat my own kid."

Ellie caught Tate's eye.

"I'm sorry," he told her again.

"It's okay," she whispered back.

Doc hurried to examine his patient and quickly came to a conclusion. "You have a broken bone, Della. We'll need to x-ray it and put a cast on. Tomorrow morning when it's dry, you can have all your friends sign it."

"Why would I want to do that?" Della frowned. Her cheeks were tear streaked and her lips orange from her Popsicle, but she hadn't lost any of her backbone.

"So folks can let you know how much they care about you. Duh." Crockett huffed as the rest of his Popsicle fell to the floor. "I wish I had a cast."

"Crockett," Della said in a hoarse voice. "You

better listen up 'cuz I'm only gonna say this once. We care about you, you turnip."

"Della," Ellie said in a chastising tone.

A sob had all eyes turning toward the door.

It was Rochelle, red nosed and teary-eyed. "It's okay. That's the nicest thing I've ever heard anyone say to him."

AFTER BREAKFAST ON Friday morning—another made by the men since Mom was still in the hospital—it was time to load stock into trailers for the one-day rodeo on Saturday. It was a local event, only an hour away, but the livestock needed to be there on Friday to settle in.

Tate was grateful for the work. It was hard to wait for more news on the medical front. He'd already checked in with Ellie to see how Della was doing. His little bull rider in training had happily gone to school, wrist in a sling, prepared to be the most popular girl on campus. Tate wished he had time to take Ellie for coffee or dinner. There just wasn't enough time.

"I need bulls," Chandler called out. He managed everything, keeping inventory of the animals being used and doing a last inspection of them. Any animal that showed signs of injury or illness wasn't allowed out to perform.

Tate and the others were kept busy moving stock to holding pens, through chutes and into trailers. The bucking bulls had to be sorted into groups that got along. As with the last rodeo Big Stomper Chomper had his own trailer because he didn't get along with anybody.

It was the same protocol for the bucking broncs. And for some of their ranch mounts, too. There were just some animals that had an attitude, and no one wanted a fight breaking out while you were rolling down the highway at fifty miles an hour.

As each trailer was loaded, it was sent off on the road with a truck escort full of cowboys. By the time lunch rolled around, there were just a few more trailers to be loaded with ranch horses and a few more cowboys doing some last-minute packing.

During that lull, Dad drove in.

"I've come from the hospital. Just wanted to check on you boys." Dad didn't smile, which was odd because he was a smiler. "According to your mother, she's having every test the hospital offers."

They suspected cancer of some sort, a fact that had shaken Tate and everyone on the Done Roamin' Ranch. "How does she look?"

"Like an angry pin cushion." Dad resettled his white cowboy hat onto his gray hair. "I've never seen her so annoyed. She told me she'll be breaking out of there on Sunday if Doc Nabidian doesn't release her."

"Ronnie and Wade are considering having two ceremonies," Tate told him. "One at the hospital and one at the church."

"Let's hope it doesn't come to that. Now, where's the man in charge?" Dad wandered off to find Chandler.

"Let's get over to Jo's and pick up our horses." Ryan tossed his competition and overnight bags into Tate's truck bed, next to their saddles. "We can practice one more time before we leave."

Tate had already loaded his stuff in the back. He climbed behind the wheel. "Sounds good." Any extra time he had with Goldie was a plus.

When they arrived at the Pierce Ranch, Tate and Ryan discovered a kink to their plans.

Jo was working in the uncovered arena with her brothers, Ty and Eric, who were Tate and Ryan's biggest threat in the Prairie Circuit.

"The plot thickens," Tate said softly as they entered the arena.

Ryan scoffed and then raised his voice, "Look who's finally putting in the work. Got you nervous, have we, fellas?"

"You beat us the last couple of weekends, Ryan, but let's see how well you do this week." Eric Pierce coiled his rope as he rode back to the cattle-release chute, smiling like he enjoyed talking smack. Which he did, same as Ryan.

"Ha!" Ryan draped his arm across Jo's shoulders. "You're wishing you would have bought Prince and Pauper. Instead you bought that pair from some fancy California outfit."

"We're always slow season starters." Ty Pierce backed his horse into the box next to the chute. "And now that Jo's helped us fine-tune our performance, our victory this weekend is assured."

Ryan didn't look happy. The sun disappeared behind a cloud.

"There's plenty of room for both our teams." Tate took the stopwatch from Jo. "The top three ropers qualify for the postseason. But we don't care if you come in second or third." Apparently he had a knack for smack, too.

"Jo, we've got time for one more run before we need to head out." Eric backed his horse into the box.

"Let's show these boys how it's done." Ty tugged his hat brim down. The silver tips on his expensive black boots glinted in the sun.

When it came to rodeo, everything about the Pierce brothers was carefully chosen to intimidate, from their stony expressions to their highfalutin presentation.

The pair made their run. They were quick. Their form perfect. Their time competitive.

"Beat that, boys." Eric dismounted and led his horse out of the arena.

"Beat that without Prince, he means," Ty said, doing the same. They went into the covered arena to cool down their horses.

Tate felt his confidence shake.

It's safer not to try.

The sun peeked past the cloud, bringing its warmth the same way Ellie brought light and happiness when Tate was with her.

"We've got this, Ry," Tate said.

"Darn straight we do." Ryan removed Jo's cowboy hat and pressed a kiss to her temple.

Jo laughed, short brown hair ruffling in the breeze. "What's happening here? I thought you'd be upset with me."

"I would never question your motives, honey."

Jo bumped Ryan with her shoulder. "I'd question yours."

Ryan let out a laugh and enveloped Jo in a hug.

Tate's heart panged with envy.

"Tate, we should go load the horses." Ryan put Jo's cowboy hat back onto her head. "We need to get on the road."

"Because you don't want my brothers to see Goldie in action?"

"That's right." Tate gave a quick nod.

"Smart." Jo led them toward the barn. "My brothers tend to be a little cocky when they believe the competition is at a disadvantage. And when they get cocky…"

"They get sloppy." Ryan swept her into his arms once more. "I love you, Jo."

Tate left them, walking to the barn and messaging Ellie.

I miss you.

It wasn't the same three words his brother had said to his fiancée, but it was close enough.

CHAPTER SIXTEEN

"MISTER TATE, do you want a cookie?" Lulu skipped toward Tate, pretty pink skirt swishing late Saturday afternoon. "We saw you win."

"It's a fortune cookie." Della ran up to Tate, hitching up her blue jeans with her good hand. Her wrist was still in a sling. "They have love fortunes and everything."

"What? Gigi's not doing love advice today?" Tate couldn't believe it. "How's your wrist, Della?"

"Good. Wanna sign it?" The little girl showed him her cast. It was covered in scribbles and doodles. "Doc says I won't be riding bulls again until summer."

"Bring that cowboy over," Gigi called.

The twins flanked him and grabbed hold of his hands.

Tate allowed himself to be led to Gigi's table. He was finally on a break, riding the high of another win.

"Ellie said we needed to keep our approach fresh." Gigi held up a basket with a batch of fortune cookies and pointed to one in particular. "So today, you buy the cookie and get a love fortune inside."

"A truly random experience, I'm sure." Tate dutifully dug out a five-dollar bill.

"For sure, for sure." Gigi kept pointing. "I saved this one for you."

Tate took what was offered, curious as to what Gigi wanted to give him.

He cracked open his cookie. His love fortune was handwritten: *Hang in there for the prize.* He shook his head. "This isn't earth shattering." He and Ellie had obstacles, to be sure. But he was determined to clear them out.

"Pish. You never appreciated encouragement when times were tough?"

"Are times going to get tough?" He thought about Buck, frowning a little.

"Likely, yes. Buck's here." Gigi put the basket down, which sent her bracelets jingling. "And when that man makes an appearance, no one ever knows what to expect."

Least of all, Tate.

Tate moved on, eating his fortune cookie and thinking about Ellie. He found her in a barbecue trailer, mixing a large bowl of coleslaw. She wore a pink Curly's BBQ T-shirt, a brown apron and an intense look of concentration. A teenage girl was collecting money from customers at the order window.

"Congratulations on another first place," Ellie said upon catching sight of him. "I told you Goldie was good."

"You told me, sunshine." Tate grinned. "Goldie pranced and everything." After every run, earning chuckles and applause from the crowd. Tate set his fortune on the counter closest to her. "I got this love fortune, but I thought you could use it more than I could."

"*Hang in there for the prize.*" Ellie gave him one of her sunny smiles. Her reddish-brown hair was in a neat braid that swayed cheerfully every time she turned his way. "Maybe we should share this fortune."

"I'd like that."

"I hope you haven't eaten. I want you to try my latest creation." Ellie dished barbecue chicken onto a roll, topped it with coleslaw and then sprinkled bite-sized chunks of pineapple on top. She set it in a sandwich tray and handed it to Tate. "You like spicy food, don't you?"

"I like anything you make."

"Foie gras?" She teased. "Liver? Beet salad?"

"For you? I'd learn to like it all." Tate took a bite. It was sweet and savory. Until it was hot. And hotter. The heat continued to build as he swallowed. "Whew." His eyes watered.

Having watched him closely, Ellie handed him a glass of water. "Too much?"

Oh, yeah. Tate tried to save face, working up a smile. "Only because I had no warning."

Ellie wasn't buying that. "I asked if you liked spicy food."

"This isn't just spicy, it's smoking hot." He ate a chunk of pineapple since his mouth was still burning. He drained the glass of water.

Ellie laughed.

The perfectness of the moment didn't escape Tate. His career was looking up. Ellie was happy. Her girls were good, apart from Della's arm. "Ellie, can I ask you something?"

"Sure. Is it about the weather? Or animal husbandry?"

"No." Tate drew a deep breath. It was time to ask her out. "Would you—"

"There's my wife!"

"THERE'S MY WIFE," Buck repeated, pointing to Ellie.

"Your *ex*-wife." Ellie corrected Buck, smile fading. She'd been sure Tate had been about to ask her out. "Hello, Buck. Who's this?"

Smiling like he'd just won the lottery, Buck stood at the window, a swanky-looking brunette standing at his shoulder. "This is Sherry. She's new at the base."

"Hi." One very short syllable was all Ellie offered.

"Buck, are you here to try Ellie's barbecue?"

Tate appeared at Buck's side at the order window. "I thought you didn't like spicy food."

"Hey, it's the roping champ." Buck hugged Tate and then tipped his cowboy hat back, grinning. "It's like the band is back together. You, me and—"

"Your *ex*." Ellie couldn't say that fast enough. "Tate, don't tease Buck about spicy food. You know he can't handle the hot stuff."

"Who says?" Buck's grin didn't waver. "Give me two beers and two of what Tate's eating and something mild for Sherry. She's in a delicate condition."

Ellie gasped. "She's pregnant."

"Hungover." Sherry looked up from her cell phone. "I'll get us a table." She walked away.

A young cowhand rushed up to Tate and spoke to him briefly. "Sorry, I've got to get back to work. Call me if you need me," he said to Ellie.

"Will do," Buck said back.

Audrey rang up Buck's order while Ellie prepared it.

A few minutes later, Ellie handed everything to Buck through the window.

Buck tucked the beer bottles under his arm and then took the food tray. "So, this is the job that's keeping you in Oklahoma. I thought your dad was sick."

"He is." Ellie recognized Buck was leading up to something. "It's going to take a long time to get Dad back to living independently. He can't drive yet."

Food and drink balanced, Buck peered at Ellie through the window. "I miss the kids, Ellie. When are you coming home?"

Never.

Ellie wanted to send Buck on his way, but there was no one behind him waiting to order food. "I can't just leave my dad."

Buck frowned. "You're here at the rodeo, aren't you?"

"Yes, but I arranged for a friend to check on him." Ellie realized where Buck was going, and it wasn't going to be pretty when Buck got there. Her hands were shaking. She tucked them into her back pockets. Custody agreements were scary things.

"I missed two weekends because you came here." Although Buck was smiling, his voice had grown cold. "And it looks like I'm going to miss the weekend after this, too."

"Not necessarily." Ellie swallowed her nerves and tried to sound composed. "The girls are here with Gigi. You can find them in the merchants' aisle. They'd love to spend time with you."

"You need to come home."

Had Ellie thought his tone was cold a moment ago? Now it was frozen, each word a jagged icicle inching under her skin. She shivered. "I can't come home yet. My father—"

"We spent a lot of time working through our custody agreement." Buck's jaw thrust out. "It feels like I need to remind you of the terms of the agreement or maybe have the court remind you of your parental obligations. Our children are mine twice a month."

Buck was good at boxing her in until she felt as if the windows were closed, and her wings were clipped.

He can't treat me like this.

Ellie drew on an inner strength. "The agreement also cites flexibility when it comes to circumstances, like family emergencies, holidays and celebrations. And let's not forget that you agreed the girls could come up here."

"But that was before you got a job, gorgeous." Buck's endearment conveyed no warmth. "Are you setting down roots here, Ellie? Because I won't stand for it."

"WILL YOU LOOK at that?" Tate said when he entered the living room at the Done Roamin' Ranch later that night, still covered in rodeo dust but needing to see his mother in person before helping unload stock. "Someone set you up the way you used to do for us boys when we were sick."

Pillows behind her on the couch. Blanket tucked in around her waist and legs. Water, cookies and the remote on the coffee table next to her.

Mom's complexion was still not entirely better,

but there was a spark in her eyes. "Turns out I don't like being babied at the hospital as much as I do at home." She patted Dad's arm. He was sleeping in the chair next to her. "The boys are back, Frank."

Dad shuddered awake. "What? Oh. How'd it go?"

"Big Chomper Stomper threw a cowboy into the dirt after two seconds and then gave us only a little trouble before heading for the exit." What a relief that had been.

What hadn't been a relief to Tate was seeing Buck act so cavalier with him and Ellie. He'd texted her on the way home, asking if she was okay. She'd sent him a thumbs-up emoji. If it wasn't so late, he'd call her to offer her the opportunity to talk if she wanted.

"And you? Did you bring home another trophy?" Mom asked.

Tate nodded. "What's the latest from the doctor?"

Outside, someone called for him.

"We have to go in for more tests on Monday." Without his cowboy hat and usual smile, Dad looked old.

"More tests," Mom grumbled. "All because a pony bit me."

"It's not the bite that's confusing the doctor," Dad said gently.

"Inconclusive and normal. I have more cultures developing than a pharmaceutical lab." Mom scoffed. "They're testing me for every killer disease in the book. I keep telling them I'm fine. But they won't believe me."

Someone called Tate's name again, this time louder.

"Better get out there." Mom shooed him away. "I'm on bedrest until I've proven I'm healthy as a horse. I need to talk to Ellie first thing in the morning about the reception dinner. *Someone* took my phone away today."

"That would be me. I won't apologize." Dad wiped a hand across his forehead. "She was threatening to call the floor manager at the hospital because they weren't speedy enough getting her released."

"Tate!" Griff burst in the living room. "Hey, Mama. Looking good. But I need the *nice* Oakley to lend a hand outside."

"I was just moving that direction." Tate kissed Mom's forehead and then turned toward the door.

"Skating out on the unload." Griff tsked. "If you do become world champion this year, there's gonna be no living with you."

CHAPTER SEVENTEEN

ELLIE BEGAN COOKING several hours before Wade and Ronnie's wedding reception. The kitchen at the community center had two stoves, two ovens, a very large refrigerator and plenty of counter space. She used every inch.

Ellie followed Mary's plan, even if it was plainer than she would have liked. The chicken and steak marinades were made first, then liberally applied and put in the refrigerator. Next came the baked potatoes, poked, rubbed with butter and salted. Off they went to the oven since hundreds had to be baked.

The work kept the worries about Buck at bay. Those same worries had plagued her sleep last night. What if he brought her back to court? What if the judge took her picking up and moving the wrong way? What if she got so distracted, she overcooked the chicken?

Ellie drank some coffee and refocused.

Gigi, Dad and the girls showed up in time to prepare the garlic bread, set up the serving trays on the buffet table and fold napkins. Gigi had prepared hundreds of cookies for a cookie-and-coffee bar.

Two hours before the wedding reception, Katie showed up with a wedding cake made by Betty's Bakery. "Are you sure this is enough of a crew to cook for a wedding?" She glanced around. "Do you want me to stay?"

Dad sat in a corner, folding napkins. Gigi, Lulu and Della were admiring the fancy decorations on the head table.

And then there was Ellie, rushing around with a big smile on her face. "Thanks. But I think we'll be fine. Once the meat and chicken are cooked, we'll just be filling serving trays for the buffet."

The time flew by. Guests began arriving. A DJ filled the building with mellow country music.

Mary entered the kitchen wearing a flowing blue dress and white cowboy boots with a matching hat. "How is everything?"

"Under control and on time," Ellie reassured her. It felt good to be bustling in a big kitchen. She'd worked two big gigs in five days. What did it say about her dreams and her future at the family ranch that she was so happy cooking for others?

She was afraid Tate was right.

Mary drew a deep breath, a look of pleasure crossing her face. "It smells just the way I like it to."

"I'm glad."

Mary came over to hug her, but Ellie held up a hand. "My jacket is dirty, and that dress looks too pretty on you to be soiled by marinade."

"Once again, you come to my rescue."

"Call me anytime. How was the wedding?" How did Tate look?

"It was so beautiful. I cried." Mary's gaze grew distant. "And now... I feel a little odd."

Ellie took her arm and led her to a chair next to Dad. "Stay here. I'll go get someone." She could hear the DJ announcing the entrance of the wedding party, received by cheers and fanfare. The bride and groom would be entering soon.

"Girls." Ellie rushed over to her daughters, who were peeking out the serving door at the proceedings. "Can you find me a cowboy, like Tate or Mr. Frank?"

"Don't panic." Mary touched Ellie's shoulder. "I just needed a moment." And she walked out, getting in line with her husband before walking up the aisle toward the long head table.

Ellie tried to catch Tate's eye, wanting to let him know that his mother wasn't quite right. But his attention was on the bride and groom making their entrance.

And then Ellie's was, too. Ronnie looked lovely. Her dress was a traditional style but a soft pink color. She and Wade glowed.

Ellie didn't think she'd looked that happy on her wedding day.

But I might if I married Tate.

The reception hall was filled with hoots and hollers.

Ellie's ears rang. She drew back, taking stock of herself. The last thing she needed was to pass out. But she wasn't lightheaded. The ringing came from the timer.

"The chicken!" Ellie ran to the oven.

She spent the next few minutes transferring large trays to warmers on the buffet line. It was just her and Dad in the kitchen now. Gigi and the twins had long since disappeared, their soiled aprons tossed over a chair with Ellie's purse.

The DJ poked his head in the kitchen. "Are you ready for dinner service?"

"Yes. Go for it." Ellie positioned herself at the kitchen door, watching as people from her past lined up to be fed.

There was her first-grade teacher, Mrs. Jackson, chatting with her second-grade teacher, Mrs. Edwards. There was Toby Stewart, who'd sold Ellie her first horse. And Coronet Blankenship, who owned the Buffalo Diner, standing with Sheriff Underwood. No one noticed Ellie. No one was *supposed* to notice Ellie. It wasn't their fault that she'd left Clementine for Texas and hadn't looked back.

I should have stayed in touch with these people.

Maybe then Tate would be more confident opening his heart to her.

Ellie replenished the chicken and meat trays and hurried back to the kitchen, only to continue to peek at the reception.

"You're lurking," her father told her. He looked drained.

"It's better than being a wedding crasher." Like Gigi and the twins, who sat at Buck's table eating dinner.

"You should be in there," Dad said. "Ronnie was your friend."

Ellie came over to kiss his cheek. "Ronnie needs me back here." But it would be nice to be a part of the festivities. Perhaps to have a dance with Tate.

Dinner dishes began to appear on the pass-through ledge. Ellie waved off several offers of help and busied herself with washing them. The cake was cut. More dishes appeared. The garter was thrown and the bouquet tossed. The dancing began.

Gigi entered the kitchen with an armload of dirty dishes. Her long, colorful skirt billowed as she walked. "The girls are dancing with Tate. I thought I'd start clearing the rest of the dishes from tables." She set them in the sink with a clatter of plates and a jangle of bracelets.

"There are more dishes?" Ellie's spirits sank. She was Cinderella, stuck behind the scenes. "I mean, yes, clear the dishes. I need to break down the dinner buffet, too." Maybe she should snag a helper or two.

Mary and Frank came trudging in, looking spent from the celebration.

"Thank heavens, it's quieter in here." Mary sat down next to Ellie's dad.

Frank pulled up a chair next to his wife. "Looks like you could use help at the sink, Ellie. Give me a second to let that music stop pounding in my head, and I'll help."

"I should have let Ronnie talk me into paper plates." Mary smiled apologetically.

"Ellie!" Tate entered the kitchen with Lulu and Della. He looked very handsome even though he'd removed his tuxedo jacket and lost his tie. "The girls want to dance with you."

The twins rushed over to Ellie, cheeks pink, smiles bright and palms sweaty. "Come on, Mom!"

"Sorry, girls." Ellie shook her head. "I'm just the help tonight. Lots left to do."

"Let me help," Tate said.

Before Ellie could turn him down, Buck burst in with a bit of alcohol-fueled swagger. His face was flushed and his eyes a bit bleary. "Looks like the party is in here." He sat down in a chair near Dad, on the other side from the Harrisons. "You do look like death warmed over, Henry."

"Are you drunk?" Dad asked him, scowling.

Buck nodded.

"You never listen, Buck." Mary shook her head, sending a glance to her husband.

Frank took her hand. "We've got several designated drivers here tonight. You won't be driving back to your hotel, Buck. You hear me?"

"Yes, sir." Buck saluted.

Gigi said something to the girls that sent them back into the main hall. And then she put an apron on, eye on the pile of dishes. "Are you here to help with clean up, Tate?"

"Yes." Tate rolled up his shirt sleeves.

"You shouldn't." Ellie moved between him and the sink. "You're in the wedding party."

"Weddings." Buck swayed in his chair. "I just proposed to Sherry."

Ellie froze, surprised, hurt, relieved. "Congratulations?"

Buck's gaze swung from Tate to her. "Before I saw Henry, I thought you moved back here to try your hand with Tate."

"No, Buck," Ellie said in a loud voice at the same time that Dad said, "She's leaving as soon as Robbie comes home."

"See? No one knows what you're doing, gorgeous." Buck wiped a hand over his face. "I didn't know that you gave up your apartment. Found that out Friday morning when I called your landlord."

"Why did you call my landlord?" Ellie demanded.

Buck ignored her. "I didn't know that you took your horses. Found that out yesterday at the rodeo when I saw Goldie. But what I do know is that I have parental rights." His voice rose. "And you can't move to Oklahoma with our girls without my permission, Ellie. And I say no!"

THERE WAS A moment of silence in the kitchen after Buck's wounded cry.

Tate was silent because he was digesting this new information about Ellie. She hadn't been entirely honest with him. She'd packed up and moved to Clementine, enrolled her kids in school, set about making repairs to her family's ranch. And all under the guise of a temporary visit to care for her father.

Oh, Ellie, what have you done?

She wasn't just rocking the family boat. She'd capsized it. Buck was going to come out here with the weight of the law behind him.

"Oh." Mom leaned into Dad. "I feel woozy."

Although her timing was suspect, Tate rushed to her side. Ellie got her a glass of water. Gigi fanned her with a clean cloth napkin.

Buck slumped in his chair, mumbling, "I've got rights."

Tate reached for Ellie's hand, whispering, "Are you okay? What can I do?"

"Don't take my side," she whispered back, releasing his hand.

She might just as well have said not to be her cowboy valentine. Tate was gutted.

"I'm fine now. It was just a dizzy spell." Mom was melting in her chair. She needed to lie down. "It's passed."

"She had one earlier," Ellie said. "She should rest."

"I'll get my truck." Tate headed for the door. "And then I'm taking you to the hospital, Mom."

"I'm not leaving yet," Mom said in a determined tone. "We can't leave Buck or his...fiancée."

Tate turned.

Buck hiccupped.

"I have something to say," Ellie said, standing tall in the middle of the kitchen, her chef's jacket stained and wisps of reddish-brown hair escaping from her braid. "After I learned that Buck was cheating on me, I moved out of the house with the girls to an apartment. I didn't cosign on that house. Buck owned it, and he'd been...hosting his lady friends there." Her cheeks flushed with the bright red color of embarrassment.

Tate gave his former foster brother a dirty look, silently vowing never to be his Switzerland again.

But Ellie wasn't done. "I went out and bought myself a truck because I wasn't on the registration for the one I was driving. Buck never involved me in those decisions or acknowledged me on the paperwork."

Buck put his elbow on one knee and rested his chin in his hand. "A man is supposed to provide for his family. That's just how it is."

Mom and Dad didn't look very happy to hear any of this. Henry looked like he was going to have another stroke. And Gigi had her arms crossed over her chest, drumming her beringed fingers on her arms while staring at Buck with deadly intent.

"The divorce was easy. *Uncontested,*" Ellie said the word succinctly. "But we had some differences over custody, didn't we, Buck?"

"You…" Buck drew himself up straighter in the chair. "You weren't a good mother. You were never home. Always at the restaurant and paying for a nanny." He pointed at Ellie, again and again. "You're why I looked elsewhere for love."

She'd been pursuing her dream.

Tate gave Buck a dark look.

And motherhood has nothing to do with love for a spouse.

Tate felt tenser than when he sat in the starting gate.

"You began wandering long before I became a chef or we had kids." Ellie didn't waste time arguing anymore, but color was high in her cheeks. This was a sensitive subject for her. "Buck made it clear to me that I could either quit my job as a head chef…" Her gaze connected with Tate's.

A head chef… Every chef's dream job.

"…or I could give him full custody and have visitation. Two weekends a month."

Tate's gut twisted. Ellie hadn't given up on a dream solely because she'd realized it was taking away from family time. She'd been told. Black-mailed, even.

"That's what I got," Buck mumbled, although his voice grew louder as he continued, "Two weekends a month. But now I've got nothing!" He hunched back down in his chair, head hanging.

"I didn't come here with a plan to move back," Ellie said, head high, green eyes glistening with tears. "I came here with all the things that mattered to me. And what I found in Clementine was what had been missing in my life the entire time I was married to you, Buck. I rediscovered love. Love for the land and ranching. Love for the family I rarely saw. And love for…" Her gaze landed on Tate. "…a man worthy of me."

That was him. Tate. But he hadn't wanted their romance to start off this way, with a bitter custody battle and unfulfilled dreams. What would that pressure do to their love? Tate imagined it would tear them apart.

He couldn't be that man for her. Not yet. Not now. His gut wasn't just twisting. He was being wrung from the inside out.

"A man worthy of you?" Buck's head still hung down, but now it swung back and forth. "That was supposed to be me."

"Yep." Henry reached out and poked Buck's shoulder again.

This time, Buck fell out of his chair.

ELLIE HAD THE worst timing.

Once more, she'd laid her feelings on the line for Tate and he'd left her hanging, waiting for an answer.

She'd expected him to say, *And that man is me!*

Hadn't he realized she'd just said she loved him?

So much for Tate ever being her cowboy valentine.

"We need to go." Gigi grabbed hold of Ellie's shoulders and gently pushed her toward the chair with their purses and coats. "Henry, get yourself up out of that chair, you troublemaker."

"I still got it." Dad grabbed hold of his walker and pushed himself to his feet, giving Ellie a lopsided smile. "I can still protect and avenge my family. Can I get a woo-woo, Gigi?"

"Do you feel like your chi is in balance, Henry?" Gigi asked.

"Darn straight."

"Woo-woo." Gigi raised her hands to the roof.

"That's woo-*hoo*," Ellie mumbled.

"Give the man his time in the spotlight," Gigi mumbled back, taking hold of Ellie's arm. "Now, let's head home."

"I can't leave," Ellie protested, digging in the heels of her Crocs. "There are dishes to be done."

"It might be better if you leave," Tate said in a kind voice while he and Frank tried to get Buck to his feet. "I'll call you later this week, and we'll talk."

"This boy has certainly filled out." Frank struggled to lift Buck.

"I can help." Ellie began to move around behind the men.

"No, thanks. Go home, sunshine," Tate said, still using that soft-as-a-hug voice. "We'll find someone to clean up or do it ourselves."

"Are you sure?" Ellie glanced again at the mountain of dishes.

Mary nodded. "We'll see you at church next week."

Ellie gave Gigi the keys to her truck, packed up her knives and went to collect the girls.

All without a word from Tate other than to say they'd talk *later this week*.

As she drove away from the community center, Ellie felt something she'd hoped never to feel again.

Her heart breaking.

"I HAVE SOMETHING to say." Tate's mother sat in the front seat on the drive home from the wedding reception.

Buck was passed out in the back seat with Dad.

His fiancée had been dancing at the wedding reception and unwilling to leave. Buck's life was a hot mess.

A hotter mess than mine. Which was saying something.

"After what just happened, we should all have something to say." Tate took the turn toward the motel Buck was staying in. "Hit me with it."

"When your father and I first began fostering teenage boys, we created a set of rules for keeping the peace in the house. Disagreements would be resolved quickly. Hugs would be given out even quicker. And when it came to romance—"

"There was a rule for that, too," Tate finished for her.

Mom nodded. "But what you may not know is the reason for the romance rule."

"Mary…" Dad shifted in the back seat. A glance in the rearview mirror showed him grimacing.

"It's time, Frank," Mom said. "Past time, really."

"I don't want to dredge up bad memories." Tate slowed as he drove through downtown proper.

"Some memories are bittersweet, honey." Mom patted his arm. "The reason for the romance rule was because I was dating your uncle Stephen when I first met your father."

Tate's jaw went slack. If it hadn't been attached to his skull, it might have fallen to his lap.

"And when I realized that my feelings were stronger for your father than for Stephen, it caused a rift in the Harrison family that persists to this day."

Dad stared out the back window, saying nothing.

"Oh" was all Tate could come up with.

"I know you have feelings for Ellie," Mom continued in a quiet voice. "Feelings that have lasted a long time. Feelings that are reciprocated."

Tate shook his head. "The last thing Ellie has time for right now is getting on the same page as me romantically." There was a relief to be found in those words. They could be *more than friends* indefinitely until Ellie's life was more stable. Until he knew for sure where he stood with her long-term.

"Tate," Mom said slowly. "I want to make sure our family code isn't an obstacle standing between you and Ellie."

"Really? But… I…" Tate still wasn't reassured. There were other things in play now. .

"It's good about the code," Dad said in a gruff voice. "Some relationships don't end up the way we'd like, on a timeline we'd like. And that's… just something you have to accept."

"I'm glad you understand." Tate spent the rest of the drive lost in thought.

So much had changed in the last week.

"There's one more thing," Dad said as they

pulled into the motel parking lot. "Ellie expected you to say something when she said she'd found a man worthy of her love. I wouldn't wait too long to let her know you feel the same way."

CHAPTER EIGHTEEN

"DAD, WE NEED to talk," Ellie said to her father the day after the wedding debacle.

She'd just returned from taking the girls to school and was pouring herself a cup of strong coffee when her father wheeled his walker toward the kitchen table and its oak captain's chairs.

Ellie hadn't slept well. Her head hurt. And her heart wasn't much better off. She felt as if she'd lost Tate somehow. For good this time? But decks had to be cleared. Decisions had to be made. Starting here. At home.

Family before romance. Isn't that the way Tate had always been?

"This sounds serious." Gigi glanced up from her phone. "I'll make Henry's egg-substitute breakfast." She popped out of her chair, blue Bohemian skirt swishing around her bare feet.

"Real men…eat *real* eggs." Dad sat too quickly in his kitchen chair, nearly falling over.

"Dad, be careful." Ellie set her mug down and hurried to fuss over him.

He waved her away. "Real eggs. When are you leaving?"

Gigi stuck her head in the fridge rather than answer, which was odd.

"Yes, Gigi." Ellie picked up her mug, suddenly curious. "When are you leaving?"

"I meant…when are both of you leaving?" Oh, Dad was in a mood that matched Ellie's this morning. He was on a roll. "I am perfectly…*capable*…" He bit the word out, scowling. "Of taking care of myself."

"That was a great sentence." Gigi took the egg substitute carton out of the refrigerator and moved to the stove. "You'll have to tell Doc Nabidian about your verbal progress."

"When are you leaving?" Dad ground out, still scowling. "Someone answer me."

"You heard me say last night that I'm planning on staying. You want me to go?" Ellie came to sit next to him. "How will you run the ranch?"

"I promised your mother." Dad panted, red faced. "The ranch goes…to Robbie."

Mom. How could you?

"Robbie doesn't want the ranch, Dad. He'd have been here by now *and* helped me make repairs if he did. He has a life outside of Clementine." And his ghosting them was probably out of a desire to avoid breaking Dad's heart. "If you don't want me here, you'll have to sell." Ellie reined in her frustration. "And I don't want to hear any more protests about my leaving to be a chef. Buck was right. But only about that. I wasn't a good mother when I was a chef. I was never home. But if I fix up the ranch and I make it more profitable, I can be here for them. And I can be here for you, too."

He frowned.

"Besides, I can do both the ranch and be present for the family. I *want* to do both." Ellie drew a deep breath and said what had been on her mind, "I can cater to satisfy my cooking passion. Granted, the scene I made last night might not be the best start to a new business venture. But I think that's a good compromise, don't you?"

His frown deepened.

Ellie placed a hand over his. "Call Robbie. But you'll see. It's me or nothing. I'll get the ranch up and running better, I swear. The twins love it here, Dad. Mom would be happy that we're so happy."

"Your mother didn't want you to be tied here," he said, his tone firm. "She wanted you to have the freedom to choose."

"And I have. She'd approve of what I'm doing, Dad." Ellie got to her feet. "She'd know how important this place and your legacy are to you. And me. Call Robbie and get your answers. But you'll see. It's me or a for-sale sign. I can do this, Dad. I can be enough for you." Her speech ended on a soft plea.

"You've always been enough," he said gruffly.

Ellie hugged him.

"And you?" Dad frowned at Gigi, who was frying his egg substitute. "When are you leaving, Miss Woo-Woo?"

Gigi pushed the edges of the sizzling egg mixture. "Well, I..." She sighed, then turned, propping her hand on her hip. "Truthfully, I want to stay, too. It's hard making ends meet living alone. I always thought my daughter Irene would be with me in my old age and I'd be surrounded by family. And now, here, that's partly come true, I can have a purpose again, selling cookies and taking care of you. All of you. Even my curmudgeonly son-in-law."

They were all quiet for a time, not looking at each other, until the smell of burning egg mixture had Gigi hopping.

She dumped the smelly mess into the trash, not looking at them.

"Irene..." Dad began. He sighed. "My wife... Ellie's mother would be happy with your decision. Both of your decisions."

Gigi clapped her hands. "I guess it's settled, then. We're all in this together."

Dad shook his finger at her. "Only if I get real eggs."

UNDER THE TRUCE, Ellie helped Dad out to the sheep-shearing shed so they could see where they stood.

Not that Dad stood. He took a seat on his walker and looked around, a light in his eyes.

"Don't look so happy. It hasn't been cleaned out since last spring, Dad." Ellie grabbed a broom and began sweeping the ten-by-twenty-foot shed. It had several electrical outlets, with shearing tools and blades stored in a wall cabinet in the corner and hooks to tether the sheep. There was a holding pen where they herded the sheep from the pasture and into a chute leading to the shed. And another chute on the opposite side where they were released after their haircuts, one that led to a different pasture.

"Lots of fond memories here." Dad smiled. His smile wasn't as lopsided as when Ellie had first arrived. "Jokes... Stubborn sheep... You were good at this."

Ellie took the compliment for what it was and thanked him. "You and Robbie were faster than me." She swept tufts of wool into a corner and then set about brushing cobwebs from the ceiling, making a mental note to spray for spiders. Thankfully, no arachnids immediately dropped on her. "I bet if we call Robbie and let him know he's off the hook when it comes to running the ranch, we'll be able to get him to commit to a weekend of sheep shearing."

Dad nodded.

Ellie told him about Tate recruiting cowboys from the Done Roamin' Ranch to help.

"You don't look at sheep ranching the way I do," Dad said bluntly, honestly. "Change is good, I suppose."

"But so is tradition. I used to sit up here and watch you shear sheep when I was little. The girls will love this." Ellie patted a small bench. The ladder that Dad had built into the wall was loose. Ellie gave each of the ladder steps a tug. "Della will want to help but—*aieee!*"

A spider with legs as long as her fingers scuttled out from behind the ladder.

Ellie stumbled back.

Dad laughed.

"It's not funny." Ellie's entire body was urging her to run.

The tarantula leaped to the ground and scurried to the corner, somehow disappearing into a crack.

"Spiders and snakes." Dad shook his head. "They'll be your favorite…animals on the ranch."

"Respectfully." Ellie poked at the hidey hole with the broom. "I disagree."

TATE SPENT THE morning with Prince, taking him for a walk on a lead rope because the gelding was bored. He'd been chewing on his stall gate. "You can't do that. You've got another week of bed rest, big guy."

"Hey, wait up." Ryan jogged over from the arena where someone had brought by a pair of bucking broncos they wanted to sell. "I think Dad and

Chandler are going to pass on those two horses. Not enough life left in them. But they did offer to put them out to pasture."

"I don't want to sound rude, but I was taking a walk to try and figure something out." What to say to Ellie when he saw her next.

"Last night, Jo and I washed dishes till the last dish was clean." Ryan waved Tate's dismissal aside. "And now I'm here to listen to all your problems. Such as why the woman who is practically your girlfriend left early and what you're going to do to win her back?"

A human listener was a much better option than an equine one. So, Tate told his brother everything—all his hesitations when it came to risking love with Ellie. It took them the entire walk out to the pasture and back to Prince's stall to run out of words.

"I listened." Ryan hugged Tate, clapping him on the back. "We hugged. And now I'm offering a solution."

Tate closed Prince's stall door, making sure the latch stuck. "I don't think I want to hear this." His brother sounded too happy.

"Come on. There's only one thing for it." Ryan headed out of the barn. "We're going to open your keepsake box."

"What?" Tate followed Ryan, if only to argue against this plan. "No. Not happening. How can this possibly help me reach for what I want with Ellie without being plagued with the fear of failure?"

"You've got to close one chapter of your life to move on with another. Isn't that what Mom said?" Ryan turned and smirked at Tate. "I think if you look in that box you'll discover what needs to be said."

Tate increased his pace, desperation fueling him. "All right. I'll do it." Quickly, like when he ripped off a bandage. "But only if you do the same."

A few minutes later, they each sat on their bunks, staring at their boxes as if a coiled rattler was about to rise from inside, fangs bared. That's what their pasts were, after all. A poison that could taint everything it touched. Love. Happiness. Success.

It's safer to try than to fail.

Tate gulped.

"What's going on?" Griff came out of the bathroom, a towel around his waist and another wrapped around his hair. He saw their boxes. Understanding dawned on his face. "Hey. No. I thought we agreed we weren't doing this. Is Mom here?" He glanced around, but no one else had come in.

"You should leave," Ryan told Griff, somber as a funeral preacher. "We've got a book to close."

Instead of making a run for it, Griff nodded slowly. "Okay. If you guys do it, I have to do it, too. Solidarity and all. Like the stolen brownies."

"Get your clothes on," Tate said.

"We'll wait," Ryan added.

In no time, Griff was dressed. He sat on his bunk with his keepsake box, long damp hair hanging to his shoulders.

Ryan and Tate reached for their flaps. Griff did the same.

"Wait!" Griff looked at the Oakley twins. "Are we sharing what we find?"

"Not if we don't want to." And without any more hesitation, Tate opened his box.

It smelled of dust and musty cardboard. The first item was a pink slip of lined paper decorated with hearts.

Be my cowboy valentine. Ellie.

Tate had added that to his box after his high school graduation. He smoothed the creases and placed it on his bunk, thinking of the way the wind playfully teased the ends of Ellie's reddish-brown hair, how her freckles stood out when she blushed, how her voice rose when she was nervous and how she threw herself wholeheartedly into a kiss. A good memory, he decided, reaching for the next item.

It was a school sweatshirt. Dearborn Elementary Bobcats. Boys medium. The logo of the school so worn that the *a* and *e* were gone. He'd never attended Dearborn. He'd picked up the sweatshirt from a school's lost and found, allowed to choose by the school secretary, who was the only one to notice he'd come to school in winter without a coat. When asked, he'd told kids, "Yes, I went to Dearborn," even though he'd had no idea where the school was. He'd worn it until he'd outgrown it. And then, he'd kept it in the pillowcase of a very flat pillow.

Ryan would be angry if he saw this, bitter that their parents didn't do right by them. But to Tate, it was a sign of kindness. A good memory, he decided, reaching deeper into the box.

There was a Polaroid photo of himself and Ryan as youngsters, screaming while sitting on either side of Santa. They'd been in kindergarten and had shown up to the community center for a free meal, gifts and a commemorative photograph with Santa. The poor guy. He'd probably volunteered to play Old Saint Nick without realizing how much childhood trauma he'd cause.

Tate smiled. That was definitely a good memory.

He reached into the box again. This time, his hands closed around a crumpled piece of paper. Tate frowned, not remembering this at all. He smoothed the creases, revealing an official document from another county. It was a copy of the paperwork to put the Oakley brothers in foster care.

Tate remembered it now. His biological mother had given it to Tate the first time she'd visited the ranch. Ryan had refused to see her.

You think I wanted to give you up? You think

your dad gave up on you? Someone took you away. She'd thrust the crumpled paper into Tate's hand and left.

Tate had gone down to the river to read the document. There'd been a scrawled note at the bottom.

Neglect and abuse reported by minor.

It had taken Tate awhile to work out what that meant. At first, he'd thought it had been someone else at school. Much as he and Ryan had tried to act like everything was fine at home, it wasn't. Kids understood that kind of thing. But eventually, Tate had worked out the meaning. Ryan had reported them after their parents had left them one time too many by Ryan's estimation.

Tate had been bitter about Ryan reporting them for a long time.

But he wasn't bitter about it now. The Done Roamin' Ranch was the best thing about their childhood, other than each other. Ryan had made a hard choice. And now, as an adult, Tate was grateful to him for it.

Tate rubbed his forehead, worrying about Ellie. She'd felt backed into a corner. Was she worried about what legal move Buck would make next? Was she considering going back to Texas?

He dug around in the box. There wasn't much left. A T-shirt from a summer day-camp program where he'd learned how to swim. A small medal he'd won in a mile-long track race, an event that he'd been afraid to compete in. Ryan had talked him into it, telling him over and over how far he could run. And a jelly jar with a hole for coins cut in the lid with a bent penny inside. It was the kind of jar that grape and strawberry jelly came in, decorated with a cartoon circus carousel. He and Ryan had both had similar jars to store their money in. But times had always been lean.

It wasn't until they came to the ranch that the boys had any real money to store there.

Tate took out the items and laid them on his bed. He opened the jar. The crushed penny was from a children's museum in Tulsa. He'd gotten it on a field trip after he moved here. It had been a gift from his foster mother, who'd chaperoned the trip for the school.

You'll pick up this penny years from now and remember how much fun you had today, she'd promised.

And Tate did remember. So many wonders for a kid to experience. There'd been a ball he'd touched that had sent the ends of his hair into the air. And an optical-illusion room where someone at the far end looked smaller than they really were. There'd been a room where they'd crushed corn to make into flour that they then cooked into tortillas. He'd never been to a museum before. He'd thought they were going to look at boring paintings of kings or presidents. But it had been a truly excellent day.

He'd kept the penny and other money in the jelly jar, a few bills and small change. And life had been good until his biological mother showed up for another visit.

This time, at their foster mother's urging, Ryan had joined them. They'd played horseshoes. He and Mom against Ryan and their foster mother. Tate remembered feeling disloyal to their foster mother because he'd chosen to play with his biological mother. But he hadn't wanted either of them to feel bad. And he knew Ryan would make their biological mother feel bad if he partnered with her.

Toward the end of the game, Mom had hugged Tate unexpectedly and whispered, "Honey, I'm saving up to get you back. Doing everything I can."

Tate nodded.

He hadn't smelled alcohol on her all day. Just the mints she kept sucking on. And he'd hoped then that she'd fixed everything that was wrong with her. He'd hoped that they could be a normal family. Tate had noticed that some kids at the ranch went back to their parents. He didn't want to go back to theirs unless things would be different.

But they were different! Mom didn't smell like

alcohol. *And she said she was holding onto what money they had to get them back.*

When the horseshoe game was over, Tate ran to his room, which at that time was in the main house. He took his jelly jar and ran back out, nearly missing Mom because she was heading for her car. Ryan and their foster mother were standing on the porch watching her go.

"Mom! Wait!" He sprinted to catch her. "Here." *He thrust the jar toward her. "When are we coming home?"*

"Oh, Tate. You're such a good, good boy." *Mom opened the jar and dumped the contents into her purse. It fell around a small flask of alcohol, the sight of which stole Tate's breath. "Hang on. I can't spend this." She held up the squished penny from the museum. "This is ruined. You shouldn't do that to money. Every cent counts, you know."*

"But Mom." Tate's heart was breaking. "When are we—"

"This means a lot to me, Tate." She'd hugged him, swinging him gently back and forth. And then she kissed his cheek.

And she must have run out of mints because Tate smelled it then. He smelled the alcohol on her breath, and he knew she'd lied to him.

Tate blinked back tears. "Mom..."

He didn't know what else to say. He didn't know how to feel.

And then Mom decided for him. "Everybody

loves you, Tate. That's important. People never leave forever if they love you. I love you. And I'll be back. Just wait and see."

He'd clutched the jelly jar with the squished penny inside to his chest as he watched her drive away. And then he'd run down to the creek, thrown the jar in, crumpled to his knees and cried.

That's where Ryan found him. Without a word, Ryan fished the jar from the shallow creek. He sat down next to Tate, put his arm over his shoulder and told him that Mom would be back, that she'd always come back for Tate because she loved him.

But what Ryan didn't say was that Mom didn't love Ryan near the same.

Or at all.

Tate had vowed then and there to change that.

I won't let Ryan down.

But what he hadn't been able to change was his weakness when it came to people leaving him behind. He'd become more proactive, expanding his roster of friends and family.

In the here and now, Tate removed the penny and set the jelly jar back inside the box. He put in the medal, the T-shirt and the sweatshirt. And then he topped it with the foster paperwork and closed that chapter of his life.

But that meant he had to look toward the future. Ellie was right. Tate gave a little of himself to everyone, which left too little for a wife, kids, his roping career or even to support the brother who'd sacrificed so much for him. He had to pick and choose his friends and loved ones. He had to create a boundary around his life. The beard wasn't enough.

His biological mother could come and go as she wanted. It was her life. Tate couldn't make her into the mother he wanted. That was Mary Harrison, his foster mom.

Tate had to believe in himself because Ryan did. Ryan always had. He'd encouraged him to do things outside of his comfort zone. Running a race, learning to rope, competing in roping. Ryan could have competed in roping alone, but he hadn't. Ryan always had Tate's back. Tate had to step it up and make sure he did the same.

I won't let him down.

Oh, that didn't mean Tate wouldn't still battle with nerves. But he'd have more command over them now.

And Ellie...

Ryan appeared beside Tate's bunk. He glanced inside Tate's box. "I waded into the river to get that jelly jar for you. And now you're throwing it away?"

"Darn right I am." Tate stood and hugged his brother. He hugged him good and hard. "Thanks. For everything. I love you, bro."

Across the room, Griff sniffed and closed up his box. He folded a piece of paper that looked like a birth certificate and stuck it in his wallet. "I don't know about you guys, but I don't ever want to do that again."

"Trash-bin run?" Tate suggested, grabbing his box.

The others agreed. They dumped their boxes into the large trash receptacle outside the garage. And then they stood for a moment, as if giving their pasts a proper send-off.

"I say we don't tell Mom we looked," Griff said, sniffing once more.

"I'm going to tell her," Tate said, heading for the main house. "She deserves the truth because she loved us when no one else would."

Ryan dogged his heels. "What are you going to do about Ellie?"

"I'm going to make things right, grab the bull by the horns, take a ride on..." Tate couldn't think of any more clichés.

"Yes, but specifically, you're going to..." Griff waited for Tate to complete the sentence.

"Make a grand, romantic gesture."

And no matter how much Ryan and Tate dogged him, Tate wouldn't share his strategy.

Because he had yet to come up with one.

CHAPTER NINETEEN

"COOKIES FOR YOUR VALENTINE!" Lulu called out. She wore a blue overalls dress that came to her knees, a pink polka-dot blouse and her sparkly pink boots. Lulu didn't look or sound like her normally chipper self.

Likewise with Della. "Love fortunes." She wore a red T-shirt with red ruffles on the sleeves, blue jeans, her sparkly pink boots, a cast free of a sling and a scowl.

Little Crockett Vavre was standing a few feet away, staring at Della with a lovesick grin.

Tate spotted the twins before they caught sight of him. He'd spent the morning herding rough-stock through chutes for the bucking-bronc events and was taking a break before the roping competition. He walked up to the girls, bent down and tilted up their cowboy hat brims. "Why so glum?"

"Mister Tate, you shaved off your beard." Lulu touched his whiskerless cheek.

"Yeah, yeah. So he shaved." Della tugged down her hat and frowned over her shoulder at her cowboy admirer. "Valentine's Day is over, and folks don't want our cookies or love fortunes. We're never going to earn enough for milkshakes today."

"Haven't you girls ever heard of St. Patrick's Day?" He took their hands and led them to Gigi's table, which was covered with her colorful blue-and-purple paisley tablecloth. "Why didn't you shift to the shamrock holiday?"

"Ah, it's my best customer. Just between you and me, I don't have a shamrock cookie cutter." Gigi reached for his hand, rings catching the sunlight. "Haven't you heard? Hearts are forever. Love has no season. *Hint, hint.*"

"For sure, for sure." Tate tipped his cowboy hat to Gigi, grinning. "You don't need to tell me twice."

"Are you gonna marry our mom?" Lulu asked. "Ever?"

"Or give her horse back?" Della stuck out her tongue at Crockett. "Ever?"

Tate motioned to Crockett and said, "I thought you guys made peace and were friends."

"Lulu told me what *frenemy* means." Crockett grinned. "I'm in it for the long haul, Mister Tate."

"Smart man." Tate patted him on the back. And then he turned to the girls. "I'm going to talk to your mom now about both things."

"Really?" Della brightened. "If she says yes, can we celebrate with milkshakes?"

"Every weekend." He winked at her.

"Now you're in for it." Gigi chuckled, tossing her thick white hair over one shoulder. "Bribing the kids before you make anything official."

"Do I need to slip you a shamrock cookie cutter, Gigi? Or take Henry for a boys' night out at The Buckboard?"

"Nope." Gigi grinned. "Welcome to the family."

Family. Tate liked the sound of that. Whistling, he headed toward the food aisle.

There was a long line at Curly's BBQ Shack. Ellie was working the booth with two teenagers—one was filling drinks and the other was taking orders and cash. Ellie was busy making sandwiches.

"Hey, Ellie." Tate poked his head in the side entrance, drawing a deep breath and taking the sight of her in. The proud set of her shoulders. The wary expression on her face when she saw him. "I'm on my lunch break and hoped we might talk."

"Can't talk now, *friend*. Everyone else in the rodeo is on lunch break, too." She didn't look at him. "And they're all hungry for hot-and-spicy barbecue."

There was a dig. Dad had been right about him needing to answer her at the wedding reception. And now he was second-guessing waiting until the rodeo to talk to her.

Tate wasn't giving up that easily. "I saw the girls and—"

"Two more with pineapple, Ellie," one of the teenagers called, giving Tate a disparaging look. "Is this the guy who ghosted you?"

"Yep. We can talk briefly after my shift is over. I brought my horse trailer to take Goldie home."

That wasn't good news. He was hoping to bring Goldie over to her ranch in the morning, along with a sparkling engagement ring. She hadn't even acknowledged that he'd shaved off his beard.

Did I overthink this?

Of course he had. He'd let Ryan and Griff help him plan how to make a grand gesture to prove his love and win Ellie back.

Mistake. Big mistake.

Think fast. He wasn't much good at thinking fast. He was good at reacting and throwing a rope.

He took a deep breath and said the first thing that came to mind. "Ellie, you look like you haven't had a break all day. You know, it's a law that you have to take a break. The whole crew can get in trouble if the law is broken."

Ellie smirked at him. Having been a head chef, she was probably more knowledgeable about employee rules and regulations than he was. Possibly, Curly had made her a manager as a workaround to the rule.

"He's not going to go away until you take a break, Ellie," said the drink-filling teenager.

"Take a break, Ellie," said the order-taking teenager. "And dump him."

"Thank you, ladies. I'll take that break, but I don't think I need any more love advice." Ellie passed them the sandwiches she'd made and then turned toward Tate, one hand on her hip.

He made a *come hither* gesture. "If any customer complains, you can blame it all on me."

"That I will, *friend*."

"I'm starting to dislike that word." He took her hand and helped her down the two steps out of the barbecue shack. "But only when it's used between us."

Ellie tugged herself free and put her hands on her hips again. "How's Mary?"

"Good. Getting the treatment she needs for her symptoms, although there are more tests and answers on the horizon." Tate didn't like that there were still so many unknowns about her condition. But at least the doctors were talking in positive terms.

"Have you heard from Ms. Alpaca?"

He nodded. "She's good, too."

"You left me hanging at the wedding."

His defensive smile came naturally, as did his subtle, downward tug of his hat brim.

I shaved for her.

"I did. But I'm not hiding how I'm feeling anymore." Tate tipped the brim back up, smile falling in the other direction. "I'm here to apologize. And to tell you I love you. I'm far from perfect and I'm going to make mistakes in this relationship, but I'm also going to work very hard at—"

"Ellie, are you almost done?" One of the teens inside called out to her.

"Almost!" She smiled at Tate ruefully and took a step toward the door. "I've got to go."

He'd blown it.

"Wait." Tate reached for a small, pink envelope. At least the color was right. He wished it was larger though. He wished it was the size of one of the banners hanging in the rodeo arena. "I should have called. I was overthinking and second-guessing. And… I'm late, but I'm trying to play catch-up. I needed to give you this."

Her brow furrowed as she took the envelope, stayed furrowed as she opened it. There was a small pink sheet of notepaper. She unfolded it, reading the message silently.

"Ellie…" her coworker called a second time.

"I love you, Ellie," Tate said softly.

A tear tracked down her cheek. And then another.

Still, she stared at his note.

He brushed the tears from her cheeks. "Is that a yes?"

More tears were falling.

"Sunshine, is that a yes?"

"I was never enough for you in high school. You always chose Buck over me. I thought you had second thoughts. I thought…" She lifted her tear-filled gaze to his and gasped for breath. "You are so…so…*late*."

"That's a yes." Tate swept her into his arms. The pink sheet of paper drifted to the ground.

Yes, I'll be your cowboy valentine. Will you be mine?
XOXO, Tate

EPILOGUE

"TODAY IS THE DAY." Tate clinked his coffee mug with Ellie's in the kitchen of her family's ranch. "Alpaca shearing. Are you ready?"

"No." Ellie cradled her coffee with both hands. "But don't tell my dad." Even now, she tried so very hard to project an image of confidence to her father. To be enough. It was only with Tate that she knew, deep down in her soul, that she was perfect for him.

"Don't tell me what?" Dad entered the kitchen, pushing his walker at breakneck speed. He'd never be mobile without a cane or walker again, but he wasn't as grouchy about life as he had been. "You're here early, Tate. Something special going on?"

"Every day I'm with Ellie is a special day." Tate lifted Ellie's left hand and kissed her fingers near his engagement ring. He and his brother had been winning consistently, and their professional future and dreams were looking bright.

"Every day with milkshakes is a special day."

Della shuffled in, yawning. Her cast was gone but not her determination to try bull riding again.

Ellie was negotiating gloves and wrist guards on Della's next ride.

Lulu wasn't far behind her twin. "Who said we were having milkshakes? For breakfast?"

"Not today's breakfast," Ellie told her. "But maybe if we're lucky, Crockett and Rochelle can bring us some later. They wanted to see our finished shearing project." Ellie and Rochelle had formed a friendship that wasn't based on being frenemies. It was unexpected but nice.

Tate cradled Ellie's hand in his and fought a smile. There was mischief in his eyes. "Are you ready?" he whispered.

Ellie bit her lip.

"They're talking about special days." Della opened the cabinet with the cereal and selected a box. "That means milkshakes."

"Weddings are special days," Lulu said, taking a different box of cereal. "When Uncle Wade got married there were no milkshakes." *Uncle Wade*. The girls had been invited to call Tate's foster brothers "Uncle."

"But our wedding could be different." Della set the cereal box on the kitchen table with more oomph than was necessary.

"That would give our wedding some woo-woo," Dad said, smiling to himself.

Gigi came in next. For once, she didn't wear a

flowing dress or skirt. She had on a pair of blue jeans and a large blue flannel shirt. Her thick, flowing white hair was in a braid. She stopped when she noticed everyone looking at her. "What? You said today was all hands on deck."

"I did. And I appreciate you taking me seriously." Ellie turned her focus back to Tate, who was chuckling again. Something was amusing him, and she wanted to know what.

Tate leaned forward to whisper in Ellie's ear. "You stayed up late watching videos of how to shear alpaca like poodles, didn't you?"

Busted.

"Shush." Ellie gently pushed him back toward his seat. "Yes, family. Today is a special day. We're shearing alpaca today. Donna's coming by later to judge our work. And tomorrow we'll have a whole crew here to help us shear sheep."

"Including Robbie," Dad said dryly.

"Including Robbie," Ellie echoed, grateful that her brother was taking days off from work to help. But so were some of Tate's foster brothers. "I'll leave you all to your breakfast. You have thirty minutes to report for alpaca duty." She stood and tugged Tate with her. "Come on, love. We've got lots to talk about."

"Wedding plans?" Lulu asked. They couldn't talk about wedding logistics enough for her.

"Milkshake surprises?" Della asked. They couldn't swing by the Sugar Freeze enough for her.

"Catering clients?" Gigi asked. She was enjoying being a part of Ellie's blossoming catering business.

"Renovation plans?" Dad asked. He'd agreed that the main house should be expanded to accommodate the addition of Tate and Gigi to their family.

Tate was going to move in after the wedding, which they'd scheduled for this summer. Gigi was going to return to Sedona after sheep-shearing to gather her things and make her move official.

Ellie's Texas lawyer had amended her custody agreement. She had legal permission to live in Oklahoma. The girls were to be sent to Buck in Texas once a month. And once a month, Buck was to visit them in Clementine. Her ex-husband had been surprisingly easy to negotiate with after a talk with his former foster father, his fiancée and his lawyer.

Things were falling into place.

Ellie laced her fingers with Tate's and tugged him toward the door, not answering anyone. She was gloriously happy every day now, but this morning something was bothering her.

Once their boots and cowboy hats were on and they were outside in the sparkling morning sunshine, Tate gently spun her into his arms. "What is it you have on your mind, sunshine?"

"I want you to promise me something." She framed his clean-shaven face in her hands, reveling in the fact that she could now see every wonderful nuance in his expression.

"Anything." Tate gazed into her eyes as if he'd happily do so all day.

"Promise me…" Ellie smoothed her thumbs along his cheekbones. "That no matter how horrific these alpacas look when I'm done, you'll agree that they look adorable. Cute. Trendsetting, even."

"Sunshine… Pinkie swear?" Smiling softly, Tate offered her his pinkie, and they shook on it. "There is no failure if you try."

And when she looked into his eyes, she knew he wouldn't tease her, not if she made an honest effort to do a good job. "Have I told you today that I love you?"

"Nope." He took her hand, led her down the path and across the ranch yard. "Are you going to tell me now?"

"I thought I'd see how long it took you to ask." She pulled him to a stop, rose up onto her toes and kissed him. "I love you, Tate. I loved you when we could only be friends. And I loved you when I knew we couldn't only be friends anymore."

"That day we almost kissed in the sheep pasture." He nodded. "I love you, Ellie. I've loved you since the first time you bossed me around. I loved you when I helped Buck win you back. And I loved you when you returned to Clementine." He glanced toward the alpaca in the paddock and the ramshackle barn behind it. "And I'm going to love you when we put our sweat equity into this place and make it look the way you dreamed it should be."

"And if it doesn't look exactly like our dreams, we'll be happy anyway," Ellie said.

"We'll be happy anyway." Tate nodded. "Because not all dreams come true, nor are they meant to look exactly how we imagined."

"Even when it comes to family…" Ellie was holding on to him tight now.

"Especially when it comes to family," he murmured before kissing her.

* * * * *